JANICE A.
THOMPSON

GONE
with the
GROOM

a cozy mystery

BARBOUR
PUBLISHING

OTHER BOOKS BY JANICE A. THOMPSON

FICTION
The Wedding Caper

NONFICTION
I Must Decrease

For more information about Janice A. Thompson, please access the author's Web site at the following Internet address: www.janiceathompson.com.

Published by Barbour Publishing, Inc., P.O. Box 719, Uhrichsville, Ohio 44683 www.barbourbooks.com

Our mission is to publish and distribute inspirational products offering exceptional value and biblical encouragement to the masses.

ecpa Member of the
Evangelical Christian
Publishers Association

Printed in the United States of America.

Consider it pure joy, my brothers,
whenever you face trials of many kinds,
because you know that the testing of your faith develops perseverance.
Perseverance must finish its work so that you may be mature
and complete, not lacking anything.
JAMES 1:2–4 NIV

DEDICATION:

To Kevin, my soon-to-be son-in-law:
Thanks for staying put.

ACKNOWLEDGMENTS:

To Megan and Kevin. How amazing, to be in the midst of planning your wedding during the writing of this book. I hope your big day—unlike the one in this story—is incident-free!

To my awesome critique partners, Martha, Marcia, and Kathleen. I can never thank you enough for the hours you've spent reading over my manuscript and offering critiques. Special thanks for being there when I needed you most—during the illness and death of my father. I've never written in crisis mode before, and I thank you for helping me through that. Thanks, Kathleen, for helping me link the book's cover with the story. What a fun idea to tie the photograph into the plotline.

To Diane Flicker, "Realtor Extraordinaire." Your knowledge (particularly about mortgage fraud) has been so helpful.

To Larry Gonzales and April Upton. I knew little of the world of pharmaceuticals and the FDA approval process until I linked up with the two of you.

To Kay. Where do I begin? You know, of course, that you're the "real" Sheila in my life. You've given me so much more than just witty sayings and funny "Sheilaisms." You're a constant source of hope, encouragement, love, and support.

To all of my amazing Barbour editors, Becky Germany, Susan Downs, JoAnne Simmons, and Kelly Williams. How can I begin to thank you for walking me through this particularly difficult season of my life? You've given me so much, and I'm eternally grateful.

To my Lord and Savior Jesus Christ. You knew ahead of time everything I would be facing during the writing of this book—and you gave me this fun, lighthearted story to craft in the midst of it all. As Sheila would say: "The future will be better tomorrow"—and all the more, with Your hand in mine.

BYE, BYE LOVE

My daughter's fiancé had always been a bit of a prankster, but disappearing two weeks before their wedding day seemed a bit much, even for him.

I received the call on a Friday morning in late January while taking my dachshund, Sasha, to the groomer. The bride-to-be sounded beside herself. I tried to make sense of Brandi's frantic words but found myself in a blur of confusion.

"Honey, would you mind repeating that?" I shut off the car and shuffled the cell phone to my left ear, hoping to hear her better. "I must've misunderstood. Did you say Scott has disappeared?"

The trembling in my daughter's high-pitched voice evolved into full-fledged sobs. I wasn't sure what to make of it all. Brandi rarely cried, at least not openly. When she finally came up for air, I heard, "Y—yes! He's gone."

"Gone?"

"N—no one has seen him." I pulled the phone away from my

ear for a moment as another round of tears spilled forth on her end. "He didn't show up for work this morning. And he missed his ten o'clock tux fitting at BJ's Formal Wear. No one has laid eyes on him. No one."

I glanced down at my watch. 11:05. "I'm sure he just overslept." I spoke in my most motherly voice. "Happens all the time."

She gave a little sniffle. "I've called his apartment ten times. Maybe eleven. And I've called his cell phone more than that. It goes straight to his voice mail. He never lets it go to his voice mail when I call. Never!"

"But you told me just yesterday he's been having trouble with his cell phone," I reminded her. "Remember?"

"Oh yeah." I could hear her voice brighten right away. "I forgot about that."

"And what about those friends of his?" I offered. "You know how they are." His buddies thrived on playing practical jokes, but since they had morphed into groomsmen, their tricks had multiplied exponentially. Surely they'd had a hand in this.

"Jason says he hasn't seen him," Brandi said with a sniffle. "None of the guys have. And his car is missing from the parking lot at his apartment. Missing, Mom. Just like he is!"

I pulled my jacket tight around me, then climbed out of the car with Sasha's leash securely clutched in my hand. The pup's feet no sooner hit the icy walkway than she began to slip and slide, carrying me along behind her. "Whoa, girl!" We both skidded along until I finally caught my footing. With a shiver, I clutched her leash in one fist and my oversized leather purse in the other, all the while using my shoulder to press the cell phone to my ear.

"D–don't worry, Brandi," I panted as the dog pulled me this

way and that. "God is in control. I'm s—sure t—there's a logical explanation for this."

"But how do you know?"

I finally got my canine companion to slow down. After a couple of deep catch-up breaths, my lungs felt frozen from the inside out—not a pleasant feeling. But no time to worry about that right now, not with my daughter in a panic. I did my best to console her.

"I don't know for sure, but let's think this through. Scott probably just decided to hit the gym before work and got carried away on the elliptical machine. He's obsessed with working out, right?"

"Yeah."

I knew this firsthand, having visited the gym myself several times over the past few weeks in preparation for the wedding day. Scott and I often ended up side by side on the elliptical machines.

"Or maybe," I suggested with a lilt in my voice, "he had a dentist appointment he forgot to tell you about. It's got to be something like that." I shivered against the cold morning air as I made my way toward the puppy spa. *Mental note: Next time, skip the trendy jacket and go straight for the full-length coat.*

"O—okay." I heard her sigh of relief. "I know you're right, Mom. You're always right."

"I'm not so sure about the 'always' part, but I am sure Scott must have a reasonable explanation for all this. I love you, babe, and I'm praying."

As Brandi clicked off, I shook my head and sighed. With my twin daughters, Brandi and Candy, both in wedding-planning mode, pandemonium had taken hold of the Peterson household over the past few weeks. It seemed the closer we got to Daughter No. 1's Big Day, the more the tensions mounted. I often wondered if we would live through this season of our lives.

And my own escapades hadn't helped the situation. My budding career as Clarksborough, PA's "Crime Fighter Extraordinaire"—this according to the editorial staff at the *Clark County Gazette*—had only added to the chaos. I smiled as I thought about the strange twists and turns my life had taken of late. Somehow, in the midst of tracking down clues, I'd managed to keep my marriage and my editing business afloat, amazing my clients and putting a cock-eyed smile on the face of my wonderful husband. Always the comedian, Warren had even taken to calling me "Agatha Annie." I didn't mind. At first.

But my sleuthing days were behind me now. Crime fighting and wedding planning were never meant to be attempted simultaneously. This, I had already learned the hard way.

I shoved the cell phone in my purse and entered Coats 'n' Tails, where I passed off an unwilling Sasha to the groomer—a twenty-something female with more tattoos than anyone should be allowed by law. I gave her the necessary instructions: Flea dip. Nail clip. Red polish. Red sweater with faux fur trim. New red collar with Austrian crystals. Be back at two o'clock.

As I turned to leave, I pondered Brandi's final words: *I know you're right, Mom. You're always right.*

Hmm. The past few weeks had given me plenty of opportunity to prove myself wrong. What I didn't need, especially now, was another shot at it.

TO KNOW HIM IS TO LOVE HIM

C at got your tongue?"

"Hmm?" I looked across the table in the Clark County Diner into the eyes of my best friend, Sheila Fleming. "What?"

"Something's got ahold of you today," Sheila said with a knowing smile. "So fess up. What's up with you? Put off by my new hairdo?"

She primped, and I let out a little giggle. I had to confess that she looked pretty suave with her new highlights and contemporary style. Quite a contrast to the usual wouldn't-dream-of-missing-my-weekly-trip-to-the-beauty-salon hairdo. Still, I had other things on my mind.

"Nah, it's not your hair that has me preoccupied," I confessed. "It's something else altogether." I wasn't sure I wanted to spill the beans just yet. Sheila could be a great source of encouragement, but she also tended to want to get to the heart of things—and I wasn't sure I was up for that today.

9

"Is this wedding related?" She took a swig from her diet soda, then looked me in the eye with a hint of suspicion. "Are they wearing you out?" Next to Warren, Sheila knew me better than anyone else, so I didn't dare withhold information one minute longer.

"It's sort of wedding related," I said. "But doesn't have anything to do with being exhausted. It's something else altogether." I feigned a smile as I glanced at my watch. 12:16. "I just have the strangest feeling, Sheila."

"About?"

"Well, Brandi called a little while ago. . . ." I went on to tell her about the groom-to-be's unexplained absence, trying not to let the fear in my voice ring through.

"That's odd." Sheila doused her french fries with ketchup and gave me a thoughtful look. "But, come on. . . Scott's always cutting up. You know how he is. Don't you think, maybe, he's just horsing around? Remember what he did a couple of months ago?"

"What's that?" I nibbled at my grilled-chicken Caesar salad, waiting for her response.

"You remember. We were all supposed to meet up at that new Italian place on the highway after church, and he never showed up. Brandi was frantic."

"Right, right. I remember now. He thought we said Lee Yu's Garden, when we really said Leonardo's."

"Yes." Sheila nibbled on her chicken sandwich with a thoughtful look on her face. "Remember what he said when Brandi finally reached him by phone?"

"Yeah." I chuckled as the memory solidified in my mind. "He said the moo goo gai pan was out of this world. And I think he also mentioned that he'd invited the waiter to church."

"Well, that. . ." Sheila said. "But don't you remember the part where he asked what was taking us so long to get there?"

Now I laughed aloud. "Yes. I'd forgotten. He really thought we were the ones who got it wrong. I remember now."

"He's a brilliant guy," Sheila said. "Probably one of the smartest young men I've ever met. But, Annie. . ." She gave me a pensive stare. "He's a little on the goofy side. Scatterbrained, even."

"Yeah, I know." My heart warmed as I thought about it. "That's one of his most endearing traits. And besides, a lot of the brilliant ones are like that."

"I can't imagine anything has happened to him." Sheila swirled another french fry in the red blob of ketchup, making an interesting little design on the plate. "Surely he's just preoccupied with something."

"I don't know. If you'd asked me that an hour ago, I might've said yes. But now. . ." I couldn't explain the knot that had consumed my belly nor how it had tightened with each passing moment. "What if something *has* happened to him?"

Sheila, who always had a funny quip for every situation, simply shook her head. She leaned in to whisper, "Are you saying you think he's on the lam?"

I nearly choked on a piece of romaine. "I—I can't imagine he would just take off like that. He doesn't have it in him to leave Brandi at the altar."

Sheila shrugged. "You know what they say, 'Love is blind, but marriage is a real eye-opener.' Maybe he got cold feet." She dove off into a story about how she'd almost skipped out on her own ceremony a gazillion years ago due to prewedding jitters.

A little shiver ran down my spine as I thought about what she'd said. Scott had been acting a little distant lately. Even Warren had commented on it. But. . .to leave out of fear? Surely not.

Just then, my cell phone rang. My heart quickened as I reached for it. Perhaps Brandi had some news about Scott. I glanced at the caller ID. *Ah. Nadine Cunningham, mother of the groom.*

"Do you mind if I take this?"

"Of course not." Sheila popped another fry into her mouth, then shifted her attention out the window—to give me a little privacy, no doubt.

I answered the call, overjoyed to hear Nadine's beautiful southern drawl rolling out from the other end of the line.

"Annie, *dah*-lin, is that you?"

"Oh, honey." A former southerner myself, I slipped into gear right away. "I'm *so* glad you called. We're just be-*side* ourselves up here."

"I just got a call from Brandi. Now, what's all this I hear about my boy leavin' that a-*dah*-ra-ble daughter of yours stranded at the altar?"

"I'm not sure *stranded* is the right word," I tried to explain. "We simply don't know where he is."

"I'll tell you where he is." A giggle made its way across the telephone line. "He's up to tricks, that's where he is. Did I ever tell you about the time I lost him in a department store when he was ten?"

"No. I don't think so."

"I had everyone in the ladies' lingerie department searchin' for him, callin' out his name."

I'd never lost a child myself, so her story intrigued me. "What happened?" I asked with bated breath.

"Ah. Just about the time we'd given up all hope, he came a leapin' out from un-*duh* one of those circular racks of nightgowns, knocking a pink satin number halfway across the aisle. Scared me to death. I still remember it like it was yesterday."

"No doubt." I reached to pick up my coffee cup and took a sip.

"I went ahead and purchased the nightie," she added. "As a courtesy to the store clerk, of course."

"Of course."

"And then there was the time he ran off and joined the circus," Nadine continued.

"Surely you jest."

"No, *dah*-lin. He was twelve. One of those small-town circus troupes came through town, and he fell in love with the idea of working with the animals—said he wanted to be a veterinarian. And that's not the only time we lost him. Did you know about the ocean research boat thingy when he was seventeen?"

"Um, no." I could honestly say I didn't.

"Yep." She barely skipped a beat. "That boy of mine was always interested in science, and he heard about those ocean research boats—you know the ones, *dah*-lin, where they research the different species of fish. . . ?"

Um, not really.

"Well, he decided he could get hired on as a fishing hand. So he headed out to sea. Just one problem. . . He forgot to *tell* any of us."

"Nadine, that's awful."

"I know. But he's a little scattered like that. Easily distracted. Always has been. His teachers always said it was because his intelligence is so high. He bores easily."

"No doubt." I didn't question that for a second but was dying to hear the end of the story. "So, what happened?"

"Ah. Good news, bad news. Turned out Scott had a *teh*-rible case of seasickness. He lasted less than a week before they sent him back on a Coast Guard ship that happened to be passin' by. Why, I thought you knew all of this."

"Nope. I think I would've remembered a story like that."

After a little giggle on her end of the line, she continued. "And he's still up to tricks, even though he's a grown man. You should see the ri-*dic*-ulous text messages he leaves on my phone, just to torment me. He's a character, that boy!"

"Well, I always knew he had a sense of humor, of course," I acknowledged. "I guess I just never figured him to do something this, well. . .bold."

"Now listen, *dah*-lin'," she said. "Brad and I are plannin' to arrive at the Philadelphia airport one week from today. I would come earlier, but I'm runnin' for city council. Did I already mention that?"

"Yes. I've been getting your e-mails," I reminded her. I'd known for weeks she was running for office in the quintessentially southern city of Milby, Georgia, which sat in the shadow of nearby Savannah. "And I've been praying for you, honey. I'm sorry to hear about all the trouble you've been having."

"Oh, it's just politics," she said. "Tit for tat. But Brad *has* been a little concerned, to be sure. You know, he retired a few months back and has devoted several hours a week to my campaign."

"I'm sure he's a great asset, and it must be a lot of fun to work together." I tried to imagine what it might be like if Warren and I worked together but quickly squelched the thought. Some things just weren't meant to be attempted during the menopause years, at least not in our neck of the woods.

"Yes, but he does tend to be a worry-wart," she said. "Someone left a note on my windshield just this *mah*-nin'. Said I'd better drop out of the race if I knew what was good for me." She let out a strained laugh. "Can you even imagine? Someone thinkin' they could intimidate Nadine Cunningham like that? Why, they just don't know me. They're messin' with a child of the King here. He's got His angels encamped around me, ready to go to war on my behalf!"

"Amen."

"Now listen, *dah*-lin," she continued. "Here's what I want you to do. Tell that beautiful bride to play along. Tell her *not* to call Scott's phone or anything like that. Why, that's just what he wants, that little rapscallion."

"Are you sure?"

"Oh, honey," she said. "I'm his mama. I've been at this for years. That boy will carry on just as long as you let him. So don't let him, ya hear?"

"I hear." A sigh of relief slipped out as I contemplated her words. "You've sure relieved my mind, Nadine. Thank you so much for calling."

"You're very welcome," she said. "After all, we're about to be mothers-in-law. . .together! Why, that's the next best thing to sis-*tuhs*!"

"I'm sure you're right."

"Give my love to the girls," she cooed. "We'll see you in a week."

"I can't wait."

And at that, I clicked off.

Sheila looked at me with an inquisitive stare. "Well?"

"Nadine certainly put things in perspective for me," I said with a shrug. "Turns out, Scott has been MIA several times over the years. And that scatterbrained issue you were referring to seems to be more exaggerated than I thought. She assures me there's nothing to worry about." I nibbled at my salad, deep in thought.

"Well, then. . ." Sheila reached to give my hand a sympathetic squeeze. "If she says there's nothing to worry about, there's nothing to worry about."

I leaned back against the booth and took another sip of my now-cold coffee. Despite Nadine's comforting words, I still couldn't rid myself of the idea that something had gone terribly wrong.

LOVE AND MARRIAGE

After lunching with Sheila, I settled back into my car, turned up the heat, and pointed myself in the direction of Clarksborough Catering. Once there, I would face the now-familiar challenge of forking over fifteen hundred dollars—the final payment for Brandi and Scott's wedding reception dinner. This wouldn't be the first time I'd reluctantly passed off a fistful of greenbacks. For weeks, Warren and I had watched money trickle through our fingers like water from a leaky faucet.

Mother-of-the-bride tip: When making payments of this magnitude for your daughter's big day, swallow hard and pinch your eyes shut. This seems to alleviate much of the pain.

As always, I pushed aside my anxieties and focused on Brandi. She was worth it. And two weeks from tomorrow, she and Scott would walk down the aisle and proclaim their love for each other in one of the prettiest Valentine's Day ceremonies ever. The exquisite Be Our Guest wedding facility would be filled with well-wishers dressed in their winter best. Red rose petals would line the aisle. Candles would offer a romantic twinkle. Brandi would look radiant in her Cinderella-style dress, and Scott would beam in his black tuxedo, white shirt, and broad, red ascot.

Scott. I wonder if he's. . . Nope, I refused to let my mind go there. *He's fine, and that's all there is to it.*

I inched my way along, careful to take the snow-banked curves at a more-than-cautious speed. As I progressed, my thoughts shifted to the wedding once again. I contemplated my new role as mother of the brides. I'd slipped into it with great excitement and overwhelming joy. Sure, there were moments when I secretly longed for a quiet tropical-island retreat, but I'd pretty much decided it could wait till after the nuptials were behind us.

No, it wasn't the mother-of-the-brides role that concerned me. . .it was that "other" role—the one Nadine had referred to: *mother-in-law.*

What was it about the word that sent a shiver down my spine? Preconceived notions? Too many bad jokes, perhaps? A universal disdain for mothers-in-law in general? The stress of wondering if I'd ever cut the mustard in this area?

Surely I was not alone. Certainly every woman with a son or daughter of marrying age had contemplated what sort of mother-in-law she would make. I know I'd spent an exorbitant amount of time dwelling on the subject, particularly over the past few days. Still, for all my fretting, I couldn't get a handle on it. Just couldn't seem to wrap my brain around the idea that I'd soon be mothering a—a—*couple.*

Would I be the overbearing sort of mother-in-law, the kind who showed up at her daughter and son-in-law's apartment uninvited, ready to advise them on every conceivable thing, particularly on the things they did not care to be advised? Would I be the elusive sort, backing out of their lives until they wondered if I'd even remembered they existed? Or would I, perhaps, find myself someplace in the middle—the angelically perfect sort who somehow managed to put everything in harmonious balance—showing up only when invited and keeping my distance when privacy called for it?

Ah, how I strived for perfection, particularly where Scott was concerned. He appeared to be ideal son-in-law material—at least on the incoming side—and deserved the very best from me.

As I rounded yet another curve in the road, my thoughts shifted backward in time to the day Brandi had first ushered him through the door of our family's home. His shoulder-length shaggy hair, dark sunglasses, heavy gold chains, and too-much-chest-hair-showing, 70s-style shirt certainly made a. . .well. . .*vivid* first impression. I thought for a few seconds there my daughter had been shopping at the Don't-Bring-This-Boy-Home-to-Mama Store of Potential Boyfriends. But what really got me was the part where he pulled off the wig and glasses, revealing short-cropped hair and a boyish freckled face, and shouted a startling, "Gotcha!"

I'd loved him from that moment on. And I knew he loved me, too, which made letting go of Brandi a little easier.

A sigh escaped my lips as I pondered my rapidly emptying nest. My girls had been living in their own apartment for ages now, and, of course, I'd always known they would one day marry. I'd prayed for their mates since they were little. But to see them both tie the knot within months of each other? I hadn't signed on for the rapid-fire plan and had no point of reference. None of my friends had walked this road before me.

Still, I had to make the best of things, not just for me and my daughters, but for the men in our lives, as well. After all, my husband and son still had to eat. Still had to wear clean clothes. I had to keep my act together—for everyone's sake.

With these thoughts still fresh on my mind, I turned my car into the driveway of Janetta Mullins, good friend and Clarksborough's number one wedding caterer. I inched my way up her drive through the dirty, tire-crunched snow mush. Just as I reached to put the car into PARK, my cell phone rang. I answered to hear Brandi's frantic voice.

"Mom, Scott just sent me a text message."

"Praise God!" My hand immediately went to my heart as relief flooded over me. "I *told* you everything was fine."

"No, Mom, it's *not* fine. Something is terribly wrong."

"What do you mean?" I shuffled the phone to the other ear to hear her better. "What did he say?"

"It was so random." She began to sniffle. "It just said, 'I'm fine, but. . .'"

"I'm fine, *but*?" I repeated. "What does that mean?"

"You tell me." She erupted in tears. "I'm fine, *but*. . .I don't want to marry you?" she offered. "I'm fine, *but*. . .I can't go through with this because I'm in love with someone else?"

"Brandi, surely you don't really believe that. Scott has never given you any indication that he's, well. . ."

"Well, no." I could hear her blowing her nose in the background. "But I don't know what to think, Mom."

"Maybe he meant, 'I'm fine, *but*. . .I'll have to miss our dinner date because I'm at an appointment,'" I offered. " 'Or, I'm fine, *but*. . . I'm having trouble with my car.' See what I mean?"

"Or, 'I'm fine, *but* I had to get away to clear my head.'" She began to cry again.

"Honey, you're speculating," I said at last. "The point is, he's fine. That's the part you should be focusing on, not the *but*."

"How can I ignore the *but*?" she pleaded. "There's no ignoring the *but*!"

After a few more consoling words on my end, we closed out the call. I was pretty sure I'd convinced her not to panic. And knowing Scott had taken the time to send the message, odd or not, gave me a certain sense of peace.

Still, in spite of my assurance, I couldn't help but worry about the *but*.

Moments later, I sat inside Janetta's kitchen, sipping a cup of hot Earl Grey tea—heavy on the cream, of course—and talking about the wedding.

"Where's that daughter of yours?" Janetta asked.

"She couldn't get away from the office. You know, she's got that new job at the real estate company. . . ."

"Oh yes. She just got her Realtor license, didn't she?"

"Yep." I couldn't help but smile. "I think she'll make a great agent." I knew the Bible said that pride was a sin, but I couldn't help myself. I thought my daughters were excellent at just about anything they attempted. And I was especially proud of Brandi for her progress in the real estate field over the past few months.

"That girl could do anything she puts her mind to," Janetta observed. "She's probably the most determined young woman I've ever met."

"That's one way to put it." In truth, Brandi was a bit on the headstrong side. Perhaps the only reason I so rarely admitted it openly was because she and I were so very much alike.

Janetta pulled out a piece of paper and put on her let's-get-down-to-business face. "Do you have a final count?" She raked her fingers through her short, spiked hair.

"Three hundred seventy."

"Wow. A few more than you'd planned." She let out a chuckle, and her hoop earrings bobbed up and down. "Does Warren know?"

"Yeah. He's prepared for the worst. When I gave him the projected costs, I based it on four hundred, so he'll actually be pleasantly surprised. And besides, we didn't want to leave anyone out. There's nothing worse than forgetting to invite someone to your daughter's wedding."

Janetta nodded, then stuck the end of the pencil in her mouth and chewed on it as she looked over the paperwork. "Hmm."

"Problem?"

She pulled the pencil out and set it on the table. "No, just going over some things in my head. The ceremony starts at seven, right?"

"Yep."

"Probably lasting about half an hour?" She gave me an inquisitive look.

"Or a little less. You know how these things go. Months of planning—and all for a service that seems to pass by in the blink of an eye."

Janetta sighed. "I wouldn't know. Never had a wedding, remember?" She leaned back in her chair and shrugged.

"Aw. I'm sorry, honey." I reached to pat her arm, remembering her before-I-came-to-Christ testimony, with its twists and turns. "Maybe you will soon."

"I'm not sure what the Lord has in mind for me, at this point in my life," she said with a sigh. "To be honest, I've been on my own for so long, I wouldn't know what to do with a man if one fell in my lap."

I couldn't help but laugh at the image she'd just presented.

"I'm pretty set in my ways," Janetta continued. "Have my own style of doing things, you know?"

"True," I said with a wink. "But I hear your son has a few matchmaking tricks up his sleeve, so I wouldn't give up on the idea altogether."

Janetta slapped her forehead. "Jakey needs to leave that alone. Besides, we're in the throes of wedding planning for your girls. I certainly don't have time to contemplate a fella for myself."

"I'm just saying. . ."

When she looked up with a pointed glare, I let it go. Then, with a shrug, Janetta went back to work on her list.

"Wedding party will be at a separate table, right? Will they be going through the buffet line, or would you like them to be served?"

"Served."

"Okay, then. . ." She read the menu aloud. "Appetizer table will include a variety of cheeses and crackers, as well as a vegetable platter and dips. Dinner will include salad with Italian dressing, breadsticks, bow tie pasta with Alfredo sauce, chicken cacciatore, and cheese tortellini. And Italian meatballs, of course—in a portobello sauce."

"Man. That sounds amazing." My mind zipped backward in time to my own wedding. What was it we'd offered our guests? Ah yes. Cake and punch. And a few of those pastel-colored mints, of course. My, how things had changed.

She looked up with a wicked grin. "Didn't mean to tempt you."

"Trust me, any mention of food is a temptation at this point," I said. "I've been at the gym every day for the past two weeks. Got to fit into that mother-of-the-bride dress. Deliberately bought it one size too small."

"Risky."

"Yeah, I know. But a great motivational tool."

"Sheila said something funny the other day," Janetta said with a chuckle.

"She's a hoot, isn't she," I agreed, even before hearing what she had to say.

"Yeah." Janetta grinned. "She said that middle age is that time in our lives when broadness of the mind and narrowness of the waist change places."

"Oh, amen to that!" After a hearty laugh, I dove into a discussion about the beautiful red dress hanging in my closet. I shared every detail, right down to the tea-length skirt and delicate fur collar.

Two *ooh*s and three *aah*s later, my countenance must've changed. Janetta gave me a curious look.

"Is everything okay with you today, Annie? You seem a little distracted."

"Yes, I'm fine." I managed a shrug. "There's just a lot going on right now—and I'm having a hard time staying focused."

She dove into a story about a wedding she'd recently catered— honing in on the part where the mother of the bride had tried to run the show.

"At least you're not like *that* gal, Annie," she said. "You're the ideal mother of the bride. Just enough interest. Just enough distance. I think Brandi and Candy are really lucky to have you."

"Thanks." I then shared a story about my own wedding, how my mother-in-law had tried to take the reins, leaving me in the dust.

After several laughs, Janetta and I finally realized we'd completely deviated from our plans. I nearly came out of my skin as I glanced at my watch. "I can't believe I've let the time slip away from me!" I shot to my feet. "I've got to pick up Sasha at the groomer's; then I need to stop off at Brandi's office for a few minutes before heading home."

Janetta walked me out to the car, where we said our good-byes. For whatever reason, as I climbed in and buckled my seatbelt, I thought about that elusive word once again, the one I'd pondered all day. . . .

Mother-in-law.

Hmm. I slipped the car into gear and headed on my way.

LOVE IS A MANY SPLENDORED THING

At five minutes after two, I picked up Sasha from the groomer. My little darling greeted me, as always, with that pitiful what-took-you-so-long look. I swept her into my arms, babbling like a toddler over her new look—particularly the frilly red sweater and sparkling new collar. After paying the harried groomer, the dog and I headed out to the car for yet another drive across icy roads. Seemed like I'd spent a lot of time behind the wheel lately, and not under the best driving conditions.

Minutes later, after dropping my canine companion off at home, I met up with Brandi at her office. She'd only been working at Norton Realty for a few weeks, and I'd been looking for an excuse to pop in, though I would have preferred to visit under better circumstances.

She met me at the door with red, moist eyes. I reached to give her a hug. "I'm sure everything is fine," I whispered. "I talked to Nadine, and she said. . ."

"I know." Brandi reached up with a slender finger to dab the tear from her heavily mascaraed lashes. "I talked to her, too. I'm just a worrywart is all. And this is a pitiful time for Scott to be pulling a stunt like this. I don't know what he's thinking."

"Just trying to get a little attention, most likely." I offered up a warm smile. "He's quite a character, after all."

Her face lit up immediately. "Yeah. That he is."

I traipsed along behind Brandi as we entered the swanky office of Clark County's most prestigious realty company. She nodded at the receptionist—a girl whose name tag read BRIDGET—and we continued on our way. I noticed that Brandi kept her face tipped to the ground, a sure sign her eyes had filled with tears again.

I never said a word, just followed behind on her heels, hoping for a quick route to her new office. We passed by several others, though none paused from their own ponderings to speak. Finally, we arrived at the tiny space Norton Realty had graciously designated for Brandi. She took a seat behind the desk, and I sat across from her, mesmerized by the fact she'd already taken the time to decorate. Typical Brandi. When she and Candy had moved into their apartment a year ago, she'd had the place spiffed up in no time at all.

"This is great, honey." I looked around in genuine awe.

"Yeah." She glanced up with a silly smirk on her face. "I still can't believe they paid my way through the licensing process." She gestured to the framed certificates on the wall. One read REAL ESTATE FUNDAMENTALS and the other, REAL ESTATE PRACTICE. Each proudly boasted her name, along with a seal from the Pennsylvania Real Estate Commission.

My heart swelled with pride. "Before you know it, you'll be their top listing agent," I bragged. "I'd bet my red hat."

"You don't have a red hat, Mom." She offered up a little giggle, the first hopeful sign I'd seen from her all day.

"True. But most women my age do."

"Good grief." She let out a giggle. "I happen to know for a fact that you have to be at least fifty to get the red hat. You're not even old enough for a pink one."

"I never looked very good in pink anyway."

She shrugged and then looked at her watch once again. "I didn't mean to get off on all that. I really wanted to talk to you, Mom. I need you."

Mom, I need you. Ah, those magic words! They set my heart ablaze, as always.

Brandi's hands trembled as she continued, and my I-wonder-what's-up antenna rose. "I'm so worried about Scott. In spite of that text message."

"I know you are. I've been a little nervous, too."

At that very moment, I noticed a photograph of Brandi and Scott on the desk. I reached to pick it up, smiling as I took note of the shirt Scott was wearing. It was one of his favorites—a navy blue T-shirt with white lettering that read, "CLEVERLY DISGUISED AS A RESPONSIBLE ADULT." *That boy.* I replaced the picture frame where I'd found it and then turned to look at my daughter.

"Talking to Nadine really helped put things in perspective for me," I said. "She's full of similar stories about Scott. This isn't the first time he's pulled off a stunt like this. Trust me. He's got quite a history. She wants to make sure you don't play into his hands, says that's exactly what he's hoping for."

"I can see her point." Brandi bit her lip, and her eyes filled at once. "But there's something I didn't tell you earlier, and I think it might be the reason Scott has disappeared. What I'm about to tell you will put his text message into perspective, too, if I'm understanding it correctly, anyway."

What in the world? My supersleuthing skills kicked in right away. *If only I had my notebook with me, I'd jot down every word she's about to say.* "What is it?"

A little tear trickled down her cheek, and her voice trembled as she spoke. "L–last night, Scott and I got into a—a—f–fight."

"A fight?" I couldn't help but chuckle. "You two don't fight. You. . .debate."

"We did last night." She let out a sigh. "We had dinner with Candy and Garrett—and the guys started doing their usual thing—teasing us about our jobs, our taste in decorating, that sort of thing."

"What's new there?"

"Nothing. But then they dove into the wedding plans, challenging some of our opinions."

"Ah."

"And then one thing led to another. Before you knew it, Candy was mad at Garrett, and I was mad at Scott. It started so innocently. . . ."

"And I'm sure it ended innocently, too," I threw in. "This was just the usual bantering, right?" I had to confess, watching the boys when they were in prime form provided hours of entertainment for the rest of us, though my daughters had taken more than their share of ribbing over the past several weeks and months as wedding preparations mounted.

"I guess. But Scott said some things about my new job that hurt my feelings. I get the feeling he doesn't think I'm very good at what I do."

"What?" I couldn't believe it. Why, he was her biggest fan.

"Anyway, we kissed and made up before parting ways," she said. "Still, I can't help but think. . ." Tears began to flow again. "I can't help but think Scott was really more upset than he let on. I called him a—a. . ."

"What, honey?"

"A male chauvinist." She leaned her head down on the desk. "He was acting like one, so that's what I called him. But I didn't mean it. He's not really like that. He was just kidding about most of it. I know that now." She looked up, eyes overflowing. "What am I going to do if I've lost him, Mom? I don't think I could live without him."

Mother-of-the-bride tip: An ounce of encouragement is worth a pound of cure. And sometimes two ounces are worth. . .well. . .two pounds.

"Brandi, you haven't lost him. That boy is so in love with you he can't see straight. And he thinks you hung the moon. I see it in his eyes every time he looks your way. I honestly don't think this has a thing to do with whatever you might have been arguing about. I don't."

"Really?"

"Really." My nervous fingers reached to straighten a cup of pencils—just for something to do. "I think Nadine was right. Maybe he's capitalizing on the fact that you had a little tiff last night and is pulling a prank. He knows how to get to you, is all."

"He sure does." Here, her face lit into a brilliant smile.

"Remember that time he told me he was being transferred to Japan?"

"Good grief, yes. How could I forget it?" I gazed across the desk at my daughter, who suddenly wore a hopeful expression once again. "You were beside yourself, if memory serves me correctly. And all for naught."

"I know, Mom. You're right. You're always right."

Ack! Those words again!

Just then, a knock at the door interrupted my train of thought. The receptionist popped her head in with a rehearsed smile. Brandi looked up, startled.

"Yes, Bridget?"

"Mr. Norton wanted you to know that his client Malcolm Pfifer is waiting in the front office. He said the three of you have a meeting in his office in five minutes."

My sleuthing antennae rose immediately. Why would Brandi's wedding photographer be meeting her here, of all places?

"Right, right." Brandi snapped to attention. "I'm sorry."

"Also, you have a call on line four," Bridget added. "I tried to page you, but there's something wrong with the intercom system again. Sorry. One of these days, we'll get everything in this office working."

"Oh, that's fine. Who is it?"

Bridget shrugged. "Some guy. Sorry, he didn't leave a name."

Brandi's eyes sparkled with joy. She turned to face me and whispered, "Scott!" She grabbed the phone and squealed a joyous, "Hello!" Her smile faded after just a few seconds—and she dove into a chat with the person on the other end about a piece of property on the far end of town.

I settled back in my chair and looked around the room. Sheila would love this place. My best friend might have crazy clothing styles, but she was keen on decorating—anything and everything. In fact, when I'd recently shared the news that I planned to lose ten pounds before Brandi's wedding, she came back with, "You know my motto: "If you can't lose it—decorate it!" She would absolutely adore this office. I couldn't wait to bring her around for a look-see. When things settled down, of course.

As Brandi hung up the phone, I realized I'd probably overstayed my welcome. I stood up and reached for my purse. "I should go now. I didn't realize you had a meeting."

"I can't believe I forgot."

As I shuffled my purse strap onto my shoulder, I asked, "So, what's up with that? Are you having more pictures done?"

"Oh no, nothing like that. Malcolm only operates his photography studio part-time. He's really more interested in real estate investments—kind of like Mr. Norton. In fact, they're good friends. And Malcolm has been buying up quite a few homes in the area and then renting them out. He's in the process of purchasing a home from one of my clients—my first client, actually. But we've run into some snags."

"I'm sure you'll get it all worked out. I'm so proud of you, honey."

Right away, her smile faded. "I hate it that my very first deal has turned out to be so complicated. And I'm on such a crazy learning curve. Maybe Scott was right. Maybe I'm no good at this real estate thing."

"Don't go there, Brandi. You know he doesn't think that."

"Still. . ." She chewed on her fingernails, a childhood habit, and then let her hands fall to the desk with a look of exasperation on her face. "Malcolm is having a doozy of a time getting financed, which has the seller pretty upset, as you might imagine."

"Strange."

"I wouldn't be stressing over this, but we owe him so much," she said with a sigh.

"Oh?" *Remind me.*

"Sure. He's the one who helped Scott plan the proposal, remember?"

"Oh, right! At the Fall Festival." Pfifer had set up one of those back-in-time photo booths, and Scott had jumped at the chance to do something memorable.

Brandi grinned as she spoke. "I still remember the look on Scott's face when he suggested we put on those hokey bride and groom costumes to have our pictures taken. I went along with it, but I secretly thought he was nuts." She let out a little chuckle, the first laugh I'd heard from her in awhile. "That wedding dress was probably just as ugly thirty or forty years ago when it was worn the first time."

"Yep. Saw the photo." Even in sepia tones, the dress left something to be desired.

"And that *suit* they made him put on!" She made a face. "It kind of reminded me of that pin-striped number Grandpa Hubert wore in his wedding picture."

"Hey now," I warned. "Your grandmother thought he looked mighty handsome."

"Still. . ." She paused for a moment, and seemed to disappear into her thoughts. "I felt like a goober posing for those shots, till Scott dropped down on one knee and put the ring on my finger."

She held out her left hand and stared at the beautiful marquise diamond, tears welling.

"Aw, honey. . ."

"Suddenly I got it," she whispered. "He'd planned the whole thing." She dabbed at her eyes. "Well, with Pfifer's help. Which is why we *have* to make this deal work for him." She looked up with a shrug. "And for my client, too, of course. I want everyone to be happy."

"Of course you do. And you will make it work. I know you will. You're the best. Don't be discouraged. Remember, 'I can do all things through Christ which strengtheneth me.' You've known that Bible verse since you were a kid."

"I know you're right, but I guess I needed the reminder. Thanks, Mom."

We wrapped up our chat, and Brandi followed me out into the hallway. I turned back to ask her one final question.

"Hey, do you want to go to the gym with me in the morning? We can go really early—before work."

"I don't know, Mom. I don't think I'm up for it."

"Okay." I gave a little shrug. "I'll try to go anyway. I'm still working on fitting into that mother-of-the-bride dress."

"Trust me, I understand."

We made our way down the hallway, passing Malcolm Pfifer as he entered Norton's office door. As I swished my way by him, he offered up a polite nod and said, "Great to see you again, Mrs. Peterson."

Brandi gave him a smile and a wave. I turned toward the lobby, then looked back to give Brandi a wink and a thumbs-up. After nodding my way, she disappeared into Norton's inner sanctum.

I headed out the door, motherly pride leading the way. Yes, with my encouragement, Brandi would surely be Norton Realty's top-selling agent before long.

CHAPTER 5

CRAZY LITTLE THING CALLED LOVE

O kay, Agatha Annie, spill your guts."

I looked up from the dishwasher into my husband's mischievous eyes.

"W—whatever do you mean?" I pressed a drinking glass into a spot on the top rack of the dishwasher.

"You hardly said a word through dinner, and that's just not like you."

Um, thanks.

He drew close and slipped his arm around my waist, planting a couple of kisses into my hair. "Something must be up. Wedding plans getting to you?"

"No, it's not that." I carried on loading the dishwasher, hoping he wouldn't press the issue. Despite his words of reassurance, I still couldn't squelch the knot that took up residence in my stomach every time I thought about Scott's disappearance. What had seemed like a harmless prank this morning felt more like a full-blown crime this evening. It wasn't just the text message, though that bothered me, too. I couldn't shake the feeling that he had run into some sort of trouble. Something was keeping him from us. No matter how you sliced it, we still had one MIA groom.

"Are you missing your work?"

"No." As much as I loved my work-from-home job as a free-lance editor, I was really glad I'd arranged my schedule so that I could have a couple of weeks off before Wedding No. 1. In fact, I don't know how I could have accomplished everything at once.

"Ah. So, it's this thing about Scott then, isn't it?" Warren tipped my chin in his hand and gazed into my eyes. "You're worried, aren't you?"

I nodded and did my best to push down the lump in my throat. "What if it's not a joke, Warren?" My words came out more rushed than I'd planned, and I couldn't seem to hide the tremor in my voice, though I tried valiantly. "What if something has happened to him? Don't you think we should call the police—see if his car has been involved in an accident or something?"

"I did that a couple of hours ago."

"You're kidding." I reached to dry my hands with a dish towel.

"Nope." Warren shook his head. "I called from the bank before I left for the afternoon. Talked to Sergeant O'Henry."

"What did he say?"

"Well, he checked the computer and said there hadn't been an accident in all of Clark County involving that particular model of SUV. I also talked to him about filing a missing-persons report."

"You did?" I gave my hubby an admiring gaze. If Warren kept this up, he might very well surpass me with his crime-fighting skills. *Hmm.* I couldn't let that happen.

"Yep. O'Henry said we have to wait twenty-four hours before we can file the paperwork. That's standard with adults. But he felt pretty confident. . .well. . ." Warren's gaze shifted a bit as he said, "He doesn't think we're dealing with any sort of foul play here."

Hmm. I looked directly into my husband's eyes, trying to understand his meaning. "He thinks Scott has cold feet, doesn't he?"

After a deep sigh, Warren nodded. "Yes. And I can't help but wonder. . ." He shook his head. "So many things don't add up here, Annie. That text message was a little on the suspicious side. And grooms don't just disappear two weeks before the big day unless they, well. . ."

I leaned my head against his chest and sighed. "I hate to even think like that. What in the world would Brandi do?"

The idea that she'd been abandoned by the man she loved seemed unfathomable. On the other hand. . . I went on to tell Warren about Brandi and Scott's tiff and shared Brandi's concerns that she might have caused his disappearance.

"I'll tell you what. . ." Warren's jaw tightened as he spoke. "If that boy has done anything to hurt Brandi, I'll—I'll. . ." He simply shook his head, and I noticed his face turning red. For a moment, he looked like a top, about to blow.

"Have you taken your blood pressure medicine?" I asked, growing nervous.

"Yes, of course." He drew in a deep breath, and the normal color returned to his face. "I'm a Christian man," he said, "but I'm also a father. If anyone ever hurt either of my girls, I don't know what I'd do."

"I understand, honey. I feel the same way."

"It's killing me to think that Brandi might get hurt." He

paused long enough to rake his fingers through his hair. "But it kills me even more to think that something bad has happened to Scott. I don't know what in the world any of us would do without him, especially Brandi." Warren's eyes moistened.

For a moment, neither of us said a word. His expression finally relaxed, and he shrugged. "For now, it's easier to believe he's just trying to pull something over on us. But just in case, I think we need to contact his parents."

"I talked to Nadine this afternoon. They're not planning to come for another week."

"Hmm." He shook his head. "Let's sleep on this and then decide whether or not we should convince them otherwise. My gut tells me his mom and dad should be here, especially if there's no word from him by the morning."

"Okay."

I finished up the dishes, then scooped some Moo-lennium Crunch ice cream into two bowls—a nightly ritual at the Peterson household, regardless of the season. In light of my hope-I-can-fit-into-that-mother-of-the-bride-dress dilemma, I opted for half a bowl. Warren and I cuddled up next to each other on the sofa, also a nightly ritual.

Not two spoonfuls into the dreamy mixture, the phone rang. Right away, my nerves kicked in. I glanced at the caller ID, relieved to see daughter Candy's cell phone number. I answered right away, doing my best to sound upbeat and positive.

"Hi, honey."

"Hey, Mom. I'm actually calling for Brandi. She's just too. . . well. . .too worked up to talk right now."

"Are you with her?" I set the ice cream bowl down on the

coffee table and focused on the conversation. "I wanted to tell her that a couple of presents arrived this afternoon—one from my great-aunt Mary in Indianapolis and another from some cousin of Scott's."

"I'll tell her. She's right here." Candy's words became breathless as she shot out the next part. "We've been cruising around town in Garrett's car. And I think we've stumbled onto a clue of sorts."

Goodness. I've birthed a whole family of crime solvers. "What's happened?"

"We've found Scott's SUV."

"What?" I sat up straight, then mouthed the words, "They found his car," to Warren. "Where was it?"

"Down the street from the pharmaceutical company where he works. It was off on a side road, all by itself. Keys were in the ignition. We drove up to McKinley and talked to the security guard. He said he hadn't seen a thing."

"That's so odd." I leaned back against the sofa, more confused than ever. "Did you call the police?"

"Yes. They're here now. They're having the car towed to the sheriff's office, so they can dust it for fingerprints. And they're searching the woods where the car was found. Not easy, in this weather."

I couldn't help but sigh as I thought about how this must be affecting my girls. "How is Brandi taking this news?"

I knew the answer even before Candy spoke it. "She's really struggling, Mom. And I think she's beyond thinking this is some sort of joke. If not for the car being found, she might think he was cruising around town with his friends or something, but now. . ."

Now everything had changed.

"There's a big mess going on at Scott's workplace," Candy reminded me. "And Brandi's worried this might have something to do with that. I guess worried would be an understatement. She's pretty much lost it."

"Do your best to keep her calm." If anyone could do that, Candy could. My girls were polar opposites in personality, but that often came in handy. I paused to think about what Candy had said about the pharmaceutical company. Though she'd made a valid point, I wasn't quite ready to let my thoughts take me in that direction just yet.

"What about his apartment?" I asked. "Have you gone by there?"

"Several times. He's not there. Brandi has a key, so we were able to get inside. . . ."

"And?"

"Nothing." She let out an exasperated sigh. "The apartment is a wreck, but then again, it always is. That boy. . ." She went off on a tangent about Scott's inability to keep anything clean, then finally halted. "I'm sorry, Mom. I just don't know what to think."

"Do you think his mom and stepfather should be called?" I asked.

"Actually, we were kind of hoping you and Dad would go ahead and take care of that. We hate to bother them, especially with everything Nadine is going through down in Georgia, but things are kind of reaching a scary point now."

Yes, they are. I changed gears, hoping to improve the tone of the conversation. "Honey, God is in control of all of this." I bounced the words off my tongue with confidence exuding from every pore. "He knows where Scott is. And He's going to get him here in time for the wedding—mark my words."

A long pause on the other end of the line let me know Candy wasn't so sure. "I hope you're right, Mom."

Hey, whatever happened to "You're always right, Mom"?

"Stay strong for your sister," I urged. "And let me know if there's anything I can do."

"Just keep praying." I could hear the catch in her throat. "Just keep praying."

"Of course." I hung up the phone and looked at Warren, my eyes wide with the realization of what we were facing. He immediately swept me into his arms.

"Looks like you have some work to do, Agatha Annie," he whispered in my ear. "Better get to it."

STAND BY ME

You know how people always say, "No news is good news"? Well, that little catchphrase doesn't offer much consolation when a family member has gone missing. No news is just that. . .no news. And "no news" is tough to take when you're sitting on the edge of your seat waiting for, well, news.

I awoke Saturday morning with the keen sense that my world was, once again, about to change. Though I dreaded putting my Agatha-Annie cap back on, I felt I had no other choice. Words from my past flitted through my brain, holding me captive to their lure: *Just the facts, ma'am. Just the facts.*

With a sigh, I eased myself from the bed—careful not to wake Warren—and reached for my spiral "sleuthing" notebook, still filled with notes from my recent crime-fighting escapades. I hated to think something had happened to Scott, but I at least had to consider the possibility. And considering the possibility meant I had to put together a plan of action—one that started with listing

43

the facts as they presented themselves.

I stole away into the kitchen, pausing long enough to open the back door so that Sasha could wriggle her way outside into the iced-over yard to do her morning business. Though it was too early for a phone call, I reached for my cell phone anyway. I needed to talk to Brandi—needed to find out if anything had transpired during the night.

Five seconds into the tearful call, I knew nothing had changed. I prayed with her before hanging up, my words rushed and heart-felt. In truth, I felt like I'd swallowed an avocado seed—the lump in my throat had grown to such enormous proportions.

Afterward, with *Just the Facts, Ma'am* leading the way, I picked up an ink pen and began to scribble some facts into my notebook.

Fact #1: Scott is a prankster. He would love nothing more than to get his family and friends stirred up two weeks before his wedding day, just for fun.

Fact #2: Scott's groomsmen are equally as rambunctious. I wouldn't put it past them to have "kidnapped" him for a few days to put one over on Brandi.

Fact #3: Scott and Brandi engaged in a lover's tiff the night before his disappearance. There is some thought that he has headed off for some time alone—to clear his head. His random text message would appear to confirm that.

Fact #4: Scott's SUV has been located near McKinley Pharmaceutical Company, where he works. No one actually saw him in or with the car. A search in the woods turned up nothing. Police have confiscated the vehicle for the time being.

I paused to chew on the end of my pen as I contemplated what Candy had said about Scott's problems at work. He *had* shared a few choice tidbits of information with us over the past few weeks, so I had some indication of the problem, though I hate to think his disappearance might have anything in the world to do with all of that. Still, I had to write down the facts—all the facts. Quickly I penned:

> *Fact #5: Scott has been working on a project for McKinley Pharmaceutical Company—handling a new heart-related drug that should receive FDA approval within weeks, if not days. Perhaps his disappearance has something to do with his job.*

The idea terrified me, but I could not leave it alone. I stared at what I'd written and grew more worried by the second. Had someone at McKinley harmed him in some way, in an attempt to thwart his efforts? Surely not.

Again, I paused to think. I drew in a few calming breaths and tried to focus on the whole picture. While all of these things rang true, none of them seemed particularly logical or even threatening. My eyes scanned the page, landing again on the words *Scott is a prankster*. I couldn't seem to let go of the idea that he was up to tricks, even now. Costly tricks—at least to his bride-to-be's emotions—but tricks nonetheless.

Just then, Warren entered the room, his wavy hair standing atop his head in a scraggly mess.

" 'Morning." He yawned, then leaned down for a good-morning kiss.

"Oh. Morning breath." I made a face, and he pulled back with a grimace.

"Sorry. I forgot." He gave me a funny look. "Not going to the gym this morning?"

"Nah. I have other things on my mind today. There will be plenty of time for that later on this week."

"Ah." He looked down at my notebook. "Any word?" When I shook my head, he said, "So. . ."

"So." I closed the notebook. "Nothing to get excited about. I was just putting my thoughts down on paper." I looked up at him with a sheepish grin, then paused for a moment before asking the question on my mind. "Hey, do you remember Scott saying something the other night about that new heart-related drug his pharmaceutical company was testing? That FDA thing?"

Warren's eyes lit up as the memory registered. "Yes. Something went wrong at the last minute, didn't it?"

"Yes."

"A handful of research patients had a bad reaction to it, if memory serves me correctly. One man almost died." Warren's brow wrinkled as he tried to remember the details.

Suddenly I remembered. "Yes, it almost destroyed his liver. I just remember that Scott seemed really worried about it a few nights ago when we had dinner. He could hardly concentrate."

"Right." My husband gazed into my eyes with suspicious curiosity. "What made you think of that?"

"I'm not sure." I stood and tucked the notebook under my arm. "I'm just thinking out loud."

"Uh-huh. Sure you are." He padded into the kitchen, opened the refrigerator door, and pulled out a package of bacon. "Hungry?"

"Always." I sighed as I looked at the bacon. "But I'm dieting, remember? I've got to fit into that dress two weeks from today."

I felt like a lightning bolt hit me as I spoke the words. Two weeks from today, exactly. We would all be decked out in our finest. But what kind of ceremony would it be, with a missing groom?

"You don't need to diet, Annie," Warren said, as he reached for the carton of eggs. "You're perfect just like you are."

Good grief. My daughter thinks I'm always right, and my husband thinks I'm perfect? Have I slipped off into the twilight zone? I mumbled a gentle, "Thank you," then smiled. There were worse things they could be saying, after all.

As Warren set about cooking bacon and eggs, I leaned my elbows against the bar and stared at him in silence. Finally, he turned my way.

"I can only hope you're thinking about calling Scott's parents."

I nodded and sighed. That man could read me like a book. "Yeah. I think they should be updated, anyway. And if they decide to fly in early, all the better."

He wiped his hands on a dishcloth and nodded in agreement. "Would you like to do the deed, or should I?"

The aroma of bacon slowly filled the room, and temptation hit right away. "I'll call them," I offered. "I don't mind." I practically sprinted from the room to fetch the portable phone. Once retrieved, I carried it into the office, as far from the scent of bacon as I could manage.

I punched in Nadine's number with some degree of apprehension. I didn't want to alarm her, but she and Brad should both be made aware of the situation. She answered on the third ring.

"Annie, *dah*-lin!"

What did we ever do without caller ID?

"Nadine, I hope I didn't wake you." I eased my way into the rolling chair behind the desk and kicked up my feet.

"Wake me? Are you joshing? I've been up for hours. There's work to be done! Never a dull moment here, honey."

No dull moments here, either. "I hate to interrupt your work, especially in light of all you're up against, but there's something I need to run by you." I then dove into the story, doing my best not to alarm her, but stating the facts as I knew them. By the end of the call, I was talking to a much more subdued Nadine.

"Brad and I will come right away, hon," she said. "Would you mind bookin' a hotel room for us?"

"Hotel?" I stammered. "No way! You will stay with us. We want you to be close by."

"Thank you, *dah*-lin." For the first time, I picked up the fear in her voice. "And, Annie. . ."

"Yes, honey?"

"Pray. Please pray."

My heart quickened as I responded, "Already have, but I'll keep it up."

We ended the call, and I padded back into the kitchen to find Warren seated at the breakfast table, a monstrous plate of bacon, fried eggs, and toast in front of him. He gestured for me to sit across from him. I smiled as I looked at the plate he had prepared for me—one hard-boiled egg, half a piece of dry toast, and one crisp slice of bacon. In light of a bit of recent elevation in blood pressure on Warren's part, I had to wonder if we might not be better off switching plates, but I didn't say so. There would be plenty of time to mother him later. Right now, I simply needed to join him for a bite to eat.

"Only one hundred and fifty calories," he bragged as he pointed to my plate. "I read the packages."

I gave him a kiss on the top of his head, then sat across from him, taking my time with the food. *Mental note: A little can go a long way when consumed slowly.*

As we ate, I filled Warren in on my phone conversation, including the part where I'd offered our home instead of a hotel. He nodded in understanding.

"I think that's a good idea. We'll want to be close. And I'll enjoy having Brad here. He and Scott are so much alike, it's uncanny."

"Particularly in light of the fact that Brad isn't his real father," I reminded him.

"Oh." The realization registered in Warren's eyes. "That's right. I'd forgotten."

Both of us grew silent after that, and my mind began to wander, as always. Where in the world was my son-in-law-to-be? And when in the world would we ever see him again?

WHEN WILL I SEE YOU AGAIN?

A nnie, *dah*-lin', I'm here!" Nadine Cunningham waved with zeal as Warren and I approached the baggage claim area at the Philadelphia airport. Brad stood at her side, clutching a couple of overstuffed rolling bags, his silver hair glistening underneath the incandescent glow of the lighting overhead and his smile as wide as the Potomac.

I sprinted their way, a little surprised at the surge of joy in my heart as Nadine and I met for a goodness-gracious-it's-good-to-see-you-again hug.

"Have you heard anything?" she asked as we pulled back to gaze into one another's eyes.

In true sisterly fashion, I brushed a loose hair from her eye. "Not a word, I'm afraid. Other than one very mysterious text message, but I think Brandi already told you about that."

"She did." Nadine shook her head, and I noticed a lone tear, which she flicked away with a cherry red fingernail. "I was hoping he would have called by now."

"Me, too," I whispered. I took her by the arm and offered a bit of encouragement. "I feel so much better now that you're here. Two heads are better than one, right?"

"Right." She gave me a reassuring smile—her bright white teeth a stark contrast to the rose-colored lipstick. "And I just know we'll find that boy—wherever he's hiding."

My heart quickened. "Do you still think he's up to tricks?"

I picked up on the I'm-not-so-sure-anymore look in her eyes, but she shrugged and said, "I'm hoping. I'd hate to think of any other options. Though, if this is a trick. . ." Her eyes narrowed slightly. "It far outdoes any of his previous ones. And it borders on cruelty, if you want my opinion."

I'd thought as much but never voiced it. And from the look on Warren's face, he'd given the matter more than a fair amount of thought. Still, I couldn't help but conclude the obvious. Scott was fun loving, not cruel.

Just then a loud bell sounded, and the baggage carousel took off running. Seconds later, luggage appeared at the top of the conveyor belt. Brad kept an eye on each bag that slipped down the ramp, while Nadine seemed to have other things on her mind. She turned to glance my way, a curious look on her face.

"I *knew* something about you had changed!" she said at last. "You've done your hair differently since I saw you last." She stepped back to give me a thorough once-over. "I love it, hon!"

"Thank you." I gave a little twirl to show off the shorter-than-usual, choppy style. "I'm trying to branch out in my old age."

"Old age, my eye." She let out a laugh that rang across the clanging of bags and raised voices of passengers. "Why, you're a good five years younger than I am."

"Really?" I almost broke the cardinal thou-shalt-not–ask-a-lady-her-age rule. Almost. But something distracted me. At that very moment, something off in the distance caught my eye. A stocky, blond fellow on the far side of the room with a camera in hand. It seemed to be pointed straight at us. *Am I seeing things? Surely he's snapping a photo of someone else.*

Odd. He appeared to be taking shots of us, whether intentional or coincidental, I couldn't tell. I gestured for Brad and Nadine to look his way, but they were distracted by their luggage, which had just made an appearance.

"Heavens, girlfriend!" I looked at the three overstuffed bags Brad pointed out, each abnormally large. "You pack like I do."

Brad let out a little snort as he reached to fetch the bags from the carousel. "No comment."

"I didn't know how long we would be stayin'." Nadine fidgeted with her oversized designer handbag, which kept slipping off her shoulder. "And I wanted to be prepared. Could be we'll stay on through the weddin'." Her eyes misted over again. "Once Scott shows up, I mean."

"He will, honey. I feel sure of it." I gave her an encouraging pat—really trying to reassure myself, as well.

As we walked to the parking garage, I kept a watchful eye on Nadine. Despite her forced smile, I could tell her thinking had changed from our first phone conversation. This wasn't another one of Scott's running-off-to-join-the-circus escapades. No, the more time elapsed, the more convinced I became. We were dealing with something of a sinister nature here.

As we approached the car, I noticed a fellow off in the distance.

Is that the same guy with the camera? I strained to see him, but a passing car blocked my view. When I looked up again, he had disappeared.

Warren popped open the trunk of our car and helped Brad with the cumbersome luggage; then we all climbed into the car for the ride home.

"As soon as we get to Clarksborough, I'd like to go by Scott's apartment," Nadine said. "If you don't mind."

"Of course we don't mind," I assured her. "And I don't think Sergeant O'Henry will, either. He's already been through the place with a fine-tooth comb and determined there was no foul play."

"Still. . . ," Nadine said. "I'd feel better if I took a look myself."

"I'll have Brandi meet us there. She has a key." Another knot consumed my stomach as I thought about the fact that his apartment would be hers soon, as well. *If* we had a wedding.

Nadine nodded, putting on her most confident face. "I just know there will be some clue as to his whereabouts," she said. "I'm sure of it."

"I pray you're right."

"Should I call O'Henry?" Warren offered. "Have him meet us there, just in case?"

"Hmm." I pondered the idea. "Maybe we could make that decision after we get there, depending on what turns up."

He nodded, but I could sense his anxiety in the way he gripped the steering wheel. I also sensed the obvious—he was uncomfortable around Scott's parents. *Easy, honey. Even if Scott is up to something, his parents aren't.*

As we headed onto the turnpike out of Philly, I took advantage of the uncomfortable silence in the car to ask Nadine about her campaign. I'd had a hard time from the get-go figuring out why she had opted to enter the world of politics.

I leaned back against the seat, ready for a long ride and detailed conversation. "Whatever made you decide to run for city council?"

The edges of her lips curled up in a smile. "Well, I stumbled onto the idea by accident, really."

"Stumbled into politics?" She probably wasn't the first with such a testimony. I'd give her story a listen, though I doubted I'd be able to concentrate for any length of time, what with my mind being in such a whirlwind and all.

Nadine nodded, and her blond hair—really, more ash-blond—rested easily against her shoulders. "I showed up at a city council meeting a few months back to protest a new policy related to the homeless," she explained. "Apparently—from what I've been told, anyway—I made such a good argument for my case that a reporter caught wind of it and spoke to me afterward. He said it jokingly, of course. . . ." She looked up at Brad with a sheepish grin. "But he said, 'Lady, you make more sense than any of those people sitting in there. Why don't *you* run for office?' "

"Quite flattering," I offered.

"Oh yes," she said. "I went home from the meeting and told Brad what he'd said, and we both had a good laugh. Can you imagine, *dah*-lin? Me? Running for city council?"

I couldn't help but laugh. Despite her polished appearance and genuine southern charm, I still couldn't picture Nadine Cunningham sitting in a dull city council meeting, even in a designer business suit with matching attaché case.

Brad interjected his thoughts as he gave her a playful wink.

"This girl of mine." He gave a little shrug. "Whenever she gets an idea, she just runs with it. If you need a Bible study teacher, she's your gal. If you need someone to head up a women's luncheon, she's the ideal candidate, trust me." His features tightened slightly at this point, as did his voice. "But I wasn't so sure about this working with the homeless thing. I still remember the day she told me she wanted to take on several hours a week at the shelter. Boggled my mind, really."

"Brad thought I was joshin'," Nadine added, "but I wasn't. I've always had such a heart for the down-and-out, and our church was putting together a program in the inner city. I wanted to be a part of it!"

Brad shrugged. "Like I said, she's quite a leader. Before you knew it, she had half the church volunteering at the homeless shelter, cooking, washing clothes, even teaching the men some worship choruses. I had no idea the woman could play the keyboard and sing." He shook his head, though the glimmer of pride never left his eyes.

"Why, there's a lot about me you don't know, then!" Nadine said with a giggle.

"No doubt. Though I have the rest of my life to figure you out." He reached over to give her a tender kiss on the cheek. "She's always taken very seriously that scripture about being salt and light."

"Why, of course I do, *dah*-lin," Nadine cooed. "How could I not, when the Lord has made it so very clear that we're to care for those less fortunate than ourselves?" Immediately, she dove into a scripture, which she quoted from memory, her eyes ablaze with excitement. " 'If you spend yourselves in behalf of the hungry. . .' " Here, she put her hand to her heart. " '. . .and satisfy the needs of the oppressed, then your light will *rise* in the darkness. . .'" Her hand lifted dramatically. "'. . .and your night will become like the noonday.'"

"Wow." This gal really knew her verses. And her speaking skills weren't bad, either. She would certainly make a fine politician, no doubt about it.

"Isaiah 58:10," she threw in with a smile. "My mandate. Truly, the mandate for us all." Again, her hand went to her heart.

Warren whispered a gentle "Amen," and I saw his shoulders relax. *Good girl, Nadine. You've won Warren over, and that's really something, current circumstances considered.*

I managed a smile, though I felt—as I so often did in her presence—that I certainly came up lacking in the evangelism department, at least in light of all of her good works.

Nadine turned to face me. "The city of Milby has been workin' to rid itself of what they call 'the homeless problem'—but they're going about it all wrong. Someone needed to set them straight."

I reached over to pat her hand. "And you're just the girl to do it." A little chuckle rose up from the back of my throat, and I gave her hand an encouraging squeeze. "Why, I think you could sell just about anything to anyone. You're a born salesperson. And God will use you to convince others to do the right thing, I feel sure of it."

"I pray you're right." She turned her attention out the window and sighed. "My intentions are good, to be sure. But I've had to remind myself that people will judge me by my actions, not my intentions. I might have a heart of gold—but so does a hard-boiled egg."

I couldn't help but laugh at the image she'd presented. "You're not a hard-boiled egg, honey. You're over easy."

Her response surprised me. "And that's not neces-*sar*-ily a good thing." She turned back with tears in her eyes. "I need to toughen up, or I'll never last." She shook her head with a disgusted look in her eye, one I'd never seen before. "I will just never understand why some people take it upon themselves to tear others down in order to build themselves up, that's all. These past few weeks, my adversaries have really come out swingin'—and it's been so ridiculous. They've got the historical society backing them up, which is such a shame. I'd hoped to win those fine folks over to my way of thinkin'."

Brad shook his head. "I told her just a week ago that I would fully support her if she decided to back out of the campaign—and I meant it. This whole thing has taken quite a toll on her emotions and her health. And if they keep this up. . ." He shook his head, clearly disgusted. To his credit, he didn't continue on with his thoughts.

I gave Nadine's fingers another light squeeze and leaned back against the car seat. "Girl, you're from the south. You are gracious, hospitable, and kind. And you're not the type to repay evil with evil."

"Which doesn't neces-*sar*-ily make me an ideal candidate for political office." She offered up a shrug. "So many of those folks are downright *de*-vious."

"I disagree. I would argue that it makes you the ideal candidate for office." My voice intensified as I grew more emotional. "Why, the city of Milby needs someone like you. You have the biggest heart in the world, and you're smart to boot."

Brad broke into raucous laughter. "Annie, if you weren't so busy planning weddings and solving crimes, we'd move you down to Georgia to take over the role of campaign manager. Heaven knows, our current one isn't doing the best job."

I squared my shoulders and gave him a determined look. "And if I weren't so busy planning weddings and solving mysteries, I'd take you up on that offer. Why, there's nothing I love more than to see a child of God step up to the plate and fill a political office. Just warms my heart."

Once I had significantly encouraged Nadine, our conversation shifted back to Scott's disappearance.

"I've been wondering if the news about Scott has hit your local papers yet." Nadine flashed a worried look.

"So far, so good," I said. "But once word gets out we've got a missing groom on our hands. . ."

Warren shook his head. "I just hope we don't end up with a media circus in our little town," he said.

"I've put Devin on phone patrol," I threw in. "Just in case. He's been told to stick to 'no comment' as a response to any and all question from media folks."

Nadine bit her lip and nodded.

"Reporters, local or national, could go a long way with a missing-groom story," Warren added, "and I hate to think of what that would do to Brandi, especially if Scott really is just taking some time away to himself."

"Is that what you're thinking?" Nadine gave him an inquisitive look.

Warren shrugged, and an uncomfortable silence filled the car once again.

Nadine gave my hand another squeeze, and unspoken words traveled between us. We spent the rest of the trip back to Clarksborough coming up with a plan of action—something to make us feel useful during the hours of waiting. As we pulled into town, I telephoned Brandi, who agreed to meet us at Scott's place, key in hand. Minutes later, we all entered the apartment.

I looked around the tiny chaotic space in horror, noticing clothes on the floor, books strewed about, and even dirty dishes on the coffee table. "Wow," I started, "this place is a. . ."

"A wreck." Warren finished my sentence for me. "Do you think the police did this?"

"Heavens, no," Nadine said with a chuckle as she looked around. "This is Scott's doing, all right. He's always been a little messy."

"A little?" Warren scratched his head.

"Yes," Nadine said. "His idea of housecleaning has always been to sweep the room with a glance." She laughed at her own pun.

Frankly, I couldn't imagine Brandi living like this. My very meticulous daughter would likely dive into housework with a vengeance as soon as they were married.

Brad shook his head. "Kind of reminds me of that prank he used to play with the vacuum cleaner when he was in his teens. What did he call it, again?"

"Crop dusting." Nadine pursed her lips, then faced me to explain. "He'd set the vacuum to work in reverse so that all of its contents would blow out onto the floor. Kind of looked like. . ." She glanced around the room. "Well, like *this*."

"Yes," Brad agreed. "Scott was always a little. . .discombob-ulated." He gestured to the clutter. "Messy. Scattered. Couldn't keep things straight. Man, you should've seen his room as a teenager."

I could only imagine, based on what I was seeing now.

"It's a wonder he did so well in school," Nadine added. "But I hear the brilliant ones—the truly brilliant ones—are often like this."

"The super-intelligent ones are always a little quirky," I concurred.

My hand went to my mouth immediately, as I realized my words could have been taken offensively. Nope. No one seemed to be bothered by little old me. They all continued to pick through the apartment in search of clues.

Though we worked at it for a while, we found nothing that seemed out of the ordinary in Scott's whole apartment.

"I guess we can nix the idea of calling O'Henry," Warren acknowledged.

I offered up a nod.

Brandi reached for a photograph on Scott's bedside table and shifted it my way. "Mom, look. Remember this? We were just talking about it yesterday afternoon."

"Oh yes." I remembered the picture well. Why, it was the very one Pfifer had taken the night Scott proposed.

"He looks so happy," she said—and tears began to flow. "*We* look so happy."

"Oh, honey." Nadine wrapped Brandi in her arms. "Scott has been deliriously happy with you. Why, you're the best thing that ever happened to that boy. So rest your mind. He hasn't. . ." Her gaze shifted to the ground. "He hasn't run off—not in the way you're thinking, anyway." She looked around the apartment with a sigh. "I'm still inclined to believe he's playing a prank, especially now that I've seen his apartment. Nothing here lends itself to the suspicious."

"I hope you're right." Brandi looked up with a feigned smile.

Warren's jaw tightened; though, to his credit, he didn't utter a word. Instead, he slipped an arm around our daughter's shoulder and planted a kiss on her forehead.

"Just wait till the two of you are on the beach in Cozumel a couple of weeks from now," Nadine said with a wink. "This whole fiasco will all be a distant memory."

"Cozumel?" Brandi's eyes lit. "Is *that* where we're going? He wouldn't tell me! I even tried to pry it out of Jason and the other guys, but they wouldn't say a word, either."

"Oh my stars!" Nadine, who'd turned white as a sheet, clamped a hand over her mouth and groaned. "I've gone and done it now, haven't I!"

Brad slipped an arm over her shoulder and gave her a peck on the cheek. "Yep, you've done it all right." He looked over at Brandi. "But she doesn't look like she's opposed to the idea of traveling to the Yucatan."

"Of course not! It sounds amazing." Brandi nodded, and I saw an expectant ray of hope in her eyes—the first happy sign all day.

Thank You for that, Lord. She needs something to look forward to.

We wrapped things up at the apartment, and I gave Sergeant O'Henry a call on my cell phone, asking if he'd be so kind as to meet us at our place later this evening for a chat. He readily agreed. Together we headed back home for some much-needed rest.

How Can You Mend a Broken Heart?

Even with the calming addition of Scott's parents—and the chatter that ensued as we met together—our nerves remained on edge all Saturday afternoon and evening. Every time the phone rang or there was a knock at the door, we all came out of our skin. And there were plenty of knocks on the door to unnerve us. Seemed like every hour or so another wedding present was delivered—adorned with ribbons and bows. Would this parade of packages ever end? Worse still, would the groom arrive on the scene in time to open them?

None of us could believe Scott remained MIA; the whole thing felt strangely surreal. Why, at any moment, I half expected him to pop in from some bizarre place where he'd been hiding all along—like the tiny closet under the stairway or out from under one of the beds, perhaps. I could imagine the grin on his face and the *Gotcha!* glimmer in his eye. I actually prayed that very thing might happen.

Sadly, the hours moved forward without a trace of the groom-to-be, and with each minute that ticked by, the creases in the foreheads of all in attendance grew that much deeper. I refused to be anything but positive and upbeat, at least in front of an audience. However, I found myself reaching for a tissue a couple of times in private. I even slipped off to my bedroom once to call Scott's cell phone, just on the off chance he might actually pick up.

No such luck.

At eight o'clock, our entire family, along with Scott's parents and Sergeant O'Henry, gathered in our living room for a powwow. Added to the mix were my son Devin's best friends—Jake Mullins and Jake's perky blond girlfriend, Nikki Rogers. The two spent most of their time together making goo-goo eyes at one another, but I still thought they might be of some assistance to us, given Nikki's job as security guard at the Clark County Savings and Loan and Jake's street savvy.

Nadine and I had taken special care to make sure Brandi had absolutely no alone time all afternoon. Even now, she sat wedged between us on the sofa, tissues in hand and eyes red and swollen. Clutched in her fist was the proposal-night photo, which she planned to pass off to O'Henry.

Warren and Brad sat across from us in the two wingback chairs, and the kids pulled in extra seating from the dining room table. Candy and Garrett, doing all they could to calm our nerves, perhaps, circulated around the room, offering everyone flavored coffees and hors d'oeuvres. The tray of mini quiches and egg rolls trembled in Candy's hand as she eased it my way. *Steady, girl.*

Devin, growing teenage boy that he was—took more than his share. I watched him load up his plate with goodies. From across the room, I gave him a silent, motherly warning with my eyes, one I'd perfected over the years. He slipped a couple of egg rolls back onto the platter with a sigh, then sat on the floor to make more room for the others.

I took one of the egg rolls just to be polite, though I doubted I'd be able to eat any of it. I thought back to Warren's meager breakfast offering this morning—dry toast and a hard-boiled egg—and my stomach growled. Had I really not eaten since then? I should be starving, but nothing sounded appealing right now.

I wrapped the egg roll in a napkin and set it on the coffee table, hoping my daughter wouldn't notice and take offense. *Mother-of-the-bride tip: When your soon-to-be-married daughter takes the time to cook for you, either (a) eat what she has provided or (b) hide it away so that she doesn't see.*

Not that Candy appeared to be paying a bit of attention to me. I noticed, instead, she shot a glance Brandi's way every few seconds with genuine concern in her eyes. *God bless those girls of mine.* Though they most often bickered like cats in a back alley, they ultimately adored each other, even after all the twin jokes they had endured.

I settled onto the sofa, draping an arm around Brandi's shoulder as Warren brought the room to attention. He led us in prayer, and then O'Henry stood to address us. The good sergeant—still in uniform after a long day's work—paced the plush beige carpet until I thought he might wear a path in it with his heavy black boots.

"I filed the missing-persons report this morning," he explained. "Had to wait twenty-four hours, you understand. State law. But it's been filed now, and the state police are aware of Scott's disappearance." He looked at Brandi. "Did you bring that photo I asked for?"

"Yes." She passed the picture off to him, and I could see the curiosity on his face.

"Is this the best picture you have? It's not very clear. And the coloring is off."

I had wondered about those same things but hadn't voiced my thoughts because I didn't want to run the risk of further upsetting Brandi. I could get another photo of Scott into O'Henry's hands, if need be. For that matter, Nadine could probably do the same.

Brandi shrugged. "I've got more at my apartment, but I like this one." She went on to explain her logic, and I could sense the passion in her voice as she told the story of the night Scott had proposed.

"We'll make do, then." O'Henry shoved it into a manila envelope and dove into a lengthy explanation about the county's policy on missing persons.

"Will they really look for him?" Brandi dabbed at her eyes with a tissue. "I mean, I know the police always get right to it on television shows, but are they really like that in the real world?"

O'Henry nodded as he took a tiny spinach quiche from the tray on the coffee table and popped it into his mouth. "I can assure you," he spoke around the bits of food, "we at the Clark County Sheriff's Office will do everything in our power to track down Scott."

"Thank you," Brandi whispered.

"We had a question about the media," Warren ventured. "How long do you think it'll be before this story leaks to the *Gazette*?"

O'Henry drew in a deep breath. "Won't be long before one of

those nosy reporters gets ahold of it. We'll be putting up missing person posters, that sort of thing. There's sure to be some media fallout."

"That's exactly what we're hoping to avoid," Warren said.

I flashed a worried look Brandi's way. She seemed to take the news in stride.

"We'll do our best to keep the story local," O'Henry spoke with assurance. "But I can't make any promises. And besides, when a person goes missing, it's always good to get their face out there in front of the public." He pulled out his steno pad. "Now, if you don't mind, there are a few questions I need to ask."

I scrambled for my pad, as well. Wouldn't hurt to jot down a few thoughts along the way, just in case.

"I understand from our earlier conversation that the two of you had a lover's spat the night before Scott disappeared." O'Henry gazed into Brandi's eyes with some degree of suspicion. For a minute there, I wanted to slap the man. How dare he!

"W—well. . ."

My daughter looked at me for moral support, but I shifted my gaze back down to the pad in my hand. *Annie, you're such a coward.*

"Look, Officer," Candy interrupted with a more-than-terse look on her face. "I think your question has an accusatory tone to it. Why don't you just come out and say what's on your mind?"

You go, Candy!

The entire roomful of us sat up a little straighter and looked at him in anticipation of his next words.

"It has entered my mind," he started, "that Scott has put together this rather complicated plan in order to escape. . . ."

"From marrying me—is that what you mean?" Brandi glanced his way, her eyes blazing with anger.

I patted her on the arm to calm her a bit. She pulled away in a huff. I couldn't say I blamed her.

"I was thinking of something less dramatic than that, actually." O'Henry's tone softened right away. "The words in his text message are pretty convincing. He's fine, *but*. . . The *but* leads me to believe he's just needing his space."

"Thanks a lot," Brandi muttered.

O'Henry shrugged, as if by way of apology. "Some men get a little nervous in the last days before their wedding and just need time to clear their heads. I'm pretty sure he will turn up in a day or two with a dozen red roses in his hand—and all will be forgiven." The smug officer folded his arms against his chest, obviously satisfied with himself for coming up with such a remarkable— though completely off-the-mark—explanation.

"You're forgetting about his car," Garrett said. "If you're suggesting he made a getaway, then he had to have made it on a bus. You've got his SUV, remember?"

"Yes, and we've dusted it for prints," O'Henry said. "So far, we haven't turned up anything. In fact, I'm not sure how the car factors into all of this. But maybe he's left town with a friend, or something like that," O'Henry suggested. "Could be he's traveling with someone."

"Are you implying another woman?" Brandi's lips tightened, and I feared for a moment she might spring out of her seat in the officer's direction. "Because if you are. . ."

"No, no. . ." O'Henry put his hands up in the air, obviously taken aback by her reaction. "I'm not saying that. I'm just saying that a coworker or friend might have offered to slip him out of town for a quiet getaway, allow him some time to clear his head and think things through or something." He reached for another quiche, then swallowed it whole.

"Ludicrous." Warren spoke the word, and everyone in the room turned to look his way.

You know, some men don't need an expansive vocabulary. In this case, one word would certainly do.

O'Henry shrugged and wiped his sticky finger on his pant leg. "I'm just guesstimating, Warren. Thinking out loud. Please don't hold me to any of this."

As our small-town-cop-turned-detective rambled on, I did my best to overlook his earlier comments. Surely he was just doing his job, turning over every stone. And who could blame him? The evidence really *did* lend itself to a runaway groom, though I hated to admit it.

In dazed curiosity, I watched as the napkin around my egg roll took on a mind of its own and began to unwrap itself. *So much for hiding the evidence.* As if on cue, O'Henry reached down and snatched it in his right hand. "Mind if I eat this?"

Before I could answer, he popped it into his mouth.

"Um, well. . ." I gave a little shrug. "I suppose not." I couldn't help but wonder what he would have done if I'd given a different answer.

Then again, I couldn't help but wonder at a number of things. One thing, in particular, plagued me tonight—like a tiny ant nibbling away at my toes. That man at the airport—the one with the camera in his hand. Who was he, and what was he up to?

I know he was taking our picture. I know it.

Just a coincidence? Maybe. Or maybe not.

Out of the corner of my eye, I watched Nadine reach for a quiche from the tray and take a bite off the edge. I looked up into her creased brow and offered up a silent prayer on her behalf.

Again, my thoughts shifted as I contemplated all she had shared with me in the car on the way home from the airport. I pondered a couple of things, in particular. *Hmm.* Was it possible? Had I overlooked something, perhaps?

I suddenly felt led to add something to my notes from earlier this morning. After making sure no one was watching, I scribbled the following into my crime-solving notebook:

Fact #6: Nadine Cunningham's political views could very well have put her family at risk. Perhaps Scott has been kidnapped in an attempt to distract her from running for office.

Yikes. I hated to consider the possibility, but there it was, staring me in the face. I looked up into Nadine's eyes, still damp and red. She gave me a woeful shrug, and my heart began to ache as I pondered the "what-ifs." What if I had to walk a mile in her shoes? What if one of my *own* had turned up missing?

Immediately I realized the truth of it: Scott Cunningham *was* one of my own—and the realization that I'd possibly already lost him nearly split my heart in two.

TEARS ON MY PILLOW

Sheila always said that experience was a wonderful thing because it enabled you to recognize a mistake when you made it again.

I couldn't help but agree. After all, I'd made plenty of mistakes, particularly over the past several months. Probably met my lifetime quota, in fact. Take, for instance, the time I'd suspected my husband of stealing a $25,000 night deposit in order to pay for our daughters' weddings. And that other time, when I left the dog tied to the flagpole at the bank because of my distraction with a suspect.

Yep, I had certainly missed the mark on more than one occasion, which was why I wanted to step very carefully into my Agatha-Annie role now, if that was what the Lord required of me. I would certainly need to ask for His thoughts on the matter before taking any steps forward.

I went to bed on Saturday night with both my cell phone and the house phone on the bedside table, just in case I received a call at some point. Sergeant O'Henry had promised to call us the minute he had any news at all, and I certainly didn't want to miss that.

As my head met the pillow, I wrestled with the Lord over Scott's disappearance, honing in on the dilemma I now faced as to whether or not God was *really* asking me to help figure all of this out versus the possibility that I had slipped over the crime-fighting edge. I lay quite still for several minutes until Warren's steady breathing assured me he had truly fallen asleep. Then I willed myself to join him. A good night's sleep. . .and the answer would come in the morning, no doubt.

Ten minutes later, I stared at the clock in frustration. Another ten passed. Then another.

Unable to rest, I finally sat up in bed and reached for my Bible, which I had nestled in between the two telephones. I snapped the little nightstand lamp on and blinked several times to rid myself of the flashing effect the bulb had on my eyes.

Call it a fluke. Call it a God-thing. But my Bible literally fell open to the fifteenth chapter of Luke—the story of the lost sheep. I felt my breath catch in my throat as I read.

> *"Suppose one of you has a hundred sheep and loses one of them. Does he not leave the ninety-nine in the open country and go after the lost sheep until he finds it? And when he finds it, he joyfully puts it on his shoulders and goes home. Then he calls his friends and neighbors together and says, 'Rejoice with me; I have found my lost sheep.'"*

Of course I knew the passage referred to a sinner in need of saving—but I couldn't help but wonder if the Lord might be trying to speak something else to me, as well. Would I drop everything in pursuit of my future son-in-law? Would I lay down my desires and insecurities and do all I could to solve this crime—if indeed it was a crime?

Of course I would.

Resolved to the idea, I turned off the light and leaned back on the pillow for a time of prayer. I sought the Lord for His direction, His timing, and a heightened sense of discernment. I asked for a strategic plan of action and the courage to see it through. Finally content, I felt my eyes grow heavy.

I awoke to the sound of Nadine rapping on my bedroom door.

"Annie, *dah*-lin?" she called out. "Are you awake?"

I popped up in the bed, startled by the interruption. It felt like I'd just fallen asleep minutes before, but the sun streaming in through the bedroom window let me know several hours had indeed passed.

Warren, never one to awaken easily, let out a snore and rolled over. I wished I could do the same but chose to tend to the needs of my guests.

"I'm awake," I called out. "Hang on." I leaped from the bed and sprinted to the door, then flung it open—hoping she had some news for me.

"I'm sorry to bother you," she whispered, "but Brad has been up for nearly an hour and is aching for some coffee. We can't seem to locate any."

"Ah." I reached for my robe and tiptoed into the hallway. As we made our way toward the kitchen, I took her hand and whispered, "I thought perhaps you'd heard from Scott."

"No." Her bloodshot eyes brimmed, and she gave my hand a gentle, sisterly squeeze. "I kept my cell phone next to the bed, but he never called."

"I did the same."

With a sigh, I led the way into the kitchen, where Brad sat at the table in his flannel pj's with the Sunday paper spread out across the table.

"Sorry to keep you waiting," I said with an apologetic smile.

He glanced up with a look of embarrassment on his face. "Don't think a thing about it. I hope she didn't wake you." He gestured to the paper, which was open to the sports page. "Hope you don't mind. I fetched it from your driveway."

"Of course not! Help yourself. My paper is your paper."

He pointed to the article about tonight's big game, and I suddenly remembered. "Super Bowl! It's Super Bowl Sunday."

"Sure is."

"Brad's favorite day of the year," Nadine interjected. "He and Scott would always. . ." She stopped herself short, then put on a determined face. "Anyway, it's his favorite day of the year, which explains why the man was up with the chickens."

With a shrug, I reached into the pantry and fished around behind the containers of flavored teas until I came up with the bag of coffee. "And don't fret over waking me. My alarm was set to go off in just a few minutes anyway. And trust me, once Warren smells the coffee brewing, he'll make an entrance."

True to form, my husband joined us minutes later, his salt-and-pepper waves sticking up this way and that. We went through our usual morning-breath kissing routine, then settled down with huge mugs of coffee to start the day.

Warren glanced through the newspaper in silence. I knew he was looking to see if the story had broken yet. Thankfully, it had not. I knew because I'd already checked. After a few minutes, he turned his attention to the sports page headline, giving Brad a cheerful thumbs-up. Then he dove into a zealous dissertation about his favorite team.

Didn't take long, however, to figure out the two men were rooting for opposite teams. *Hmm. Might be problematic.*

No sooner had we emptied the coffeepot than Devin staggered into the room in a bit of an early morning stupor. The wrinkles in his cheek let me know he'd only just crawled out of bed—and probably not to spend time with us, if I had to guess.

" 'Mornin', son," I ventured.

He rubbed at his eyes and grunted in response, then moved in the direction of the coffeepot, which he found to be empty. "W–what? No coffee?" My typically easygoing son turned to me with panic in his eyes.

You know, it doesn't take much to get a twenty-first-century eighteen-year-old male riled up. Just try taking away his morning coffee. Like father, like son, I guess. When I was eighteen, I hardly knew what the stuff was. But kids these days. . .

I sprang from my seat and started another pot, and Devin eventually joined us at the table. Within minutes, Nadine had him laughing and talking—about football, no less. What was it about this amazing woman? She seemed to be able to weave some sort of spell over us all. Even football foes were ready to sign a truce when she was on the job.

I smiled as I realized the truth of it: Her constituents would be just as taken by her as the rest of us—if she ever made it to office.

The men went on talking about the Super Bowl game once again, and I turned my thoughts to Scott's disappearance. Nadine grew silent, and I couldn't help but notice her expression shifted from overtly serious to a near-whimsical look. *Is that a glimmer in her eye?*

"Thinking about something?" I asked as I reached to touch her hand.

"Mm-hmm." With a lilt in her voice, she went on to tell us a rather humorous story about a time when Scott had rigged the handheld sprayer on their sink so that she got hit in the face with a forceful spray when she turned the water on.

I had to laugh, only because Devin had once done the same thing to me.

"He's always been a real card," Nadine said with a smile. "Did I ever tell you about the time he put our cat into the dryer for a spin?"

"Um, no."

"He was only six at the time," she explained. "And it didn't really hurt the little kitty, leastways not that we could tell." Her lips pursed as she thought about it a bit longer. "Though, to be quite honest, Fluffy did appear to have a bit of an equi-*lib*-rium problem after that. As I recall, he was always runnin' into things."

I chuckled at the irony of the name *Fluffy,* and Devin let out a snort of laughter. Eventually, we all joined in.

As if out of sympathy for poor Fluffy, Sasha made an appearance at the table. I looked down into her woeful face, realizing she was overdue for a trip to the backyard. I stood and opened the back door, noting that we'd had a serious snowfall overnight. "Heavens!" I turned back to look at Warren. "If it's this bad in the back, I'll bet the driveway is iced over."

"It is," Brad agreed. "I nearly broke my neck trying to snag the morning paper."

Warren let out a sigh. "I'll have to deal with it. I can't miss church this morning. I'm teaching Sunday school, remember?"

"Ah, that's right. I'd forgotten." As Sasha made her way back inside, I turned to close the door. Just then, something from across the yard caught my attention. *What in the world?*

A dark-haired man—stick-figure tall and thin—shot across the back of our snow-covered yard, headed for the gate on the side of the house. *Oh no, you don't!* I sprang out into the snow, my robe flapping in the February wind and my house shoes cutting out a path for all to see.

"Annie, what are you doing?" Warren hollered. He stepped out onto the back porch, slipping and sliding every which way.

I rounded the edge of the house, never pausing to answer. I had to catch up with the stranger, if it was the last thing I did. "W—wait! Stop!" I cried out at the top of my lungs, but the bitter cold air caught the words in my throat.

Just then, Sasha raced beyond me, barking like a maniac. *You go, Sasha!* She managed to catch the edge of the fellow's trousers in her teeth, snarling like a dachshund possessed. Just as the fellow reached the gate, he managed to shake her loose. He slammed the gate shut, but Sasha, clever little thing that she was, managed to squeeze underneath it, wriggling through the snow like a gopher in a bed of mulch. I could hear her yapping all the way across the front lawn.

"Annie!" Warren appeared behind me, just as the fellow disappeared from view. "What in the world? Who are you chasing?"

I doubled over, the cold air now biting all the way down into my lungs and my feet icy cold and wet from the snow. "D—didn't you s—see h—him?"

"Him?" Warren's dazed expression reflected his clueless state. "I didn't see a thing—except you, sprinting like a high school track star."

I gave him a thanks-for-the-compliment grin, still panting. "Thanks. But I'm not as fast as I used to be. Maybe a few more days at the gym. . ." I looked again toward the gate for signs of Sasha's return. No such luck. I could still hear her barking off in the distance.

"I'll get her," Warren offered. "You get back in the house and change into something warm. We don't need you catching your death. . ." He paused as he gave the words a second thought. "We don't need you sick."

"Okay." I stumbled back through my markings in the snow and found Devin, Nadine, and Brad waiting for me on the back porch, their eyes bugged so wide I could almost see myself in them.

"Mom?" Devin gave me that has-my-mother-lost-her-mind-again look. I opted to ignore him.

"*Dah*-lin, you've got to be freezing." Nadine slipped an arm around my shoulders. "Get in here, and I'll refill your cup with hot coffee."

Everyone spent the next several minutes questioning, consoling, and warming me. When my teeth finally stopped chattering, I looked at them all with pleading in my eyes. I had to make them understand—I simply *had* to. "There really *was* someone there," I explained. "I promise."

"No need to say anything else, Annie." Warren entered the back door with a cold and very wet dachshund in his arms, handed her off to Devin, then gripped my hand. "I found his tracks in the snow. Lots of 'em. Must've been a big guy, gauging from his boot prints."

"He was." I nodded emphatically. "He was huge. Six foot three, maybe. Or six foot four!" Funny, the longer I thought about him, the taller he grew.

We debated for several minutes over whether or not to call Sergeant O'Henry, finally opting not to bother him, at least not yet.

"Could've been someone looking for shelter from the cold," Brad offered.

"Or maybe the paper delivery boy got mixed up?" Nadine suggested.

Neither sounded—or felt—right. I knew what I had seen. That man was here to spy on us. No doubt in my mind. A little shiver ran down my spine as the truth settled in. Just the thought of someone prowling around in my backyard unnerved me.

Warren glanced at the wall clock and groaned. "I can't believe it's this late. I still have to get dressed for church." He gave me a look that asked, *Are you still coming with me?* I answered with a nod. If ever I needed my brothers and sisters in the Lord, today was the day.

"We'll all go," Brad chimed in. "I think it would be wrong not to."

"I agree," Nadine added, giving me a pat on the shoulder.

They all raced from the room to dress for church, but I couldn't seem to move. Instead, I leaned back in my seat, dumped another tablespoon of flavored creamer into my coffee, and pondered all that had happened. I thought back to my middle-of-the-night prayer vigil, where the Lord had given me a clear go-ahead to jump aboard the Agatha-Annie train.

Another shiver rippled down my back as I reflected on the prowler once again. This was *one* train I wasn't so sure I wanted to board.

CRYING IN THE CHAPEL

Later that morning, Sheila met me in the foyer of the church, her eyes full of questions. With no explanation at all, she took me by the arm and pulled me away from my family for a one-word discussion. "Well?"

"Well, what?" I pulled off my gloves and shook them dry.

"You know what." As she leaned in close to whisper the words, one of her long dangly earrings caught in her fur collar. She wriggled it free, then got down to business. "Has there been any word from Scott?"

When I shook my head, Sheila headed off with outstretched arms to greet Nadine, as if they'd known each other for years. I could scarcely imagine these two women as potential buddies, but Nadine seemed to take to my eclectic friend right away, even going so far as to offer a gracious compliment about Sheila's black sequined jacket.

"Don't you love it?" Sheila turned in an animated circle so that we could all see the intricate beadwork on the back. "I just bought it yesterday."

"*Dah*-lin, it's divine!" Nadine cooed. "These teal sequins are *pre*-cious, and your broomstick skirt is so colorful! You must tell me where you shop, so that I'll know where to go while I'm here. Why, I do believe an outfit like that would really suit my effervescent campaign strategy."

Sheila dove into a lengthy discussion about a local dress shop, and Nadine countered with a political story. Within minutes, I'd been completely factored out of the equation.

Not that I minded. I turned my attention to the sanctuary, where the opening music let me know the service was about to begin.

Sheila clamped a hand over her mouth as she glanced through the open door. "I can't believe I'm standing out here. I'm going to miss my entrance."

Oh no, oh no. Don't tell me you're going to sing special music. Not this morning. . .

"I've been commissioned by the women's ministry to announce the upcoming Valentine's banquet." She turned to face Nadine, her voice now laced with assurance. "But don't you fret. We've taken Brandi and Scott's wedding into consideration. The church's banquet will be held the night before, on February 13. We don't want anything to interfere with the big day!"

Nadine's eyes filled with tears right away, and Sheila realized at once what she'd done. "Oh m—my," she stammered. "I'd forgotten that Scott was. . .well. . ." Clamping a hand to her mouth seemed to be her only option. Well, that, and sprinting up the center aisle of the church, out of view.

"She means well." I gave a little shrug, unable to think of anything else to say.

Nadine dabbed at her eyes, then took me by the arm. "I think your friend is *dah*-lin'."

On our way to the pew, we passed Candy and Garrett, who were engrossed in a conversation with Pastor Miller. He nodded my way and whispered, "I'm praying," as I passed. I thanked him and took my seat.

Once we'd all settled in, I looked around the sanctuary. There seemed to be fewer people here than usual—probably the bad weather. But one new worshipper caught my eye—a strikingly handsome Asian gentleman in his early thirties sat alone in one of the pews to our right. He stared down at the bulletin in his hand, looking a little uncomfortable with his surroundings.

"Hey," I gestured across the room but kept my voice low as I leaned in to Warren. "Isn't that the guy Scott pointed out to us last week? The waiter from Lee Yu's Garden?"

Warren looked over, then nodded. "Yes. I can't remember his name. Started with a T, I think."

A little shiver ran down my spine as I looked at the fellow. Was he somehow involved in Scott's disappearance? It seemed a little too convenient that he'd made his appearance just days before the chaos began. All throughout the service, I tried to remember the guy's name. Tai? Nah, that wasn't it. Tim? Too plain. As soon as the service ended, I shot his way to reintroduce myself. "Annie Peterson," I said with a friendly nod. "We met last week."

"Ah." He nodded and then extended his hand my direction for a firm shake. "Tomi Yu," he reminded me. He glanced around the room, looking a little lost. "Is Scott here this morning? I really need to tell him something."

For a moment, I contemplated telling him about Scott's absence but then decided against it, just in case he'd come to spy on us. "Oh?" It was the only word I could muster, in light of the fact that my crime-fighting antennae had shot straight up into the air at his mention of Scott's name. Somehow I just knew this fellow was about to give me a critical piece of information.

Tomi's eyes narrowed, and he leaned in close to share his story. "I've been looking for Scott for days. Something kind of odd happened at the restaurant the other evening. A man stopped by, asking a lot of questions about Scott. . . ."

"No kidding. What did he look like?" I reached in my purse for my notebook. "Did he happen to be a really tall man?" Visions of this morning's prowler shot through my mind.

Tomi had just opened his mouth to answer when Sheila appeared at my side, all atwitter about tonight's upcoming Super Bowl game. She dove into an exaggerated tale about one of the players, and I watched out of the corner of my eye as a fellow parishioner distracted Tomi, pulling him into a different conversation altogether.

When the moment was right, I clutched Sheila by the arm and looked directly into her eyes. "Sheila, I love you, but I was right in the middle of something."

"Well." She put her hands on her hips and stared at me in disbelief. "I do apologize." She glanced Tomi's way, then looked back at me. "Let me guess. Solving crimes again or ordering take-out for tonight's football crowd?"

"W–what?"

She gestured to her right. "That's Tomi Yu, right? His father owns Lee Yu's Garden. . . ."

"He's the owner's *son*?" I looked back at Tomi with newfound admiration. "He's not just a waiter?"

"Of course not. I've known the Yus for years." Sheila paused to giggle at her inadvertent alliteration, then forged ahead. "Orin and I love their kung pao chicken. It's the best in Clark County. And their shrimp fried rice is great, too." Her eyes blazed with excitement. "That's why I was so excited to hear Scott had invited Tomi to church. We'd been praying for the Yus for years." She chuckled as she realized she'd said it again.

"Goodness."

She leaned in to whisper with a gleam in her eye. "The family is quite well-off, and Lee is about to retire, which sets Tomi in line to take over the family business. Though I hear he would rather go away to medical school."

"Medical school?" I glanced his way once again, trying to figure his age. Thirty-two, maybe. Or thirty-three. "Isn't he a little old for. . ."

"He never had the opportunity to finish his schooling, and I think he's always regretted it. His family needed him to help run the business. And he's been very loyal. But it's time to shine now, don't you think?"

"Um, sure."

"There's only so long you can go on working in your family's restaurant before you finally have to do something for yourself."

"I guess." Funny, all this talk about Chinese food was making me hungry.

As if on cue, Warren appeared at my side, with Nadine and

Brad nearby. "We were thinking about stopping off for a bite to eat on the way home so that no one has to cook or wash dishes," he offered.

"Mmm." I nodded with zeal. "Let's do. And I believe I know just the place."

CHAPTER 11

HEARTBREAK HOTEL

Our lunch at Lee Yu's Garden proved yummy, but—from a sleuthing standpoint, anyway—entirely unproductive. Our waitress was a tiny little thing, probably still in her teens. She wore her hair pulled back in a ponytail, and her wire-rimmed spectacles kept slipping down her nose. She informed us that the Yus were away on a Caribbean cruise. Even Tomi deserted us, opting instead for lunch at Pastor Miller's house with Devin, Jake, and some of the other guys. I couldn't help but wonder what they were talking about over there. Tonight's game, perhaps?

We arrived home—full of Chinese food and unusually somber. Unlike the prior two days, no one spoke much of Scott's disappearance. It was almost as if everyone had slipped off into a state of denial. Or perhaps the truth, in all its ugliness, had finally registered at last.

I checked the answering machine to discover a couple of messages from a reporter at a Philadelphia news station. I wouldn't be returning them.

Sasha let out a yelp, getting my attention. I opened the back door to let her out, and a wave of cold air hit me. As it did, I thought back to this morning's incident. Watching that eerily tall fellow sprint across my lawn had sent a wave of fear through me. Even now, I trembled as I gazed down at his tracks in the snow.

I eased my way out into the yard, away from my guests, for another look. "Wow." Mammoth prints created a jagged path through the snow. If I hadn't seen the man with my own eyes—if I had to go solely off these prints—I'd have to say we were dealing with Bigfoot, here. Or, at the very least, his cousin.

I let my mind wander a minute, though the shivering threatened to overtake my thoughts. The man at the airport—the one taking our pictures. Had he followed us home from Philadelphia, perhaps? Was he lingering nearby, hoping for a chance to. . .

To what? Skate across my backyard?

Hmm. I buttoned my jacket to protect myself from the cold as I pondered the possibilities. Had the man followed Nadine all the way from Georgia to Clarksborough, PA?

Nah. Much as I wanted to paste together a workable conclusion, I had to admit the man in the airport was much shorter than our prowler. And, if memory served me correctly, his hair was a lot lighter. *Mental note: Next time someone snaps your photo from across the room, pay closer attention to what he is wearing.*

I eventually made my way back into the house, noting that everyone had slipped off to their respective rooms—probably to nap. I doubted I could sleep, what with Big Foot loose in our neighborhood and all, but I decided to give it a try. As I crawled under the covers to get warm, Warren tried to instigate a chat.

"You're worried, aren't you?"

I grunted my response, afraid that if I truly spoke my mind, tears would come.

"Annie, look at me."

I shook my head and turned my face to the wall. I didn't feel like speaking to him. I didn't feel like speaking to anyone. I just wanted to go to sleep and wake up again to find the past few days had only been a horrible dream.

"Come on, Annie. I think we need to talk."

"I'm tired, honey. I'd really like to rest."

He leaned over to give me a tender kiss on the cheek, and my eyes filled with tears right away. For the first time, I truly contemplated the cold, hard facts. If Scott didn't return within the next several days, there would be no wedding. My daughter would have no groom. I would have no son-in-law.

If he didn't come back at all. . .

A lump filled my throat, and tears trickled down my cheeks in painful silence. I couldn't fathom the idea that he had been taken from us forever. It was unthinkable. It was. . .

Ludicrous. Yes, ludicrous—the very word Warren had used last night with Sergeant O'Henry. I knew in my gut we would see Scott again. The only thing I couldn't say with any degree of certainty was when.

I felt Warren's hand on my back and could hear his whispered prayer. He asked the Lord to move mightily on behalf of our family and prayed for protection over our son-in-law-to-be. *God bless that husband of mine.* He certainly knew what to do to win me over. I allowed him to finish his heartfelt plea to the Almighty on Scott's behalf; then I rolled over in the bed to cradle into his outstretched arms. He somehow managed to dry my tears and convince me God hadn't fallen off His throne.

It took some doing, but I finally drifted off to sleep. I dreamed the strangest thing: Big Foot, Sheila, Nadine, and I were seated together on a jumbo jet, headed for the Caribbean, where we would join Mr. and Mrs. Yu on a crime-fighting cruise. Once onboard the cruise liner, every passenger became either a witness or a suspect. And the fine folks from McKinley Pharmaceuticals were there, as well—handing out prescriptions right and left. Malcolm Pfifer snapped photographs at will, all the while, a devilish smile on his face.

Funny how it all seemed to make perfect sense when I was asleep.

The sound of Warren's alarm woke me. I rubbed my eyes, took note of my monstrous headache, and looked his way. "What time is it?"

"Almost time for the pregame show." With sleep still in his eyes, he bounded from the bed like a kid on his first day of summer vacation. "The kids should be here soon, and I need to make sure Brad is awake. I can't wait to see the look on his face when his team loses."

At the mention of the word *kids*, my heart quickened. One kid would be missing. One who genuinely loved football. My thoughts shifted back to my dream. I'd spent the last hour or so searching the Caribbean for my future son-in-law but hadn't been able to locate him.

Where are you, Scott? When are you coming back to us?

Warren stopped cold at the door, then turned back to me with a sigh. "I can't believe I almost got excited about a football game when. . ." He didn't finish the sentence. Didn't have to. Instead, he rubbed the sleep out of his eyes and gave me an imploring look.

"Enjoy your game," I whispered. "Scott would want you to."

I spent the next few coming-awake minutes engaged in a phone call with Sergeant O'Henry, during which I told him about Big Foot and answered another round of questions. To my disappointment, he informed me there had been no change in the situation. He had gone over Scott's car inside and out, but nothing suspicious turned up—at least nothing he could point to. And except for the comments about the mess he'd found in Scott's apartment, there didn't seem to be anything amiss there, either.

I hung up from the call, determined to cease my worrying. If Scott had truly skipped town, prewedding jitters were to blame— nothing more. He would return. Soon. Why, he was probably sitting in a hotel room somewhere nearby, watching the pregame show, just like. . .

Just like the people he loves.

With a sigh, I went back to work. Nadine and I spent the next hour or so preparing for this evening's football-cheering crowd. Chips. Dips. Pretzels. Meatballs. Sodas. The usual stuff.

By the time the pregame show ended, Nadine had gravitated toward her laptop to check e-mails. "Just in case Scott has sent a note," she confided.

Brad, Warren, Devin, Garrett, and Jake gathered in the living room to watch the game, though the mood in the room was far more reserved than usual. The fellas pretended to be interested in the various plays, but I could see the distraction in their eyes, particularly in Warren's. He gazed up at Brandi on more than one occasion, and I could read his expression all too well. He was worried about her. I was, too.

I eased my way down onto a chair at the breakfast table, exhausted. Brandi, Candy, and Nikki joined me for some girl talk. Brandi's eyes were red from all the crying she'd been doing, and her mascara had run down her cheeks, leaving tiny black rivers. Taking her by the hand, I offered up a reassuring look.

Mother-of-the-bride tip: When the bride-to-be is beside herself, sometimes words are unnecessary.

The house phone rang out with what seemed to be a louder-than-usual ring, and everyone in the room jolted. I rose to answer it, hands trembling. I was surprised—albeit a little disappointed—to hear my mother's voice on the other end of the phone. I had hoped it would be Scott.

She started off the conversation with a rousing, "Annie, honey!" Ah, a true Mississippi lady if I ever heard one. I relished the sound of her beautiful voice, still quintessentially southern.

"Hi, Mom."

The anticipation in the room immediately eased, and everyone went back to watching the game.

"How are things going, Annie?" My mother's usually soft voice seemed a bit edgier tonight.

At once, I felt a catch in my throat. I tried to answer but couldn't. Realization set in right away. In the midst of the chaos, I'd forgotten to call my parents and tell them about Scott's disappearance. They didn't even know.

Shame washed over me afresh. How could I have forgotten? Had I really been that busy? That preoccupied? Why, Mom and Dad would be arriving in a little more than a week—thinking they were coming for a wedding. Now I had to tell them. . .

"I felt led to pray for you today." She interrupted my thoughts. "What's going on up there?" I couldn't help but smile as Mom referred to Pennsylvania as "up there." Of course, from where she sat in Jackson, Mississippi, "up there" did seem to make sense. Still, I always felt as if I must be sitting at the top of a high-rise when she called.

I also had to marvel at her uncanny ability to know when something had gone wrong, even without being told. She might be getting older, but her spiritual discernment was as "in tune" as ever.

I went on to tell her the whole story, anxious to hear her take on things. When I finished, I could hear the emotion in her voice.

"I *knew* something had happened. I just knew it." After a moment's pause, she said, "Daddy and I weren't going to leave until Thursday morning, but we'll go ahead and hit the road tomorrow."

Yikes! Tomorrow? Nadine and Brad were sleeping in our spare room. Where would my parents stay? Hmm. We could use the sleeper-sofa option, I suppose. But how could I put an elderly couple on a sleeper sofa—especially after they'd driven all the way up from Mississippi in midwinter? Perhaps a different plan was in order.

"Drive carefully, Mom," I admonished. "And keep your cell phone charged, in case you need to make a call. Do you have roadside assistance?"

"Well, of course we do. So don't you fret. Daddy and I will find some place to stop to sleep in Roanoke, then head out again early

Tuesday morning. We'll probably get to your place late Tuesday afternoon. How does that sound?"

"Sounds great. I really need you, Mom."

Why did those words sound so familiar? Ah yes, just today Brandi had used them with me. *I really need you, Mom.* Ah, how they made a mother's heart sing.

I ended the call, then turned my attention back to the men in the living room. The halftime show had begun, and everyone in the place seemed more than a little put off by the performances.

"It's just not what it used to be," Warren mumbled.

"Amen to that," Brad echoed.

The two men dove into a lengthy chat about their respective teams, and the heat in the room rose substantially as Brad—alone in his principles—challenged the others with a daring, "Let's just see who comes out smelling like a rose at the end of the night." I couldn't help but smile, wondering if Scott would have joined in the fray. My daughter's fiancé was a lot like his stepdad, though they obviously shared different views on football teams.

Not that it mattered. At the end of the night, every man in the place turned a woeful eye to Brad, shook his hand, and congratulated him. . .on smelling like a rose.

Rainy Days and Mondays

On Sunday night, when I lay down to sleep, my mind wouldn't rest. Despite *everything* that had happened over the previous day or two, I still couldn't shake the idea that Scott might have simply skipped town to avoid getting married, just as O'Henry had suggested.

I'd never voiced this idea, naturally, but it wouldn't leave me alone. Instead, I'd contemplated it in the wee hours of the night, when everything was still and silent. I'd thought about it when looking into Brandi's pain-filled eyes. I'd wondered about it every single time I thought about that photograph Pfifer had taken on the night of the proposal. And I'd stumbled over it every time the words, "I'm fine, *but. . .*" waltzed through my mind.

Did Scott have cold feet? Had he simply walked away, overwhelmed by the idea of entering into marriage?

I rolled over in the bed and stared at Warren, deep in thought. Sure, there were things about married life that were tough—

like sharing a queen-size bed with someone who snored like a buzz saw every time he rolled over on his back. And yes, there were other things, like the funny habits he'd acquired through the years, habits that tended to shred the nerves like a block of cheddar cheese scraping up against a handheld grater. Leaving the toilet seat up. Eating with his mouth open. Blowing his nose too loudly.

Love and marriage. They went together like a horse and carriage, right? I mean, horses and carriages were two completely different things—things that, in and of themselves, might not function well on their own. Okay, maybe the horse could function on its own, but the carriage? Unless someone pulled it. . .

Hmm. Brandi *was* a little abrasive, a little controlling; this I had to admit. Had she played the role of the horse too well? Had Scott reached his limit with being pulled around?

Nah. Surely not. As tough as she could be, her genteel side made her more Arabian show horse than surly stallion.

On and on, I wrestled with my thoughts. By midnight, I'd convinced myself Scott had slipped away for some alone time, as O'Henry had suggested. By one in the morning, I'd shifted gears, settling on the idea that this was a prank—that Scott would return with a sheepish grin on his face and a fistful of red roses for Brandi. By two, fear had set in, and I wondered if Scott might have disappeared. . .forever. What if we never heard from him again? By three, I'd settled on the one thing that—at that point anyway—simply wouldn't leave me alone: Something was going on at McKinley Pharmaceuticals—something that required my attention. But, in order to *give* it my full attention, I had to shift into sleuthing gear.

Sheila, witty woman that she was, always said opportunities looked bigger going than coming. Kind of like my backside. Certainly, I'd missed more than a few opportunities over the past few days, but no more would whiz past me. No, Agatha Annie was on the job, and she wouldn't allow anything to slip by her again.

I awoke after a near-sleepless night with a specific plan in mind. I would visit the offices of McKinley Pharmaceuticals where Scott worked, to see if I could drum up any not-yet-revealed information that might lead me to discovering his whereabouts. Surely his good friend—what was the man's name again? Ah yes, Bob Kendricks. Surely Bob Kendricks would be able to advise me. I shrugged off my earlier commitment to go to the gym. That could wait till another day, right? Scott's workplace called out to me, and I must answer.

"I really want to go with you," Warren confided, "but I can't miss any more days at the bank."

"It's okay," I assured him. "I'll be fine on my own."

"Just be careful." He gave me a fatherly frown. "Promise me." After I nodded, he turned to face Brad and Nadine. "If you two want to drop me off at the bank, you can use my car for the rest of the day."

"Sounds great." The relief in Brad's voice was evident. "I don't think I could sit still. I want to track down some of Scott's friends and pay them a little visit. Do a little man-to-man chatting."

"Good idea," we all agreed.

Moments later, we all parted ways, agreeing to meet back at the house by midafternoon to discuss dinner plans.

Before backing out of the driveway, I telephoned Sheila on my cell phone.

Now, most of my friends answer with a *Hello*—or something similar—but not Sheila. Oh no. She answered with, "You're at it again, aren't you, Annie?"

I leaned back against the seat and groaned before responding with, "What are you talking about?"

"I knew it yesterday when I saw you in church. You've got that look in your eye. You just haven't been the same since you took those Internet courses a couple of months back."

"Sheila, please," I started.

"No," she interrupted. "The people at www.investigativeskills. com have ruined you for a normal life. Nothing but adventure will do now."

"What's wrong with adventure?" I challenged. When she tried to debate, I dove into an explanation of my plans for the morning, and, as always, she had a bit of advice to offer.

"Well, as long as you're sure it's the Lord's leading, I'll go along with it," she said. "But I want you to be extracareful with this one, Annie. Something about all of this just feels. . .scary."

I took her words quite seriously. The woman might have quirky taste in clothing and makeup, but her discernment skills were dead-on.

"I don't know why I feel the Lord is prompting me to play a role in finding Scott," I admitted with a bit of chagrin. "I'm completely unqualified."

A *humph* sound bounced across the phone line. "Girl!" Sheila spurted. "I shouldn't have to tell you this, but you leave me no choice. God doesn't call the qualified. He qualifies the called."

"Wow. Is that an original?" I opened my notebook and jotted the phrase down, in case I ever needed the reminder.

"Heavens, I don't know," she said. "I just know that I say it a lot. God is in the business of teaching us how to do the very things we don't know how to do. If we *could* do those things ourselves, we wouldn't need Him. So He does the undoable, and all *we* have to do is sit back and recognize that *we're* not the ones doing it—*He* is. Make sense?"

"Um. . .sure."

"I'll tell you what my Mama used to say," Sheila continued, undaunted. The excitement in her voice grew as she spoke. "The task *ahead* of you is never as great as the Power *behind* you."

"Wow." She went on to provide me with a few more words of wisdom, likely derived from a host of e-mail forwards, and then dove into a hearty prayer for my safety. She also prayed for God's favor, something I genuinely coveted, particularly when it came to today's visit to Scott's workplace.

"Oh, one last thing!" Sheila caught me just as I started to hang up. "I don't suppose you saw the *Gazette* this morning."

"No. Why?"

"Hmm. Well, there's an article about Scott's disappearance."

"Great." I'd hoped we could avoid the media at least another day or two, but with missing-person posters now going up, they were sure to catch wind of the story. "Pray for Warren then," I said. "He's going to have a hard time with this. And pray that things with the media don't get out of control—for Brandi's sake. For all of our sakes."

"I'm praying, Annie." Sheila clicked off with her usual well wishes, and I put the car into gear and headed out onto the icy roads. I hated to be out on a day like today but really felt I had no choice. I had to make the lengthy drive to McKinley Pharmaceuticals.

I arrived some twenty minutes later, surprised to find the parking lot full of vehicles in every make, model, and color. I'm not sure why, but I'd thought the poor weather might have been a deterrent for some to go to work. Must be something pressing to bring this many folks out on a day like today. I pulled up to the security gate and was met by an elderly man with a clipboard in his hand. His name tag read CLARK.

" 'Mornin'." He raked his fingers through his silver curls and gave me a curious once-over. "Can I help you?"

"Um, yes. I'm here to see... Well, I'm here because..." I shook my head and tried again. "I am here to see Mr. Bob Kendricks."

"Is he expecting you?"

"Well, no, but I feel sure he will see me. My name is Annie Peterson. He works with my future son-in-law, and I need to talk with him about something personal."

"Hmm." The fellow rubbed his chin. "I'll have to give him a call; then I'll need to see your ID." As he picked up his phone to call inside the building, I prayed Bob would see me. We'd never met in person, though I'd heard his name time and again from Scott.

Moments later, the security guard reached out his hand and muttered the words, "ID, please." I placed my Pennsylvania driver's license in his hand and waited until he jotted down the number.

"Have a nice day!" he said, then pressed a button to open the gate.

I eased my way into the parking lot, settling on a visitors-only spot near the door.

After exiting the car, I slipped and slid all the way to the front door, where I was greeted by a receptionist. I quickly explained my goal—to speak to Bob Kendricks—and after double-checking my identification, she handed me a clip-on visitor's pass and allowed me to continue.

"Mr. Kendricks is expecting you," she said. "His office is on the third floor, room 316."

Moments later, I arrived at his door. After a brief introduction on my part, I settled into a chair by his desk.

"It's good to meet you, Mrs. Peterson." He offered up a warm smile. "Though I feel like I already know you. I've heard so much about your family from Scott. He seems to think you Petersons hung the moon."

"He's too kind." I felt my cheeks flush pink but forged ahead. "But we all love him, too. In fact, he's the reason I've come to talk to you today. My daughter Brandi had planned to come with me, but she's got a new job at a Realtor's office and can't break away."

"Oh yes. I know all about that. Brandi is. . ." Kendricks never got a chance to finish, as the phone rang out. As he excused himself and lit into a conversation with the person on the other end of the line, I took a moment to observe the room. Very stark. No pictures on the wall. I glanced at his desk. Tidy. Maybe a little too tidy.

Kendricks wrapped up his call, then dove into a story about how he and his wife had been trying to sell their house for months. "Arlene's been dreaming of spending our golden years traveling the country in an RV. But this whole process of selling a house isn't as easy as it seems."

Traveling the country in an RV sounded horrible to me, but what did I know? I smiled and nodded, doing my best to be polite. "I really wanted to talk to you about Scott."

"Where is that kid, anyway?" he asked. "We've missed him around the office the last couple of days. I hope he's not sick or anything."

"No." My gaze shifted to the ground. "Well. . .not that I know of. He's, um. . ." Clearly, he hadn't read the morning paper. I looked into the older gentleman's kind eyes and finally came out with it. "It's been three days since anyone in the family has heard from him."

"What?" The look of shock registered in his eyes immediately.

"We're not sure what's going on." I spoke in hushed tones as he stood and closed the door of his tiny office. "We've racked our brains trying to figure it out. Sergeant O'Henry from the sheriff's office will be coming by later today to talk to you—or anyone else who might have information, for that matter. We're all hoping you guys can offer some insight."

Bob's face suddenly lit up—and for a moment, I saw a flicker of hope in his eyes. "Come on now. This is *Scott* we're talking about. You know what a jokester he is. He's probably out fishing somewhere with the guys and just didn't want you to know."

"That's what we thought at first," I said with a shake of my head, "but we're not so sure now. No one has heard from him."

"Not even Jason? That guy is always calling up here, distracting Scott from his work. He's a real character—and I don't necessarily mean that in a good way." He gave a little shrug.

I knew Jason well. Even though he was in his late twenties, he still had more of a high school mentality than a grown-up one. "We've talked to him several times, and he's made it clear he has nothing to do with this. But Scott's parents are paying him a little visit today, just in case."

"Ah."

My supersleuthing skills kicked in right away as the fellow's left eyebrow began to twitch. Surely this man knew more than he was saying, but. . .what?

A tightening in my gut signaled a problem. I shouldn't have skipped breakfast—not on a day like today. I needed protein—or at the very least, artificial sweetener—to garner up the courage to ask the all-important question. "Mr. Kendricks, is there something happening at McKinley Pharmaceuticals that I need to know about?" I finally managed.

"Well. . ." He glanced toward the closed door—a fact I took into consideration. I reached for my sleuthing notebook to jot down a few notes as he continued. "Yeah, actually. There's a lot going on around here right now." Bob's face paled a bit as he continued on—a little softer now. "Have you heard Scott talk about HD-387?"

Bingo. "Actually, he did tell us a little about that. FDA approval is just days away, isn't that right?"

Bob's brow wrinkled. "We're close. But there have been a few. . . problems. And to be honest. . ." His lips tightened, and the wrinkles between his brows deepened. "Scott has managed to get on the wrong side of a few of our higher-ups."

"Oh?" I prayed the *thump-thumping* in my heart wasn't audible.

"Yes." Bob looked toward the door, as if he expected to be interrupted at any moment. "As much as Scott would like to see the drug pass FDA approval, he knows that it hasn't done very well in the clinical research and testing phase." Kendricks' voice softened, and he glanced down at the desk, then up at me. "I shouldn't be telling you any of this."

I forged ahead, undaunted. "I remember hearing that a couple

of patients had suffered fairly significant reactions to HD-387."
I jotted down some notes but eventually looked up as he spoke.

"Yes." Bob's voice grew more hushed by the moment. "Some of our superiors were keen on the idea of. . ." He paused, then shook his head. "Anyway, Scott wasn't willing to play along. He didn't want to see the drug hit the market if it had produced marked reactions in patients. He said he wouldn't have been able to live with himself."

I continued to write, looking up in concern. "So where does the company stand with all of this? Right now, I mean."

Bob shook his head. "It's complicated to explain, but our ability to prove the drug's negative side effects has been minimized." A look of genuine concern flooded his face. "One day we could prove there were problems, the next day. . ." He let out a lingering sigh. "Let's just say the drug is going to pass FDA approval—and soon. Unless Scott returns quickly and gets back on the case. Even then, it might pass approval, but I'd feel better, knowing he was back on the job."

"Hmm." The whole thing made me feel a bit nauseous. To think Scott might be in jeopardy because of all of this really un-nerved me.

Bob gave a limp shrug. "Anyway, I'd like to assume his dis-appearance is completely unrelated to anything going on at work." He managed a strained smile. "I'm sure he'll be back. Soon. With his tail tucked between his legs, no doubt—and probably with a story of all the fish he caught."

'Nough said. "Okay, well, thanks for your time." I stood and extended my hand. "Please let me know if you hear anything."

"I will." He gave me his card, and I quickly entered his

number into my cell phone. I turned back for one last comment. "You should be getting a call from Sergeant O'Henry at the Clark County Sheriff's Office. We gave him your contact information. Hope that's okay."

Kendricks' face paled, but he managed a nod.

I made my way out of his office and back through the crowd of McKinley employees. Many looked stressed, I noted with my www.investigativeskills.com-savvy eyes. A few even gave me a suspicious look as I traveled back through the room.

A little shiver scuttled down my spine as I hit the parking lot. For whatever reason, my visit to McKinley hadn't settled my nerves. If anything, it had agitated them.

Ain't That a Kick in the Head?

Late Monday evening, O'Henry telephoned to say he had paid a visit to the pharmaceutical company. I didn't ask for specifics, and he didn't offer them. To be honest, I wasn't sure how much Bob Kendricks had shared with the good sergeant and didn't want to overstep my bounds.

"I guess you saw the story in the paper," O'Henry said with a sigh.

"I read it when I got home this afternoon," I told him. "But it seemed pretty basic. Just the facts."

"We're lucky. So far."

His words sent a little shiver down my spine.

After ending the call, I settled on a plan for my parents' arrival, but "said plan" presented a few unavoidable complications. How could I convince Devin to thoroughly clean his bedroom and then offer to give it up for the next week and a half so that his grandparents would have a comfortable place to stay? I broached the subject with a bribe in hand—homemade chocolate-chip cookies, still warm from the oven.

"Are you kidding, Mom?" He ignored the cookies, crossed his arms at his chest, and leaned against the kitchen wall. "I'm gonna end up on the couch, and that's not fair. I still have to get up for school every day. *Every day.* I'll be miserable."

I gave him my let's-don't-talk-about-this-right-now look just as Nadine piped up. "Don't be silly," she said. "Brad and I will go to a hotel. Then your parents can stay in the guest room. We don't mind a bit."

I turned to face her. "Well, *I* mind. I need you. Please don't leave me now. And, Devin. . ." I turned to face him. "You don't have to sleep on the couch. In fact, you won't be in the living room, at all. You'll be in the office on the sleeper sofa. You can have the whole room to yourself."

Devin's expression softened, as it so often did when he realized he couldn't possibly win whatever battle he happened to be fighting at the time. "Fine. I'll clean my room. But I don't have to clean my closet, do I? That would take hours. Days, even."

"Are you sure you're not related to Scott?" Nadine asked with a smile.

After Devin shrugged, I gave him a little warning. "Just make sure the dirty tennis shoe smell has been eliminated. Give it your best shot, anyway."

After snagging a couple of cookies from the platter in my hand, he huffed off to his room to begin the process of making it company ready. I turned to face Nadine and Brad, doing my best to hold it together. "I can't bear the thought of you leaving right now. And I think you'll love my mom. In fact, I know you will."

I felt the edges of my lips turn up. "She's a true southerner, just like you. She'll make grits for breakfast the very first morning—watch and see. And we'll have sweet tea in abundance all day long. She's very therapeutic. And my dad is a hoot."

"Mmm." Nadine smiled. "Can't wait."

Neither could I, to be honest—though I could feel the girth of my hips increasing at the very thought of all those calories I'd surely consume. At times like this, a girl just needed her mama.

The next day dawned bright and sunny. No sign of a fresh snowfall, thankfully, and the mounds of snow from prior days appeared to be dissipating. I longed for some time at the gym, but there was no time today, not with so much going on. I could always go tomorrow, right?

O'Henry called midmorning, as always. Every time I saw the number on the caller ID, my heart skipped a beat. I prayed he would have good news. Sadly, this morning's story was the same as always. "Nothing to share, Mrs. Peterson," he said with a weary voice.

After many assurances on his part that the Clark County Sheriff's Office was on the job, I thanked him for his good work and returned to preparing my house for more company.

By late afternoon, my parents had arrived—travel weary but otherwise in good spirits. My dad eased his way out of the driver's seat, looking more hunched over than I remembered—and considerably stiffer. Hopefully it was just the long road trip. I took one look at my mother sitting in the front passenger seat with her stylish silver hair and pink lipstick and had to smile. Sheila had nothing on my Mississippi mama.

I bounded to the car, swung wide the passenger door, and

reached to give her a warm hug. At once, the scent of roses accosted me. Nothing new there. My mom had emerged from the womb smelling of tea rose. It often took days to get her scent out of my sweaters and jackets after a good hug.

We practically melted into each other's arms.

"Have you heard from Scott yet?" Mom shifted her legs over the edge of the seat and then stretched her way to a standing position. "I've prayed all the way from Mississippi to Pennsylvania—lifted that boy's name up before the Almighty more times than I could count." She let out a little giggle. "I suppose the Lord is mighty tired of my repetition by now. I must sound like a broken record."

"No." I shook my head and did my best not to let the tears come. "We haven't heard a word. And you keep praying, Mom. I have it on good authority the Lord never grows tired of hearing from you."

Dad came around to our side of the car and wrapped me in his arms. Funny, even after all these years, he still smelled of the same spicy aftershave he'd always worn. Not that he had shaved. His whiskery chin let me know right away he'd avoided the razor for a couple of days—something he often did while traveling. I knew he loved the reprieve, but I also knew my mom hated it. Just one more thing they could bicker over.

"Did you have any trouble on the road?" I asked.

My mother rolled her eyes, and her carefully manicured brows arched. I sensed what was coming. My parents had developed un-deniable "signals" when a dispute was on its way, and the rolled-eye bit was usually a strong indicator of trouble. "We got turned around in Roanoke when we were leaving the hotel. Your father refused to stop and ask directions. I didn't think we'd ever make it back onto the interstate. Other than that, everything was fine."

"Now, Lillian." My father ran his fingers through the tiny ring of hair around the outer perimeter of his head and gave her a not-in-front-of-the-children look.

"Hubert, you know it's true." Mother clutched her overnight bag—the one I knew contained her skin-care products and makeup—and gave him the usual rolled-eye glance.

They dove into a discussion about his inability to read a road map, and at once, I thought of a bumper sticker Sheila and I had seen in a quirky little store just a few weeks ago: How Many Roads Must a Man Travel Down Before He Admits He Is Lost? I'd secretly purchased it for Warren but had never actually garnered up the courage to give it to him. Perhaps while my parents were here, I could slip it to my mother, just for fun.

Mom leaned over to whisper something in my ear that made me smile: "Thank goodness your father doesn't have the RV bug, like so many people our age. We'd end up lost every day of our lives."

I couldn't help but laugh aloud, though I did my best to squelch it quickly.

Warren approached, bundled in his heavy winter coat, to help with the bags, and within minutes we were all safe inside the house—traveling woes behind us. Brad and Warren helped my parents into Devin's room with their stuff, and at once my mother pinched her nose.

"What in the world is that dizzying ar-o-ma?" She gazed around the room, like a hound dog tracking its prey.

"Sorry." I gave a little shrug. "Devin's tennis shoes. We removed them from the room last night—put them in the garage, in fact—but there's a lingering odor."

"Ah." She nodded in understanding. "I remember those days well." She dove into a story about my older brother, Nick, and his penchant for leaving dirty clothes and food products in his room for weeks on end when he was a teen. Of course, that was decades ago. Nick was a grandpa now. In fact, his four-year-old grandson, Shawn, was supposed to be the ring bearer in Brandi and Scott's wedding.

"Good grief!" I slapped myself in the head. "I haven't even called Nick and Katie to tell them Scott's missing."

"We called them on the way up here." My father gave me a reassuring pat on the arm. "They want you to know they're praying, and they still have every intention of coming, regardless."

You know, *regardless* is a mighty depressing word sometimes.

My mother went to work, unpacking her bags with great zeal, hanging up her nicer things right away, and putting her carefully folded silk undergarments in a drawer Devin had emptied just for this occasion. When her suitcase was nearly empty, she reached into a side pocket and pulled out a plastic bag. "We stopped at the most wonderful gift shop in Roanoke."

"Really?"

"Mm-hmm." She pulled out the large block of nutty fudge. "See? I remembered!"

She broke off a piece and extended her hand with a smile. "It's loaded with walnuts. Your favorite."

My mouth began to water at once, but common sense quickly took over. I'd never fit into that mother-of-the-bride dress if I blew it at every available opportunity. "Actually, I'm dieting." I gave her a woeful smile, hoping she'd take the hint.

"Nonsense." She pressed the delectable delight into my hand

with a wicked grin. "A little never hurt anyone."

At once, I thought of Sheila. What was it she always said at times like these? Ah yes. *"Opportunity may knock once, but temptation bangs on your front door forever."*

With a sigh, I reached for a tiny piece and popped it into my mouth. Might as well nibble a little now, as opposed to eating the whole thing later.

"That's enough, Mom," I scolded after swallowing a tiny bite. "Hide it away so that I can't find it."

"As you wish."

Minutes later, we settled in the kitchen to update my parents and to introduce them properly to Nadine and Brad. Talk about two peas in a pod. My mother and Nadine hit it off at once. The drawl was so thick in the room you could have sliced through it with a butter knife. The womenfolk put the menfolk to work right away, unloading my parents' car of wedding gifts.

"We just purchased some *luv*-ly things for the happy couple!" My mom clamped a hand over her mouth and looked at my dad out of the corner of her eye. "Just a few things."

"A few things, my eye." My dad headed off to the car to unload what turned out to be six or seven large gift boxes. Truly, my mother knew how to shop. I wasn't sure where to put the gifts. The dining room was already filled to overflowing with boxes bearing white ribbons and bows.

"Put them in the office," I suggested at last. "Just leave a path so that Devin can get to the sofa bed."

About an hour later, Brandi came in the front door with a small, plain envelope in her hand. She greeted her grandmother with tears and a shaky, "I'm so glad you're here, Grandma." My mother wrapped her in a loving embrace, offering quiet reassurances. After a moment, Brandi snapped to attention and seemed to remember the envelope, which she passed off to Nadine.

"What is this?" Nadine gave the envelope a once-over with some degree of suspicion.

Brandi shrugged. "I dunno. Found it taped to the front door. Your name is written on it."

My supersleuthing abilities kicked in right away. There had been nothing taped to the door when my parents arrived, less than an hour ago. I definitely would have taken note of that.

Nadine stared at the crazy thing for a good sixty seconds before ripping it open. Inside, she found a handwritten note. Confusion filled her eyes as she read.

"What does it say?" Brandi leaned over her shoulder, trying to sneak a peek. "Is it about Scott?"

Everyone sat up a little straighter in their chairs in anticipation of her answer.

Nadine's slow nod did little to squelch the knot in my stomach. "This is the strangest thing." She laid the paper on the table so we could all see the chicken scratchings.

"It says, 'Am I welcome at the wedding?'"

Brandi's hands began to shake as she echoed Nadine's words. "Am I welcome at the wedding?" She looked over at me, confusion registering in her eyes, and then read it aloud again. "Am I welcome at the wedding?"

We all sat in silence for a moment, trying to process it.

Brandi's eyes grew large. "Maybe it's from Scott," she reasoned. "Maybe he thinks I won't be able to forgive him for leaving me at the altar."

Wow. That was the first time I'd heard her speak those words. They sounded just awful, particularly when I contemplated the fact that she'd actually given that idea serious thought.

We all shook our heads in tandem. "Doesn't make sense," I argued. "He would know better than that."

"Yes, but who in the world would think they weren't welcome at the wedding?" Brandi asked.

"Someone's not welcome?" Devin asked as he entered the room. He reached to open the fridge, pulled out the milk container, and pulled the top off. *Oh no you don't, son. Not in front of. . .*

He took a swig straight from the jug, wiped his mouth, and stared at us all like we were crazy. "Who did you forget to invite?"

"No one." Brandi shrugged and tossed the note on the table. "We invited absolutely everyone we've ever been connected to. And every relative we could think of, even the ones we haven't heard from in decades. It's crazy to think we might've left someone out."

"Crazier still to think. . ." I shook my head. I hated to say the words aloud but forged ahead. "Would someone kidnap a groom because they'd been overlooked? Or felt excluded in some way?"

"Come on. That's just nuts." Devin took another swig from the milk container, wiped his mouth with the back of his hand, and then looked at us with heady authority, as if he'd just given a speech before the UN. "There's more to it than that. There's got to be."

"Why in the world would they address the envelope to Nadine?" Brandi looked at her future mother-in-law with an odd expression. "Hardly anyone even knows you're in town, right?"

"Right." Nadine shook her head. "This is all too strange."

"Scott's buddies know we're here." Brad's words, though soft, shook the room. "And if you don't mind my saying so, they were acting a little strange yesterday when we paid them a visit, especially that Jason fellow. There's something he's not telling us."

"But Jason is a groomsman." I racked my brain, trying to figure this out. "The note was from someone who feels left out."

The chatter in the room escalated, each person having his or her opinion. I did my best to take it all in without question but—when no one was looking—slipped off to my bedroom to add one more thing to my notebook.

Fact #7: We've left someone out of the equation. I'm not sure who—or why—but I have no doubt time will reveal the truth.

Raindrops Keep Fallin' on My Head

True to my promise, Mother made grits for breakfast on Wednesday morning. She loaded them with butter, then topped them off with more-than-adequate amounts of sugar and cinnamon. I devoured a small bowl of the yummies with great zeal, hoping against hope that I'd eventually make it to the gym to work them off.

Nadine oohed and aahed and even asked for seconds. If I had her figure, I might've done the same. Brad finished off his second helping with a dollop of honey on top. And Warren, well, Warren—poor northern boy that he was—picked his way through his tiny first helping, doing his best to smile. *God bless you, Warren Peterson.* I wasn't sure when I'd ever seen my mother happier—or more fulfilled. Funny, it didn't take much to make some people smile.

After Warren headed off to the bank, the phone started ringing. It didn't stop for over two hours. Journalists from all over the state. Wedding vendors. Well-meaning friends from church.

Pastor Miller. Sheila, informing me that the fine women of our Sunday school class would be bringing by food every night this week. "So that you won't have to bother with cooking for all of your guests." I swallowed hard as the truth registered. The church only delivered food to families in need. Did we really qualify?

Yes, I had to admit. We did. And secretly, I thanked God for the faithfulness of my friends at Clarksborough Community Church. They knew just how to sweep in and help when help was really needed. Hard as it was to accept, we really *were* in need right now—and they were happy to do all they could to assist. Accepting their help was just part of the process, I reasoned.

Finally, just about the time I thought my ear was worn out from all the calls, Bob Kendricks telephoned from McKinley Pharmaceuticals and asked if I could meet him later in the week for a one-on-one chat. His call took me aback. Something in his voice triggered an uneasiness in me, though I couldn't pinpoint the reason for it. I agreed to meet him at our local diner at noon the next day.

After dealing with wedding details, I picked up the phone to punch in Brandi's number. She picked up on the fourth ring with a brusque, "Hello?"

"Hi, honey." I deviated for a moment, chatting about the weather—icy rain predicted, with no chance of letting up any-time soon—and anything else I could think of before revealing the reason for my call. "Your wedding photographer called. Again." I hated to bother her with this news, especially in light of everything she was going through, but I couldn't help it. "He's upped the deposit amount to a thousand dollars total. Says we misunderstood his first quote of five hundred. Do you think that's possible? Didn't we get it in writing?"

"I don't know." She sounded scattered, distracted. "Maybe. I can't remember."

"I didn't know what to tell him."

Brandi groaned. "Mom, this is crazy. If Scott doesn't come back. . ."

Mother-of-the-bride tip: Stick to the topic at hand to avoid a bridal breakdown.

"He's coming back, so we need to stay focused on the plans, including deposit amounts."

I could hear the weariness in her voice as she continued on, undaunted by my forced cheerfulness. "But let's say he *doesn't* come back," she argued. "Do you really want to fork over an additional five hundred dollars to a photographer for a wedding that might not even take place? It just doesn't make any sense. And Pfifer wouldn't refund you. I know he wouldn't. That's just the way he is, trust me."

Hmm. Whatever happened to "Pfifer is the one responsible for my engagement?"

Much as I hated to admit that the wedding was in jeopardy, I *had* called Brandi today to get her take on financial matters. Malcolm Pfifer wasn't the only one asking for money. The DJ had telephoned, as well as the fine folks at the Be Our Guest wedding facility, wanting a final head count so that they could tally up the bill. The lady who operated the chocolate fountain—something Brandi had dreamed of having for ages—had called to confirm the time and location. And Janetta Mullins, our beloved caterer, had telephoned to ask if I thought it was okay for her to start shopping for some of the food items soon.

I'd managed to stall a couple of the vendors—without sharing the whole truth, mind you. But Pfifer. . . He was a tough sell.

"I'm having my own problems with him," Brandi admitted.

"What do you mean?"

"Well, I told you that he was Mr. Norton's client, right?"

"Right."

Brandi dove off into a lengthy story about Pfifer's inability to obtain financing and how that had affected the seller. She then went on to talk about the wording of the contract and mentioned something about a side deal.

"Norton writes these contracts every day," she explained. "And I know he knows what he's doing, but this just feels odd to me." She paused, and I started to add my thoughts, but she dove in again before I could. "Pfifer's an investor. He buys properties all the time. Shouldn't have any trouble getting financed. But he's buying up several properties at once, so I guess that's why it's so complicated. Trust me. . . ." I could hear the tension in her voice. "This real estate thing is a lot harder than it looks. My client is beside himself. He's afraid the deal is going to fall through, and to be honest. . ." Here, she let out an exaggerated sigh. "I can't blame him. I'm worried, too. And this is the *last* thing I need to be dealing with right now. The very last."

"You're right, honey." I did my best to console her. "Can't you pass this off to someone else?"

"I wish." Another groan escaped from the back of her throat. "I've already upset Mr. Norton."

"What do you mean?" I hated to think her boss had become frustrated with her already. Why, she'd hardly had a chance to prove herself.

"He and Malcolm are such good friends, and they're really pushing me to keep the seller happy—which means I have to use stall tactics. And I think we are all aware of the fact that I don't do stall tactics well. My patience is superthin, especially the past several days."

"Of course."

"And trust me. . .I'd like to keep the seller happy. Someone needs to. He's already moved out of his house and thinks he's going to be closing any day now. I'm the one who has to tell him Pfifer's having trouble getting his funding."

"Sounds like a mess."

"It is," Brandi confided. Her voice softened a little. "There's really a lot more to it than that, but you get the idea." She grew quiet for a moment, then said, "Why is it that bad things always seem to happen one on top of the other?"

"Ya got me." I'd often wondered the same thing myself but had finally settled on the idea that bad things were probably less destructive to the psyche when they came in rapid-fire succession. For example, if you were going through three or four traumas at any particular time, just one of them would not take you down, because you would be so distracted by all of the others that you wouldn't have time to get overwhelmed with just one.

Somehow it all made sense in my mind—and Sheila would probably get it, too—but I figured I'd better not bother Brandi with my explanation.

"Have you heard from O'Henry?" I asked, in the hopes of changing gears. "I think I missed a call from him this morning."

"Yeah." A deep, painful sigh on her end caught me off-guard. "He calls at least twice a day. The sheriff's office is really on the ball; I have to give it to them. O'Henry has arranged a search party for this Saturday. From what he said, half the town will be there. We're meeting in the church at eight in the morning, then. . ." Her voice broke.

"Then what, honey?"

"Combing the woods." I could hear the break in her voice. "As many as are willing to, anyway. There will be search dogs, brought in from Philadelphia. And a local flight school has volunteered one of their planes to do an aerial." The crying began in earnest now. "O'Henry has asked. . .for an item of Scott's. . .c—clothes so the dog can track his s—scent."

My heart nearly broke as she shared the details. "What can we do to help?" I asked, stepping into practical-mother gear as quickly as possible.

"Call people, I guess. And pray, Mom."

"I have been, honey. But that's a great idea. We should all get together for an actual prayer meeting first. How would you feel about that? Maybe in the fellowship hall?"

"Yes. I'd like that."

"Okay. Well, I'll call Pastor Miller this afternoon and see if we can set something up."

❧

I gave Pastor Miller a call, in the hopes of setting up a prayer meeting. After his initial approval, Sheila latched onto the idea, offering to provide food and coffee for all who attended. "People just pray better when their stomachs are full," she said. I had to agree.

The rest of the day seemed to pass at lightening speed. At

some point along the way, I tried to call Tomi Yu at the restaurant so that we could finish our chat from last week. Sadly, his father informed me he was away from the restaurant for a few days. I'd have to remember to track him down later. There were some lingering questions in my mind that wouldn't leave me alone. Frustrated, I pulled out my notebook and began to write:

> Fact #8: Tomi Yu will play a role in leading me to the perpetrator.

I wasn't sure how I knew, but somehow I did.

Late that night, I called my mother and Nadine into a secret meeting.

"We have to make a decision about the wedding plans," I started. "I feel like we're stuck—can't move forward, can't move back. And the wedding vendors don't like hanging in limbo. We've got to come up with some sort of a plan. Do we move forward, or do we. . ."

"We move forward." Nadine's lips tightened. "There *will* be a wedding, and we *will* want to have everything in place—for Brandi's sake, *and* for Scott's."

My mother quickly agreed, and we settled on a plan. Over the next few days, they would forge ahead with wedding plans—decorating, finalizing details—and I would continue on with my investigation, drumming up new clues. I would also be in charge of keeping Brandi positive and upbeat.

To be honest, I wasn't sure who had the tougher job.

CHAPTER 15

ALLEY OOP

I must admit I knew little about the world of pharmaceuticals. I did know enough to know you shouldn't mix your medications. And—through Sheila, who once made this mistake—I learned that one should never, under any circumstances, take a sleeping pill and a laxative on the same night. But when it came to the high-powered world of FDA drug approval, I was a fish out of water.

Or, in this case, a prescription out of a bottle.

I telephoned Bob Kendricks early Thursday morning to confirm our lunch meeting at the Clark County Diner. I knew he would be far more likely to open up and talk in a neutral location, and there was no place more neutral in all of Clark County than our local diner.

"Are you sure you don't want me to go with you?" My mother offered her services as I prepared to leave for the meeting.

I grabbed my notebook and gave a little shrug. I knew she didn't really want to come with me. She and Nadine had already settled on heading to the local craft store to make a few purchases for the wedding reception and then meeting up with Brandi and Candy for lunch at the Burger Barn. I was tickled to pass off some of the decorating to Nadine, who seemed to excel at it. I'd come to the conclusion the woman could do pretty much anything she set her mind to.

"I should be fine," I said. "But don't worry, if anything goes wrong, I'll have my cell phone with me."

Ten minutes later, I entered the diner, shrugged off my heavy coat, and looked around for Bob. He waved at me from a booth near the window. I scooted past the hostess and inched my way through the lunch crowd to greet him. I was a little startled by his strained expression, and the trembling in his hand as he extended it for a shake set my nerves on edge right away.

I inched my way into the booth and laid my purse and coat at my side. "How are you today, Bob?" I pushed the plastic-coated menu aside and focused on the gentleman who sat across from me.

He shook his head, face chalky white. "Not so good." He shot an anxious look around the room, as if he half expected someone to be watching us.

I tried to make eye contact with him—not an easy task, since he seemed to be looking everywhere except into my eyes. "Have problems escalated at work?"

He nodded, and the crease in his brow deepened. "This whole FDA thing is spinning out of control." Again, he looked around the room. Finally, his gaze landed on me. "I'm taking a huge chance by meeting with you." He shook his head. "To be honest, I'm not even sure why I'm here. I just feel like maybe. . ."

"What, Bob?"

"Well, I . . ."

"You're thinking Scott's disappearance is in some way con-nected to everything you're going through at the company."

"Yes." His frustration seemed to intensify. "I pray I'm wrong. But if there's even a chance it has anything to do with us. . ." He gazed at the table. "I probably should've told O'Henry most of this," he muttered, "but I'm so worried about losing my job. I just can't risk that. Not now. Not with everything I'm going through at home."

"Hmm." I pulled out my notebook and began to ask him some pointed questions. "If you don't mind. . ." I rolled the point of my ballpoint pen across the page to get the ink to flow. "Please start at the beginning. I want to make sure I understand the whole process—everything from A to Z."

He drew in a deep breath and nodded. "Whenever a company has a new drug, they fill out an application with the FDA. The form is called an NDA—a New Drug Application."

"Okay." I scribbled down every word.

"Quite a bit of data is gathered at this point," he explained. "Animal studies. Human clinical trials."

"Right." Sounded plenty complicated to me, but I did my best to keep up.

Thankfully, the waitress appeared at our table, pencil in hand. She provided a nice distraction. "Have you decided what you'd like yet?"

Bob picked up the menu and scanned it for a second before muttering, "Club sandwich, extra mayo. Coffee. Black."

I opted for the grilled chicken Caesar salad and a diet soda, though to be honest, I was still pretty full after that amazing breakfast.

The waitress had no sooner turned away than Bob continued his explanation.

"Most of what goes into that application has to do with the drug's safety," he explained. And we also have to provide evidence that the drug will be effective for its intended use. Each drug is then classified, and medical reviewers evaluate the submissions." He gave a little shrug. "I'm oversimplifying, but you get the idea."

"Okay." I appreciated his oversimplification. I was having enough trouble following, as it was.

"The primary thing, of course, is human safety." His eyes narrowed, and I could tell he was deep in thought. "The FDA wants to know how the drug is absorbed, metabolized, excreted—that sort of thing."

More details than I cared to know, thank you. I continued to scribble down as much as I could, though I felt a little lost.

"Data is collected at every stage," he continued. "Good and bad." Another sweeping glance around the room let me know his nerves were on edge. "Chemists are involved, of course, and the drug sponsor—in this case, McKinley Pharmaceuticals—has to be perfectly clear about any potential for human risk. Then, of course, there's documentation for how any risks might be monitored. All of this works in stages—one, two, and three."

I looked up just as the waitress approached with our drinks in hand. I waited until she'd stepped away before asking the question on my mind. "With everything so detailed, it's hard to imagine anything slipping through the cracks."

He took a swig from his coffee cup, then set it back down. "The whole world of drug research is complicated. And the people who produce the drugs generally have the right motivation. The goal is always to create drugs that will help people. And this one. . ."

"HD-387?"

He immediately tried to shush me, then whispered, "Yes. It has amazing potential to help people with heart-related issues. And the side effects, at least from our earlier studies, are minimal. Manageable." He paused. "Well, at least in most people. When a couple of our research patients reacted badly. . ." He shook his head. "Well, disappointment would be an understatement. We'd spent years preparing, testing, filing paperwork." He gave me a pleading look. "And there's really no way to tell for sure if the patients were genuinely reacting to the drug or if something else was going on. You know?"

"Mm-hmm." I looked up from my page into his eyes.

"Most of the clinical research proved that the drug was effective and safe. It's just such a shame. . . ."

"Let me ask you a question." I hated to interrupt the man but felt impressed to ask about something. "Don't all incoming drugs go through this rigmarole?"

"Yes."

"And surely all of them—at least *most* of them—have some noticeable side effects. Some more serious than others, I'd imagine."

"Right."

"So, what's the problem with just putting all your cards on the table? Wouldn't everything just be factored into the overall equation?"

"This was our in-office argument all along. All of the evidence needs to be considered, of course. And the general consensus was that the drug would have met FDA approval, regardless. Even in light of the problems we'd seen in research. The complications would have been listed on the "possible side effects" page that every patient receives when he or she picks up a prescription at the pharmacy."

"Right."

"Problem is. . ." He looked up as the waitress approached with my salad in hand. She put it down on the table and headed off to fetch his sandwich. "Problem is," Bob now whispered, "the company is in fairly serious financial trouble. I can't tell you how important it is that we get approval for that drug. Dozens of people stand to lose their jobs, otherwise—everyone from chemists to drug reps."

"Wow."

"You have no idea." He pursed his lips for a moment before continuing. "There's so much money involved—from Point A to Point Z. And the company just forked over a small fortune to a high-dollar firm they've chosen to name the drug."

Aha. "So it won't be HD-387 forever, then?" I pushed the salad aside and penciled his words into my notebook. "By the time it hits the market, it will have a *real* name?"

"Right." At that moment, his cell phone rang. He glanced at the caller ID, and the wrinkles around his mouth deepened further. "Do you mind if I take this? It's my wife."

"Of course not." I nibbled at my salad as he answered.

I did my best not to eavesdrop as he entered into a rather intense conversation with his wife. She was clearly upset about something; but it was none of my business, so I tried to focus on other things, like the fact that McKinley Pharmaceutical Company was in financial trouble. That meant Scott's job was likely in jeopardy. But why his sudden disappearance? Was it possible someone had kidnapped him to shut him up? To keep him from making a big deal out of something that might not be a big deal? I couldn't wrap my head around it, though the words "I'm fine, *but*. . ." still filled my stomach with butterflies.

Bob clicked his cell phone shut and gave me an aggravated look. "Sorry about that. Trouble on the home front. Why is it that calamities always seem to happen one on top of the other?"

"My daughter just asked me that same thing." I proceeded to give him my thoughts on it, but he seemed too distracted to take me seriously. Moments later, he glanced up at the waitress, who appeared with his sandwich in hand.

"Here you go, sir."

The plate had barely touched the table before he dove right in. "Sorry, I'm in a hurry."

I shrugged and continued to nibble at my salad, though it didn't quite hit the spot. Since Scott's disappearance, nothing tasted good anymore—except my mother's cooking, of course. And now that I thought about it, that walnut fudge had certainly hit the spot, though she'd done such a great job of hiding it away that I hadn't been able to locate it since the day of her arrival.

The meal came to an abrupt end a few minutes later when Bob received another call. After spending a couple more minutes on the phone, he turned his attention back to me. "I have something for you."

"Oh?"

He reached down for his briefcase and opened it with only

the tiniest slit of an opening. With his fingertips, he pulled out a manila folder.

"Read these when you can. But you didn't get them from me. Understand?"

I gave a nervous nod, trying all the while to swallow the growing lump in my throat. Then I shoved the envelope into my notebook.

Kendricks quickly paid the bill, mouthed a strained good-bye, and shuffled out of the diner into the afternoon cold.

I made what started out to be a quick trip to the ladies' room, where I hoped to snag a look at the contents of the envelope. As I slipped inside the first tiny stall, all of the things we had discussed at the table raced through my brain. I couldn't get over the fact that Bob had been willing to share so much information. I prayed the Lord would protect him. I also prayed the Lord would guide me, now that I was privy to "said information." The very last thing I needed right now was to find myself enmeshed in an FDA drug-approval attempt gone awry.

I opened my notebook and pulled out the manila envelope. What I found almost took my breath away. *No way.* Several letters between Kendricks and a man who called himself John Smith.

John Smith?

I quickly skimmed their correspondence. From what I could gather, "said John Smith" was a clinical-research patient from the Philadelphia area. According to one of the letters, he had been hospitalized in ICU at one of Philly's more prominent hospitals with congestive heart failure last spring. Due to his terminal condition, he'd been admitted to the research program. Things had gone well—at first. Then HD-387 had started to turn on him.

"This is the man," I whispered. "This is the one who nearly died from the medication." I shoved the envelope back into my notebook, completely unsure of what to do next.

A funny sound emitted from my cell phone, distracting me. Odd. Didn't sound like the usual ring. I reached inside my purse for the phone and opened it to find a text message from an unfamiliar number. The words were cryptic, strange.

"In the dark." I read them aloud, unable to make sense of them. "In the dark?" I looked at the phone number again, puzzled by the fact that it seemed familiar. Where had I seen it before?

Just then, realization hit. "Scott! That's Scott's number!" I swung back my arm to look at the phone once more, but as I did, it slid from my fingers and landed with a splash in the commode below.

I glanced down, horrified as I realized my dilemma.

Hmm. I stared at the beautiful silver phone—my latest toy— and groaned. *What to do, what to do. . .*

As always, Sheila's lyrical voice floated through my head. What was it she always said at times like this? *Ah yes. "The only substitute for good manners is fast reflexes."*

I couldn't agree more.

In one swift move, I plunged my hand into the toilet, snagged the phone, and bolted from the stall. Heading to the closest sink, I scrubbed my hands with soap and water like there was no tomorrow.

Finally, when all was said and done, I stared at the soggy phone, which still rested on the edge of the sink. I grabbed a couple of paper towels and wrapped them around it, dabbing till the crazy thing appeared dry. Then I opened it and did my best to dry it from the inside out. Finally, when I was sure I'd removed all hint of the toilet water aroma, I attempted to turn it on. I had to read the cryptic message once more, to make sure I had it right.

You know, a funny thing happens to a cell phone when it's been submerged in toilet water. The screen still lights up, but not in the way you'd expect. A kaleidoscope of colors greeted me—blues, greens, and reds, all dancing about in colorful array.

"Wow, that's pretty." Not very practical, but lovely, to be sure. I waited to see if the usual welcome screen would eventually greet me. "Come on, come on."

No such luck.

The screen was gone.

The text message was gone.

My address book was gone.

"Great." I'd never memorized a phone number in my life. Everything I needed was stored in that phone. *Everything.*

"Now what?" In one klutzy move, I'd lost my only clue to Scott's whereabouts and cut off my communication with the outside world. How in the world would I maintain my supersleuth status now?

I Just Called to Say I Love You

I arrived home and hid the manila envelope in my underwear drawer. I figured no one would bother looking through my granny panties for any sort of evidence. I couldn't stop thinking about everything Bob had said, and what I'd read in those letters. Were the folks at McKinley somehow responsible for Scott's disappearance?

I'd have to pray about that, for sure. And I'd also have to pray about whether or not to pass those letters off to O'Henry. I telephoned Warren to let him know about my adventurous day, and he let me know right off that I needed to share every detail with the good sergeant. He was especially concerned about the text message and asked me several times, "Annie, are you sure it was from Scott? Are you absolutely sure?"

To be honest, the more time passed, the less sure I became. I hadn't gotten a good look at the number, had I? It looked like Scott's, but had I really seen what I thought I'd seen? Oh, if only

I could have the phone back in its preimmersed condition, even for a moment!

Later that evening, Nadine and my mother met me in the kitchen with identical looks on their faces that screamed, "You're never going to believe this!"

I stared them down, waiting to see who would crack first.

"We were at the craft store," my mother started.

"And there was this man. . . ." Nadine's eyes grew wide.

"He followed us from aisle to aisle."

"And then I noticed he had a camera."

"He was taking her picture." Mom gestured to Nadine. "He was taking *our* picture."

Aha. "What did he look like?" I asked. "Was he tall?" *Our prowler, perhaps?*

"No." My mother shook her head. "He was a short fellow. Light brown hair. With a beard. Maybe in his thirties."

Ah. The man at the airport, then.

"And when we left the craft store, we went to lunch with the girls," Nadine added. "He turned up there, too."

"At the Burger Barn? He followed you into the restaurant?"

"Yes." Nadine's hands trembled. "He sat three tables away, but I could tell he was listening in on our conversation. He was even taking notes."

"Was he eating?"

"No, ma'am." My mother's voice grew more animated. "Didn't eat a thing. Just sat there with his notepad on the table, writing things down."

"What did you do?"

My mother smiled. "Well, I did what any true southern lady

would do. I marched right up to him, asked him what in the world he thought he was doing, and told him we didn't appreciate being spied on. Then I informed him that we had friends in high places and that if he knew what was good for him, he would skedaddle."

"Oh my." I couldn't help but wonder at the fellow's reaction.

"You've never seen anyone move so fast." Nadine brushed a loose blond hair from her eye. "He shot out of the restaurant without speaking to anyone. Not a word." She gave me a wistful look. "Annie, I think I know what this is about."

"You do?"

"Yes. I've been worried all along that my opponents would send their cronies after me, and apparently they've done just that. I think they're trying to scare me."

"Do you think they would go so far as to. . ."

She looked down at the table and shook her head. "I don't know. I can't imagine it. Can you?" She looked up with a shrug. "It just doesn't make sense."

Just then, the house phone let out a piercing ring, startling us all. These days, it didn't take much to get our nerves on edge. Brandi's anxious voice greeted me as I answered it. "Mom, can you and Nadine come to Scott's place right away?"

"What's happened?"

"It might be nothing," she said, "but I'd feel better if you came by. And bring Dad, too. I've asked O'Henry to join us."

"You've got it." I was happy to hear O'Henry would be joining us. I couldn't wait to tell him about my text message from Scott. I also wondered if I shouldn't go ahead and tell him about the letters I'd received.

On the other hand, Bob Kendricks was counting on my silence in that area.

What a dilemma.

Less than ten minutes later, we all entered Scott's still-messy apartment. My thoughts could hardly keep up with my ever-increasing heart rate. *Lord, calm my spirit. And give me wisdom.*

"You need to hear this phone message," Brandi said. "It's brand-new. I know, because I've been checking every day." She reached to turn on the answering machine, weeding her way through a couple of messages before landing on the one she wanted us to hear. A man's voice, unfamiliar and very deep, greeted us.

"Scott, I got your message. Listen, I don't know about this whole wedding thing—if I should come or not. I. . ." Here the man stumbled over his words. "I don't rightly figure I deserve to come, all things considered. But if you want me there. . .well. . ."

The message ended abruptly. Brandi started the message over again, and this time, I took notes as the man's voice kicked in.

"Scott, I got your message. Listen, I don't know about this whole wedding thing—if I should come or not. I—I don't rightly figure I deserve to come, all things considered. But if you want me there. . .well. . ."

Brandi turned off the machine, then looked up at all of us with terror in her eyes.

O'Henry pulled out his tablet and pen and looked my daughter in the eye. "Is the voice familiar?"

"No."

"Are you sure?" he asked. "One of his friends? Coworkers?"

"Honestly, I've never heard it before in my life."

"Strange." He scribbled a few words onto his notepad.

From the other side of the room, tremulous words took us all by surprise. "I recognize that voice." We all turned to look at Nadine.

"Excuse me?" O'Henry asked.

She nodded, her face as white as a ghost. "I know that voice as well as I know my own."

"You do?" I reached for my notebook, sure she was on to something. "Who is it, honey?"

"My ex-husband. Otis."

"Whoa. Are you sure?" I asked.

With eyes as wide as saucers, Nadine nodded. "Oh yes. That voice still sends a shiver down my spine, even after all these years."

"But. . ." Brandi shook her head, clearly confused. "I don't get it. Why would he call Scott?" She looked at all of us, palms raised in frustration. "You heard the message. It sounded like Otis had already received an invitation to the wedding. That doesn't make sense to me. Scott hardly ever talked about his dad—not in a positive way, anyhow. And we never discussed inviting him to the wedding. I don't even think Scott would've known how to reach him."

I jotted down a few notes, then looked over at Brandi. "Maybe Scott was trying to make amends with his father and didn't want to tell you about it, for fear it wouldn't go the way he hoped."

"Or maybe he and his father had already made amends, but Otis assumed you wouldn't take to the idea of him showing up at your wedding," O'Henry tried.

"None of this makes sense to me," Nadine said. "Otis and Scott haven't communicated since Scott was seven years old."

"Can you tell us more about that?" O'Henry asked.

Nadine's eyes took on a faraway look, but I could see the anger register. *Odd.* This was the first time I'd ever seen Nadine display this kind of emotion.

"My ex-husband dropped off the face of the earth when Scott was five," she started. "When I didn't hear from him for nearly two years, I had to make some tough decisions. Then, by the time he dropped by the house—in a drunken stupor, I might add—I'd already filed for divorce. He told me he was living in his car. Wasn't sure I believed him, but I handed him some cash and sent him on his way—with a promise from him that he wouldn't show up again till he'd sobered up."

Wow. I'd heard Scott refer to his deadbeat dad but had no details—till now. And how interesting that Nadine had such compassion on Milby's homeless community, in light of all she'd been through with her ex.

"I'm just so confused." The bewildered look on Brandi's face continued as she pushed aside a laundry basket and sat on the sofa.

I paced the floor, thoughts reeling. Finally, I paused to ask a question. "Nadine, what does Otis look like?"

"Goodness." She sat on the sofa next to Brandi with a thoughtful look on her face. "Remember, it's been nearly twenty years since I've seen him." Her eyes narrowed as she reflected on it. "That last time I saw him, he was in such bad shape physically—from the alcohol. Quite a contrast to the tall, dark, and handsome man I'd married."

"Tall, dark, and handsome?" I drew in a breath and faced her. "How tall?"

"Oh, I don't know. Probably a little taller than Scott. Maybe six foot two? Or even six foot three."

Bingo. "Hair color?"

"Dark brown, when I knew him. I'd imagine he's probably turned gray by now."

Or not.

"Thin as a rail?" I asked. "With exceptionally large feet?"

"Annie, what are you thinking?" No sooner had she asked the question than Nadine clamped a hand over her mouth. "The man in the backyard? It was Otis?"

"Had to be." I paced the room, trying to piece together the evidence in my head. "He somehow figured out you were staying at my house. And he's the one. . ." I looked up to face them all as the truth registered. "He's the one who left the note on the door. He wanted your permission to attend the wedding."

"Oh my goodness." Nadine stood and began to pace with me. Her brow wrinkled as she spoke. "I don't think I can stomach seeing the man again. I really don't. You all have no idea how awful he is. What a mess. . ."

"Maybe he's changed." Warren, who had remained silent till now, finally decided to interject his thoughts on the matter. "Maybe he's ready to face you and Scott after all these years because he feels the time is right."

"Or maybe. . ." I looked up from my notebook to face the others. "Maybe that's what he *wants* us to think. Maybe he's the one responsible for Scott's disappearance."

O'Henry gave me a thoughtful nod and muttered, "That's what I was thinking, too."

I allowed my thoughts to travel in several different directions at once. Surely Otis had come to town for some specific reason. Would he want to hurt Scott—perhaps to get back at Nadine for something that happened years ago? Or was he genuinely interested in mending their relationship, as the phone message indicated?

After an extended conversation, we finished up at Scott's apartment, then headed home. Once there, my mother made her way to the fridge to warm up some of the goodies the church ladies had brought over. I managed to swallow a few bites of a nondescript casserole but couldn't really focus on food. Not tonight.

My mom offered to fetch the hidden package of fudge, but even that didn't sound good to me. "You need to eat to keep up your strength, Annie," she scolded.

"Sorry, nothing tastes right. And besides, I'm supposed to be. . ."

"I know, I know. . . You're on a diet." She turned to me with a chuckle. "Now me. . .*my* idea of a balanced diet is a cookie in each hand."

God bless that mother of mine. I got so tickled that I couldn't stop laughing for a good sixty seconds.

Later, as I crawled into bed, I reached over to click on the bedside table lamp. Reaching for my notebook, I pondered this evening's turn of events. As much as I hated to admit it, I had to add one more fact to my ever-growing list.

Fact #9: Scott's father has arrived on the scene at the very time his son has disappeared. Coincidence?

Only time would tell.

I leaned back against the headboard, deep in thought. Suddenly, reality hit. In all that had happened tonight, I'd somehow forgotten to tell O'Henry about the text message. And I'd totally forgotten about the letters.

Hmm. There would be plenty of time to deal with those things. Tomorrow.

BRIDGE OVER TROUBLED WATER

If people prayed better with food in their stomachs, as Sheila suggested, they must pray exceptionally well after eating my mother's grits.

The entire town of Clarksborough, minus only a few, met together at the church on Saturday morning at eight o'clock for a prayer meeting before the search-and-rescue mission. Overnight, another rainstorm had blown through, leaving icy roads and muddy fields in its wake. Just what we needed on a day like today.

Although I was accustomed to seeing many people from the community together in one place during our annual picnics and parades, it was quite a sight to see them all crammed into the gymnasium at the church—and all in support of our family.

Janetta Mullins, darling woman that she was, turned up with a huge breakfast casserole. Instead of gushing over it, as I might've been prone to do under other circumstances, I simply nodded and whispered a gentle, "Thank you." She nodded back with tears in her eyes.

Jake, her youngest son, arrived moments later with Nikki at his side, as always. Nikki rushed to Brandi right away, trying to make herself useful. Within minutes, I noticed the two girls huddled together, tears flowing.

Candy and Garrett arrived on the scene with a tray of coffee cakes in hand, which Candy had baked from scratch. I gave her a kiss on the cheek and thanked her for being such a great sister. Right away, tears filled her eyes. She didn't say a word. She didn't have to.

Sheila worked to oversee the food tables, scurrying about like a mother hen, fussing over her brood. My mom, never one to let others take charge at a church event, made herself useful in the kitchen, stirring the monstrous pan of grits and making coffee. In spite of all the people, the room remained eerily quiet. Somber, even.

Our men—Warren, Brad, and my father, anyway—went off in search of Pastor Miller. Once located, he entered the room, prayed over our food, and we dove right in.

As I sat there, observing the room full of people I loved, I couldn't help but think about Scott. I wondered if he knew just how many people cared about him. Wondered if he realized there was a gaping hole in each of our hearts since his disappearance. Wondered if he'd had anything to eat this morning, or if. . .

No. Stop it, Annie. Don't think like that.

We settled down to eat, and many of my northern friends nibbled at small helpings of grits for the first time in their lives. Most couldn't seem to figure out what they were, but a brave few dove in headfirst, ready to face the challenge. The expressions on most of their faces were priceless. I only wished I'd had a camera on hand.

Afterward, we all gathered in a circle around the room, joining hands. Pastor Miller said a few kind words, then led in prayer. One by one, the people in the circle began to pray. I was taken aback by their passion for Scott and Brandi. *Thank You, Lord, for these amazing people.* Men, women, and children prayed with great gusto, pleading with the Almighty to return Scott to his rightful owner. Well, rightful *earthly* owner. Many times during the prayer, I opened my eyes just enough to catch a peek at Brandi, who swiped at her tears every few seconds.

At nine o'clock, just about the time things were winding down, Sergeant O'Henry made his entrance. I managed to catch him before anyone else could and shared the news about the text message. He gave me a curious look and wrote the words *In the dark* in his notebook.

"Any idea what it means?" he asked me.

"None." I offered up a shrug. "Though I've lost quite a bit of sleep trying to figure it out. I wondered at first if it wasn't sent at night. Maybe he was literally in the dark while writing it. You know?"

"Do you think. . ." O'Henry leaned down to whisper the next part in my ear, "he's in the dark where their relationship is concerned? Having second thoughts?"

I had to admit, the idea had occurred to me. "I don't know." I shook my head, determined to be positive. "I think there's more to it than that. But it just doesn't make sense—at least not yet."

"Does Brandi know?"

"I told her this morning."

"What's her take on this?"

"She didn't know what to think," I said with a shrug. "And you know how she is. She's afraid to get her hopes up."

"Can't say I blame her there." O'Henry closed his notebook and turned to face the crowd. He clapped his hands together.

"Could I have your attention, everyone?" He went on to give instructions. I watched Brandi out of the corner of my eye as the good sergeant told us where to go and what to do. My daughter's lower lip quivered—a family trait. But she managed to dry her eyes when people were watching. *Ah, being strong today, are we? Good for you, Brandi. Good for you.*

The next several hours, we all worked in shifts, searching for Scott. The weather made things especially difficult, but no one complained. They wouldn't dare. Not when our task was so great. Mother and Sheila set up stations on various street corners where people could stop and get cups of coffee or hot chocolate. God bless those women. What had I ever done to deserve them?

Though we combed every wooded area, every park, every field. . .though we left not a stone or a bench unturned in all of Clark County. . .there was no sign of Scott anywhere. Even with the help of the aerial search planes hovering over us, the day ended on a somber note. We wrapped up the search at two o'clock, discouraged and frozen through and through.

Afterward, Warren and I went for a drive alone. We needed the time together as a couple, but we also needed to do something else. I had to replace my phone—the sooner the better. I was lost without it.

We pulled onto Main Street, turning toward the center of

town. Clarksborough didn't boast many local businesses, but the community had recently welcomed Mobile Mania—a slightly overpriced national cell phone provider. They took over the empty shop where Polly's Pet Store used to reside. The room still had a lingering kitty litter odor, one the new proprietors hadn't been able to wash away, but the locals didn't mind—at least not those of us who owned pets.

Warren pulled up to the only empty spot, which happened to be directly in front of Pfifer's Photography, Mobile Mania's next-door neighbor. The CLOSED sign hung on the front door of the photography studio, and I could see through the window to the unlit room inside. Probably for the best. If Malcolm had seen us, he probably would've asked for the additional deposit money.

After exiting the car, something caught my eye, distracting me a bit. I paused at the window of the photography studio long enough to ogle over an exquisite photograph of a smiling bride and groom. Just looking at it broke my heart.

"Don't focus on that, Annie." Warren took me by the arm and guided me toward the cell phone store.

Once inside, I settled on a small, blue jazzy-looking phone with all sorts of cool features, most of which I'd probably never figure out. Purchasing a phone midcontract appeared to be costly, but I had no choice, really. And another piece of bad news awaited me. With the chip in my old phone completely destroyed by the submersion, there was no way to transfer data to the new one. I'd have to enter every single phone number manually. What a pain.

We arrived home to find everyone napping. I took the opportunity to slip off into the office to locate some of the missing phone numbers. Not an easy task.

I started with Sheila. Now, Sheila had been my best friend for as long as I could remember, but I'd never actually known the woman's phone number. Whenever I wanted to call her, I just opened my cell phone, punched in *S* and clicked *OK* when her name appeared. Easy enough. But today, I found myself in a quandary. She could probably provide many of the numbers I needed, but I had to locate her number first.

After letting me stumble around in the dark awhile, Warren finally appeared with the church's phone directory. *Bless you, Warren!* I found Sheila's information within and quickly entered her number into my new phone. Thankfully, the church directory also had several of the other numbers on my list—including my own children's—but a few were still lacking.

I called Brandi to get the numbers for the wedding vendors. The exhaustion in her voice rang through, and she didn't even try to hold back on the emotion as we talked. I could tell she was reaching the breaking point.

"One week from today, Mom." She just kept saying those words. "One week from today, I'm supposed to marry Scott. And I can't find him to marry him—even with everyone in town helping me track him down."

I managed to redirect her thinking, discussing my gratitude to the many people who had come out to help search this morning. We talked at length about Jason and the other groomsmen, who had outdone themselves today, searching for hours on end. Surely they would not have gone to such trouble if they were playing a prank. Right? Eventually, I shifted the conversation to a discussion about the wedding vendors, and within a few minutes, I'd entered several more numbers into my phone.

I didn't let things end there, however. I took several minutes at the end of the call to console Brandi, even praying with her before we hung up.

Now came the hard part. I had to talk to my mother. I waited till we were all seated around the dinner table, eating some of the Chinese food Sheila had brought over from Lee Yu's Garden, to approach her.

"Mom, I know this is embarrassing, but what is your phone number?" I swallowed a mouthful of moo goo gai pan and waited for her reply.

"Excuse me?" My mother looked stunned, and who could blame her? She was the type who'd probably memorized every phone number she'd ever dialed.

I did my best to explain as I took another bite. "I had to replace my cell phone, and I don't have your number."

She stared at me for a good minute, fork suspended in midair, as if trying to figure out how anyone in her bloodline could possibly live without good memorization skills.

"This might be the twenty-first century," she said as she put her fork down, "but memorizing phone numbers is still essential. Why, what would you do if. . ." She went off on a tangent, naming several rather far-fetched scenarios. The only one she left out was the one that applied. *What if you dropped your cell phone in a public toilet and had to replace it with a new one?*

By the time the conversation ended, I realized she still hadn't given me her number. But I'd grown weary with the discussion and decided I'd wait till later and get it from my father, who'd managed to sit in silence through the whole meal with the tiniest hint of a smile on his face. I knew he loved it when my mom got wound up like that.

We rose from the table, and I started to do the dishes when Warren, ever the hero, swept in to offer his assistance. "Don't you ladies worry about doing the dishes tonight," he said. "The men will take care of it."

I didn't argue, though it did seem a bit ironic that he'd offered on a night when we'd eaten takeout. There weren't many dishes to load into the dishwasher, after all. Still, if he wanted to play the knight-in-shining-armor card, I'd let him.

Brad joined Warren in clearing the table, but my dad headed off to the den, probably anxious to turn on the sports channel. My mother stopped him just as he rounded the corner.

"Hubert, where are you going?"

"Oh, I thought I'd. . ." He gestured toward the television.

She pointed him back in the direction of the kitchen with a brusque, "No man has ever been shot while doing the dishes."

Yep. Southern charm at its best, even though I questioned the validity of her statement.

Perhaps there was more of my mama in me than I dared admit.

I spent the better part of the evening jotting down my thoughts in my notebook and contemplating the overall picture. I had my suspicions but still wasn't ready to point a finger at anyone yet. Not when there was so much investigative work yet to be done.

Later that night, just after I'd crawled into bed and flipped off the bedside table light, I thought back over Scott's cryptic text message. *In the dark.*

I whispered the words, trying to make sense of them. "In the dark."

For the first time, I allowed myself to think the worst. Perhaps that message from Scott was his last message. . .ever. One last cry for help. Maybe he'd not only been kidnapped, maybe he'd been. . ."

No. I wouldn't let myself go there. "He's in the dark," I whispered.

And so was I. In fact, tonight, I felt as if it just might swallow me whole.

CHAPTER 18

I WILL FOLLOW HIM

Sheila once tried to tell me there was a fine line between a hobby and mental illness. I hadn't taken her seriously till lately. Now I had to wonder if she wasn't right. Had I really gone too far with this crime-fighting thing? Had my "hobby" caused me to slip off the edge? Surely only over-the-edge people stayed up half the night, tossing and turning.

The next morning, I entered the sanctuary of Clarksborough Community Church and headed straight to the fifth pew on the left, the usual spot for the Peterson family. I tried to focus on the people around me, nodding at several who spoke words of comfort and encouragement, but I couldn't seem to think clearly enough to engage them in actual conversation.

All night long, I'd forced myself not to think about the cryptic text message, finally convincing myself the whole thing had been a mistake. But this morning, I'd awakened with a sick feeling in the pit of my stomach. The message had something to do with

Scott's disappearance. I knew it. I just knew it.

My nerves were as bundled as the cords and cables behind my computer desk, even after praying with Warren one-on-one. Even now, as I took my seat in the familiar comfort of my church's sanctuary, I prayed for God's peace to envelop me. I didn't want anything to keep me from experiencing His presence today. I needed to spend time with Him, to hear His voice.

As I scooted into my seat, Sheila came huffing my way, a look of disgust on her face. "Honestly," she said. "Some people are kind, polite, and sweet-spirited—until you try to sit in their pew."

"Excuse me?" For a moment, I thought she was referring to me, but she gestured to our right, instead. I looked that way, tickled to see Tomi Yu seated there, alongside an older couple that I guessed to be his parents. Down a few feet from them sat a familiar persnickety woman with a sour look on her face and spindly arms crossed at her chest.

"Etta Mae Caldwell." Sheila's lips tightened as she said the name. "She's been sitting in the same pew for fifty-five years, and I guess she figures she owns it. She had the nerve to tell me her tithe checks have more than covered the cost of it. Can you believe that?"

"You're joking."

"Nope. But the Yu family needed a place to sit—and it had to be close to the front because Mr. Yu has a slight hearing loss." Sheila shook her head in disgust. "You wouldn't believe what I had to go through to get Etta to move down a few feet. I tell you. . . We nearly had words."

"Oh my."

"Yes." Sheila squared her shoulders. "But I refuse to have a battle of wits with an unarmed person."

She dove off into an animated play-by-play of the story, and I did my best to follow along. However, the Yu family kept me slightly distracted. Out of the corner of my eye, I watched as Tomi spoke with his parents, even gesturing around the sanctuary to share his enthusiasm for the place. I hated to cut Sheila off mid-sentence, but with so many unanswered questions, I needed to get to work.

"Excuse me, honey." I stood and inched around her, making my way to the opposite side of the sanctuary.

I could hear Sheila's, "Well, I never!" all the way across the room but chose to ignore it. Instead, I marched right up to Tomi with a courageous smile and introduced myself to his parents. His mother, a lovely woman named Sumey, seemed to take to me right away. His father, Lee, was a bit more reserved.

After a little chitchat, I worked up the courage to broach the subject at hand. "Can I ask you a question?" I looked directly into Tomi's eyes.

"Of course."

"Last week, you started to tell me something about Scott. You said a man had come into your restaurant, asking questions about him. We never got to finish that conversation. I tried to call you at the restaurant this week, but you'd gone out of town."

"Ah, yes. Sorry about that, but I had interviews at a couple of colleges." Tomi paused for a moment, then picked up where he'd left off last week. "I remember now. A man stopped by, looking for Scott. Said they were supposed to have lunch together and started asking a lot of questions about that place where Scott works. A pharmaceutical company, I think."

"That's right. McKinley Pharmaceuticals."

"Yes, that's it. He seemed to know a lot about Scott and his coworkers—things that I didn't even know at the time."

Whoa. "Interesting. Was it a really tall man with big feet?"

"Hmm." Tomi didn't answer for a minute. I could almost see the wheels in his head clicking. "Average height, I'd say. And I never noticed his feet."

Hmm. Maybe the man at the airport? "Blond?"

"Nope. Kind of a light brown, I guess you'd say."

Great. Someone else to factor in. "And Scott wasn't there?" I asked.

"No. I hadn't seen him since that first time he'd come in." Tomi smiled. "You know that story, right? He ended up at our place one Sunday a couple of months back when he was supposed to go to Leonardo's."

"Yeah." I shrugged. "He's a little goofy like that."

"Maybe," Tomi said, "And I guess you could call it a mistake. But I thank God every day for that mistake. If Scott hadn't come in when he did. . ." He shook his head, and his eyes misted over. "To be honest, I was at a crossroad that day. I honestly believe his visit was. . ." The crease in his forehead wrinkled. "What do you call it again—a divine appointment?"

"Wow."

"Yes. I needed answers, and he just sort of appeared—out of the blue."

"Wish he'd do the same right now." The sigh that followed just kind of slipped out on its own.

"Me, too." Tomi reached to squeeze my hand. "I've been praying for him every day. And I'm sorry we couldn't be here yesterday to help with the search, but we had to keep the restaurant open. My parents. . ."—he gestured their way—"are really dependent on me, and I need to be there for them."

"Of course. I understand completely."

At that moment, the worship music began, and I excused myself to join my family on the other side of the aisle. As the service progressed, I thought about what Tomi had said, focusing on the part where someone had come to the restaurant looking for Scott. Someone who wanted to know about his work. Someone who seemed to know a lot about Scott.

Pastor Miller began his message with a familiar scripture from Psalm 27. With great zeal, he read, " 'The Lord is my light and my salvation—whom shall I fear? The Lord is the stronghold of my life; of whom shall I be afraid?' "

Wow. That certainly got my attention. I needed that reminder, today of all days. In spite of everything, what did I really have to fear, as long as the Lord was my light and my salvation? I needed—no, I wanted—to push all fears aside and move forward. But how?

Pastor Miller immediately went to another one of my favorite passages from Psalm 139. " 'If I say, "Surely the darkness will hide me and the light become night around me," even the darkness will not be dark to you; the night will shine like the day, for darkness is as light to you.' "

Okay. I was starting to notice a resounding theme here. Light versus dark. Hope versus hopelessness. Coincidence? I could hardly imagine it. No, the Lord surely had something in mind for me this morning, and I'd better be paying attention.

Pastor Miller began to share with great zeal about a "dark" period in his life—when his oldest daughter had passed away at the tender age of seven. With a tremor in his voice, he shared how he and his wife had felt swallowed by the darkness in the weeks following her death. Then he went on to tell the story of how the Lord had used those passages from the book of Psalms to minister to them, to bring hope.

I was in need of an infusion of hope right now myself, so I hung on his every word. By the end of the message, my resolve had returned, along with my courage. I wouldn't let the enemy of my soul defeat me with smoke and mirrors. I would allow God's light to shine on the situation and point me in the right direction.

And I would do it all with His hand in mine.

DON'T BE CRUEL

Monday morning, Nadine and I sat together at the breakfast table as my mother scurried around, waiting on us hand and foot. I knew it somehow made her feel better to be put to work, so I didn't scold her for tidying up after she fed us. We were well into an all-too-familiar conversation about the wedding—whether or not to cancel it—when Brad entered the room.

"Nadine, could I talk to you for a minute?"

She looked up, and I could see the fear in her eyes. "What's happened?"

"I just got a call from Edwards."

She looked my way and said, "My campaign manager."

Brad continued on, clearly a man with something on his mind. "I think there's something you need to see."

He approached the table with her laptop in his hands. "Edwards told me to check out the Savannah paper online, told me I'd want to see the headline." Brad turned the computer screen to face us, and Nadine gasped as she read the words, PERSONAL ISSUES CLOUD CUNNINGHAM'S RUN FOR CITY COUNCIL IN NEARBY MILBY.

"What in the world?" Nadine pulled the computer closer to read the article aloud. The piece focused primarily on Scott's disappearance and Nadine's emergency visit to the state of Pennsylvania. Several questions were raised as to the timing.

"What do they think—that I deliberately had my son disappear just to garner attention?" Nadine looked up from the computer, a look of horror on her face. "As if *that* would make anyone want to vote for me. And where in the world are they gettin' all of this information anyway? Who are they talkin' to?"

Brad's face paled. "Keep reading."

We all turned our gaze back to the computer, and before long, we were all talking over one another. "Otis Fuller." Nadine's faced reddened. "My *ex-husband* is talkin' to the media? Why?"

There, off to the side, was a photo of "said Otis Fuller." Big Foot. In the flesh. Though not quite as intimidating as I'd remembered.

"What in the world does he think he's doing, stickin' his nose in this?" Nadine asked. "He hasn't seen Scott for over twenty years, and he suddenly shows up and becomes an expert in parentin' and politics? It's not right, I tell you."

"Keep reading," Brad encouraged her.

By the end of the article, everything was crystal clear. Otis Fuller was here in Clarksborough. Had been for two weeks. He'd already made one appearance—albeit briefly—in my backyard. And he'd made another today—in the Savannah paper.

But why? Why had he come? Was it possible he'd come to town to respond to Scott's wedding invitation in person? Had he come out of curiosity, or had he. . .

A shiver ran down my spine as the possibilities surfaced. Did Otis have something to do with Scott's disappearance? Was he working with Nadine's political opponents, perhaps?

While the others in the room dove into a heated discussion, I took advantage of the opportunity to read through the article again. There was more here than met the eye, I felt sure. *Yes.* I paused as I read this sentence: *Nadine Cunningham has clearly proven that she cannot even manage or maintain her own home and family. How can we trust her to manage the affairs of our city?*

I read on, focusing on Otis's words. Oddly, they didn't sound negative at all, though the reporter had certainly done a good job of twisting them to sound bad. I paused when I read his thoughts concerning Scott: *I haven't seen my son in years, and I'm devastated to learn he is missing now, just when I've finally returned.*

"Nadine. . ." I looked up into her tear-stained eyes. "I'm not sure what to make of all of this, but why don't we track down Otis and ask him a few questions firsthand?"

"W—what?" She shook her head, and fear registered in her eyes. "You don't understand. I don't want to see him again. Not now, not *ev*-er."

"Even if he's. . ." I didn't finish, for fear she would crumble right before our eyes. "What would it hurt to figure out where he's staying, at the very least? He's got to be nearby. We've only got the one bed-and-breakfast here in Clarksborough, but there are a couple of motels out on the highway we could check."

"That man *ne*-vuh had money for a motel, let a-*lone* a bed-and-breakfast," she argued.

"It's been over twenty years, Nadine." Brad reached to touch her arm, and she sighed.

"Fine." She looked up into her husband's eyes. "But come with us. Please."

I glanced across the room at my parents. "Mom, can you hold down the fort while we're gone? Devin's due in from school at three thirty, and the seamstress is supposed to call at some point this afternoon about the alterations on Brandi's wedding dress. Oh, and I also got a note from the delivery guy. He tried to drop off a package on Saturday—another wedding present, no doubt— but no one was home. I'm afraid he's going to try to stop back by this afternoon."

"Well, of course!" my mother said with the wave of a hand. "Never you mind about all that. You just go off and do your crime solving. I'll stay here with your father and make some chicken and dumplings for our dinner tonight."

"But we've got all that food the people from church brought over," I tried to argue.

"Poo." She ushered me on out of the room. "Nothing's as good as my homemade chicken and dumplings, and you know it."

No argument there. Except the glaring one that faced me every time I opened my closet door and stared at that mother-of-the-bride dress.

I didn't have any time to worry about that at the moment, however. Not with a crime to solve. There would be plenty of time to count calories later.

Nadine, Brad, and I bundled up in our heaviest clothes. According to the weather report, another cold front appeared to be heading our way. Just what we needed. I managed to get the car started. *Thank you, Warren, for parking it in the garage overnight.* Then we were on our way.

I stopped first at the Clarksborough Bed-and-Breakfast on the outskirts of town. The place was relatively new—and not at all the sort of lodging I fancied a kidnapper staying in, but one could never be too sure. After a few words with Nita Fleming, the gal who ran the inn and who, coincidentally, sat next to me in Sunday school last week, I got my answer. No one matching Otis's description had been seen coming or going from the Clarksborough Bed-and-Breakfast. If she saw anyone matching that description, she would give me a call right away.

Undaunted, I turned the car out toward the highway. Perhaps answers would come at one of the nearby motels. I'd never stayed at either, but they boasted comfortable rooms at affordable rates. I found out exactly what that meant at the first place—EZ Travel. The manager met me at the front desk with a broad smile on his face—until he learned I wasn't there to check in. He shifted gears immediately and informed me he couldn't give me any information about his customers. Brad tried to argue, but to no avail. We left with no usable information.

The final place was a little farther away—approximately fifteen minutes on a good day. But today, with the roads in such terrible condition, those fifteen minutes swelled to thirty. By the time we arrived at The Happy Hideaway, we were badly shaken and in need of a restroom. Nadine headed off in search of the ladies' room, and I put my best foot forward with the young woman behind the desk. At first, she seemed amiable, even compassionate.

"I'm looking for a man," I started.

"Aren't we all, honey." She gave a little giggle.

"Well, the one I'm looking for is tall," I explained. "About six three, with dark hair."

"You like 'em a lot taller than I do, then!" She let out a chuckle. "I'm into shorter guys with blond hair."

I quickly explained myself. "No, see. . .I'm looking for a *particular* man who might be a guest at your hotel. His name is Otis Fuller."

"Ah, I understand." Her brow wrinkled, and she looked toward the back office. "Well, I'm not supposed to. . ."

"I just need to find him is all," I said. "I'm not going to hurt him or anything. Look at me." I couldn't help but laugh. "What kind of damage could I do to a man that size anyway? I'm only five four!"

"True, true." She turned to her computer. "What was his name again?"

Just then, her manager approached from the back room, with the remnants of what looked to be a powdered-sugar doughnut on his upper lip. "What's the trouble, Elaine?"

"Oh, nothing, sir."

"Can I help you?" He turned to face me, and a sinking feeling came over me.

Five minutes later, I knew I was out of luck. I gave up on convincing the manager, accepted the young woman's shrug as a silent apology, and turned my attention to Nadine, who had finally joined us, after quite some time in the restroom.

"My head is killin' me," she said. "All this talk about Otis is giving me a migraine. I think I need to take some aspirin."

She and Brad headed off to the car in search of her purse, but I lingered behind a bit. Call it instinct. Call it a prompting. Something just wouldn't let me leave. Not yet, anyway.

"Hey, lady." I heard a man's voice off to my left. I turned to see a short, chubby fellow with a newspaper in hand, sipping a cup of coffee.

"Yes?"

"You looking for a really tall guy? Got dark hair. Really thin?" The man's scraggly beard drew my attention. He could certainly use a shave.

"Yes! Do you know him?"

"Don't really *know* him," the guy said with a shrug, "but he's staying here, all right. Had breakfast with him this morning." He gestured to the microwave and the coffeemaker. "They've got a free continental breakfast here." He looked toward the front desk and then whispered, "If that's what you want to call stale muffins and burnt coffee."

"Do you know what room he's in?"

The guy shrugged. "We ain't pals or anything like that. I just said I had breakfast with him. Maybe he's already gone by now. I dunno."

I scribbled a brief note on a piece of paper and passed it off to the man, who promised he would give it to Otis, if he saw him again.

Then, with exhaustion and anxiety fighting over every pore in my body, I set out on the road toward home, ready for a much-needed nap. After that—I vowed—I'd make a trip to the gym for an extensive workout. I was, after all, days overdue.

Puppy Love

We arrived home at three fifteen to find my mother in a panic. I could hear her shrill cries all the way across the house. I sprinted down the hallway and into Devin's room—a.k.a. my mom and dad's quarters—where I was met by a rather startling scene. "W—what in the world?"

My mother's small overnight case lay open on the floor, the medicines from inside spilled out all over the floor. Sasha sat nearby, curled up in a tight ball, eyes squinted shut.

"Tell me she didn't."

"She did." My mother gestured to the tube of muscle-rub cream, partially chewed up. "But that's not the worst of it. Look." She pointed to a small mound of tiny white pills on the carpet near the edge of the bed and the open prescription bottle nearby. "Your father's heart medication."

"No!" For a moment, I wasn't sure what to do, which way to turn. Should I be more worried about the fact that my father was missing a few of his heart pills or concerned for the dog that had apparently eaten them?

"We can always call your father's doctor for a refill, if need be," Mom assured me with the wave of a hand. "But I think Sasha might need to be looked at. Heaven only knows how many she swallowed."

"Let's try to figure out how many. There's got to be a way."

Sasha's eyes opened and closed several times, and she appeared fidgety. *Hurry, Annie. Hurry.* We called Dad into the room, and together we counted through the pills we found on the carpet.

"There were sixty pills in the bottle when you had the prescription filled last week," I noted. "How many have you taken since?"

"Well. . ." He sat on the edge of the bed and scratched his chin. "I take one a day. Except on Sunday—I forgot to take one last Sunday. Remember, hon?" He looked at my mom for reassurance. "I told you. I went to bed early that night and plumb forgot."

"Yes, I remember."

After a little more conversation and theorizing, we finally concluded there must be two pills missing from the bottle. Sasha peeked one eye open, but I wasn't convinced. Was she just acting odd, having been caught doing something bad, or truly ill?

"What do you think, Mom?" I asked. "Do you think that's enough to hurt her? Should I take her in to the vet's office?"

"Of course you should!" My father was the first to take action. "By golly, these pills are strong. And the side effects are nothing to laugh at, either." He pulled out the paperwork for his medication and began to read. "Says here the medication can cause dry mouth, dizziness, drowsiness, constipation, headache, decreased sexual ability. . . ." He paused before adding, "Don't think we need to worry about that one."

"Hubert, please." My mother turned beet red.

Dad forged ahead, undeterred. "Also causes upset stomach, vomiting. . ." On and on he went, but I didn't need to hear any more. I quickly summarized that Sasha must, indeed, be rushed to the vet—and the sooner, the better.

Nadine, still nursing a headache, decided to remain behind with Brad.

"Devin should be here any minute," I told her. "Just don't let him go out again, okay? The roads are awful."

My father offered to drive, and I chose—albeit against my better judgment—to let him, so that I could hold Sasha on my lap. We climbed into my parents' car and headed out onto the icy roads.

"Oh, Hubert, be careful!" my mother moaned. "You're not used to driving in weather like this."

"Hush, woman."

My father was never one to mince words, but this time, I was on his side. My mom's anxiety was only making things worse.

Not that I was in better shape.

I directed my dad from one street corner to the next, till we finally reached the veterinarian's office. I sprang from the car with the listless pup in my arms. *Hang on, Sasha. Hang on.*

Once inside, the lady at the front desk listened to my frantic ramblings, took one look at Sasha and, bypassing all other animals in the place, set us up in an examining room right away. The vet joined us seconds later, a worried look on his face.

"What's wrong with my favorite patient?" Dr. Andrews asked.

I couldn't seem to speak past the lump in my throat. Thankfully, my parents took the lead.

"She ate two of these." My mother pressed the pill bottle into the vet's hands.

"They're 250 milligrams," my father added. "Do you think she's swallowed enough to do much damage?"

"More than enough." Dr. Andrews flew into gear. "We'll need to pump her stomach right away."

"Pump her stomach?" For a moment, the room started to spin. Of all things, we didn't need this. Not now.

"Yes," the veterinarian said. "Hopefully, not much of the medicine has hit her bloodstream. If it has. . ." He shook his head, then spoke with the wave of a hand. "You folks will have to have a seat in the waiting room." He scooped my droopy, doe-eyed baby up into his arms and headed for the door. "I'll take good care of her; I promise."

As he disappeared from view, I leaned into my father's outstretched arms and began to cry. How could this be happening? "I can't lose her." Others might not understand, but I couldn't bear the thought of losing my canine companion, especially not now, with so many other things going on.

"Hush now." My dad pulled me close. "She's going to be fine."

I took a couple of minutes to gain my composure, then reached for my cell phone. Much as I hated to bother Warren at the bank, I needed to let him know. I wouldn't bother the girls with the news, particularly not Brandi. I certainly didn't want her to think my worries over the dog somehow superseded my worries over our missing groom.

Warren didn't take the news well, which really surprised me. I knew he cared for the dog but never dreamed he was this attached.

I could scarcely make out his words as he said, "P—please keep me posted."

Wow. He does love her. I knew it!

About fifteen minutes later, the vet emerged, a perplexed look on his face.

I leaped from my seat. "How is she?"

"Resting comfortably." He ushered us back into the examining room. "Though I'm a bit confused."

"Confused?"

"It's a good thing we opted to pump her stomach." His eyes narrowed as he grew more serious. "I doubt she would have made it otherwise."

My heart twisted in pain as the reality hit. "Y—you got it? The medicine?"

"Well, that's the strange thing." He offered up a shrug. "I couldn't find any trace of medication in her stomach—unless the capsules had already dissolved, which would really surprise me, given the amount of time here. And her symptoms didn't necessarily lend themselves toward medical overdose."

"But you said. . ."

"What I found. . ."—he gave us the oddest look—"was approximately three ounces of thick dark chocolate, along with at least a tablespoon or so of walnuts."

"Oh no!" I clamped a hand over my mouth and turned to face my mother.

"The fudge!" she whispered. "I forgot I'd stuck it in the overnight bag to hide it from you!"

My dad let out a little grunt, and the doctor shook his head.

"It's a mighty good thing you brought Sasha in when you did.

Dogs have a very low tolerance for chocolate—and nuts. Either one could've been deadly in that quantity."

"Oh my goodness." I dropped into a chair. "It's a miracle." I looked up at my dad. "But what about those pills?"

He gave a shrug, and a blank expression covered his face. For a moment. Then, with the snap of his fingers, he seemed to remember something. "Oh, that's right! I took *two* pills last Monday to make up for the one I missed on Sunday. And I've already taken today's dose. So I guess that accounts for the missing tablets." He gave me a satisfied look, as if that solved everything. My mother, always needing the last word, punched him in the arm.

"Honestly," she said. "You're a grown man, Hubert. You need to remember how and when to take your medicine."

"Still. . ." I reached to give my dad a hug, "if it hadn't been for this mix-up, we wouldn't have known about the fudge." I looked up at the vet, curious about something. "It does seem odd that we didn't even notice the wrapper on the floor, though."

"Not so odd." The vet shrugged. "She ate that, too."

At this point, Doc Andrews asked some pointed questions about Sasha's behavior. He thumbed through her chart as he spoke, looking up at me on occasion. "I remember the last time you were here we spoke about Sasha's battle with SAD."

"SAD?" My parents spoke in unison.

"Separation Anxiety Disorder," the vet replied with a nod. "Sasha has a terrible case of it. I'd suggested to Annie that she try a couple of different things." He gave me a look that said, "Well, did you do the things I asked?"

I shrugged. "I've been a little busy." *Major understatement. Seriously.* The man had no idea.

"Well, I'd have to say her behaviors are still indicative of a dog trying to garner attention," Dr. Andrews said. "And this will only get worse over time. As I said before, I'd recommend behavioral training. There are people who can come to your home to train you one-on-one, or you can sign her up for classes at Coats 'n' Tails. They're pretty reasonable, and they do a fine job."

"I just don't have time for. . ." I started to explain.

"Or. . ." His face lit up, as if he'd just had an "aha" moment. "Maybe this would do the trick." He called for his assistant over the intercom, then added, "And bring in Copper."

"Copper? Hasn't she been through enough?" I asked. "Why give her copper? Is she low on minerals, too?"

"No, not that kind of copper." He flashed a suspicious grin.

The assistant opened the door and entered with a Sasha look-alike in her arms.

"What in the world?" I asked. This couldn't be my little girl. Why, this dachshund was considerably larger, with slightly darker red coloring.

"This is Copper," Dr. Andrews explained. "We've had a sign posted in the front office for weeks. Someone dropped him off here in the middle of the night ages ago. He's looking for a home."

"Oh no." I put my hands up in the air and backed away. "I couldn't. You don't understand. It's just that I. . ."

"He's had all of his shots," the vet said, "and he's not very old. Maybe six months or so. And he's clearly a purebred. Look at his features."

Sure enough, the little fellow had beautiful markings, right down to the hint of a mask on his face and the black tip on his tail.

"From what we can gather, based on his coloring, at least one of his parents was a black and tan and the other a red," the vet explained.

My dad scooped the lovable pooch into his arms, and the dachshund started licking him all over the face.

"Well, you sure are a friendly fellow, aren't you!" my dad said.

"Hubert," my mother warned.

"Dad, don't even think about it," I echoed. "Warren would. . ."

At that moment, the door opened again and another vet technician entered the room with Sasha in her arms. I smiled at the sight of my baby and reached to take her into my arms. She glanced over at the other dog, and her tail began to wag.

"Don't get your hopes up," I whispered in her ear.

"But, Annie. . ." My father's pleading eyes took me back a bit. He'd never been a dog lover, not that I could remember. Whatever in the world possessed him now was beyond me. The unfamiliar pooch was adorable, to be sure, but I didn't have time to think about any of this right now.

"Dr. Andrews, thanks for thinking of me." I pointed to the male dachshund, which seemed to have taken a liking to my dad's aftershave. "It's just not a good time for us. We're in the middle of a, uh, situation."

"I understand." He let out a little sigh, then reached to take the pooch from my dad, who suddenly looked as if he'd had the wind knocked out of his sails. "I'm sure this little guy will find the perfect place before too long."

"Of course he will." I let my gaze shift back to the hyper pup once more. No matter how tempting, I couldn't consider it. Not now. Not with so much on my plate.

As we headed to the front office to pay the bill, Doc Andrews reached to touch my arm. "It's a good thing you brought Sasha in, Annie. It's always better to be safe than sorry. And that heart medication of your father's is strong stuff. Just one or two pills would have been enough to. . .well. . ."

I nodded and swallowed hard. "I can't thank you enough," I whispered.

"Just promise me you'll think about Copper," he said with a nod. "Might be a fair exchange. And I might give some thought to trimming back your next bill." With a wink, he left the room.

As we pulled away from the vet's office, I couldn't stop thinking about everything that had happened, particularly Dr. Andrews's comments about the potency of my father's heart medication. For some reason, thinking about that got me to thinking about HD-387. Thinking about HD-387 got me to thinking about Bob Kendricks. And thinking about Bob Kendricks got me to thinking about Scott.

Whether I wanted to admit it or not, I was faced with the missing groom every which way I turned, even at the vet's office.

As I slipped behind the wheel to make the drive home, I had the strangest feeling come over me. *Heart medication. Potent.*

At once, I thought of those letters in my underwear drawer. Had Sasha's "accident" led me to yet another clue?

TWIST AND SHOUT

Early Tuesday morning, I decided to pay Brandi a visit at Norton Realty. I wanted to bring her up to speed. Wanted to ask some pointed questions about Scott's relationship, if any, with Otis. I also wanted to get her take on the FDA situation at McKinley Pharmaceuticals. Perhaps with my daughter's help, I could come up with some answers that would lead me closer to discovering Scott's whereabouts.

I arrived at Brandi's office at ten fifteen, stunned to find Bob Kendricks inside. *What in the world is he doing here?* Had he come by to share the same information with Brandi that he had already shared with me, perhaps? Had something else happened that I needed to know about?

As soon as Bob saw me, he extended his hand. "Mrs. Peterson, this is a pleasant surprise. Always good to see you."

I reached to grasp his hand, giving it a firm shake. "A happy coincidence, I'm sure. And it's good to see you, too, Bob."

Brandi looked back and forth between the two of us, a dazed expression on her face. "You two know each other?"

I nodded. "We just met last week for the first time. Remember that day I went to the pharmaceutical company to see if I could drum up any clues?"

"Yes."

"I told you I'd met with some of Scott's coworkers."

A smile lit her face. "Ah. Makes sense now." She closed the door to her office, and I could sense a bit of strain in her voice as she spoke. "Bob and I were just wrapping up a meeting. . . ."

"Right." For a moment, I half expected her to dive into a story about McKinley Pharmaceuticals, but that's not what happened at all. Instead, Brandi shifted into a story that took me completely by surprise.

"Bob is the client I told you about, Mom."

"W—what?" I looked at him, confused.

"Yes." With my www.investigativeskills.com know-how in place, I noted that the sadness in her eyes didn't quite match the forced smile she flashed our way. "You know that deal I've been telling you about? The one that's gone sour?"

"Yes."

"I've told you how sorry I've felt for the seller, right?"

"Yes, of course." I remembered it all too well. I just had no clue Bob Kendricks was "said seller." Suddenly, it all made sense—his comment about trouble on the home front. He'd meant a *literal* home front. And that call from his Realtor. . . It'd been Brandi?

"Why didn't you tell me?" I turned Bob's way, hoping he wouldn't mind the question.

"I started to, that day at the office," he began. "Then you told me what had happened with Scott, and I got distracted. The next time we met—at the diner—we just had too much to talk about. After all, your family's been put through the wringer," he explained. "And I didn't want to burden you with any of my problems. Besides. . ." He looked at Brandi with a shrug. "Brandi is your daughter. I didn't want you to think that she. . ."

"I'm sure he was just being kind, Mom." Brandi offered. "He probably didn't want you to know what a loser I am. Although, I wouldn't blame him for spreading the word. I'm on a terrible learning curve here, that's for sure."

"Don't be so hard on yourself." Kendricks looked conflicted as the words spilled forth, but I didn't ask any questions. Instead, I took concise mental notes—for later reference.

"So, how did you two meet?" I asked, opting for a chatty approach.

"At the Fall Festival," Bob explained. "I was there with my wife."

"And I was there with Scott." Brandi looked my way. "You remember, Mom. The same night Scott proposed."

"Right."

"I was standing in line, waiting to get some barbecue, talking to my wife about traveling in our RV," Bob offered.

"And I happened to overhear his wife say that she was ready to sell their house and hit the road."

He smiled. "I'm set to retire in a few months, and my wife and I had this harebrained idea that we'd spend a few years traveling America in our RV. Hit at least one or two parks in every state—that sort of thing."

Ah yes. I remembered him mentioning it that day at the office.

"Anyway, I had just started to work here at the time," Brandi added, "and was nearly through with my classes. I wasn't quite ready for clients yet, but they were willing to wait till I was." She gave a woeful shrug. "I'm grateful, especially in light of the mess it's all turned out to be."

Bob pursed his lips and didn't say anything for a second. Then he turned to Brandi and said, "Well, I should probably get back to the office. Lots going on there."

After he made his way out the door, Brandi came back in the room, sat at her desk, and immediately leaned her forehead down on the desk and groaned.

"Anything I can help with?" I tried.

Her muffled voice was barely intelligible. "Not unless you want to offer me a job." She looked up at me with tears in her eyes.

"What in the world is happening, Brandi?"

She spent the next twenty minutes trying to explain the ins and outs of a real estate faux pas—one in which she found herself completely enmeshed. Bob and his wife had already moved out of their house and into the RV—this at the insistence of the buyer, Malcolm Pfifer, who—even though he did not yet own the house—had already located renters to put in it.

"He said it would be a great idea," Brandi moaned. "Said we were closing in a few days, anyway."

"But you didn't."

"No. And Mr. Norton is representing Pfifer. You know?" She gave me a frantic look that screamed, *Shouldn't I be able to trust my boss?* Then, she added aloud, "He positively assured me the closing would happen within days. But days have turned into weeks, and Bob and his wife still don't have their money. There's been no closing—or even a hint of a closing."

"What a nightmare for those poor people." I could hardly imagine losing my home like that.

"Yes. I've called the mortgage company several times, and they're apparently having trouble getting Pfifer funded because he's buying so many properties at once. Maybe he'll never get financed. I don't know."

Yikes.

"I feel just awful for Bob and his wife." Brandi shook her head, clearly defeated. "They don't even have the option of moving back into their house, now that renters are living there."

"But it's their house, right? It's not sold yet."

"Right, but it's more complicated than that. The renters are great people, and they're stuck in the middle of this, just like the Kendrickses."

"Who's collecting the rent money?" I asked, reaching for my notebook. "Where's it going?"

"The first month, the Kendrickses were given the rent money—to cover their mortgage. That was Norton's idea. Felt odd to me, but he told me this kind of thing is done all the time. But this month. . ." She shook her head, and I could see the anger there. "It's already the tenth, and no one has offered the Kendrickses anything. The renters paid Pfifer directly. I know, because Norton authorized it. He says they're going to pass the money on to Bob and his wife, but I'm not so sure."

"Let me get this straight." I looked into her bloodshot eyes. "Are you saying that Pfifer is acting as landlord of a house he doesn't even own yet?"

"Yes."

"But. . ."

I stopped when she clutched her forehead in her hands and groaned once more. "I know, I know," she muttered. "We're all shaking our heads, wondering how we got here."

"Just doesn't sound kosher to me. How in the world could he do that? Don't the Kendrickses have clear title?" I jotted down everything she told me, writing as fast as I could.

"Yes, thank goodness." The crease in Brandi's brow deepened. "And we could get the renters out, if we really wanted to. But, as I said, they're great people. So, we keep hoping the deal will go through. Every day, Norton tells me we're going to close "tomorrow"—but tomorrow never comes. I mean, it comes, but there's no closing. And every day, the Kendrickses get their hopes up, thinking they're going to a closing." She bit her lip, and a little tear made its way down her cheek. "Mom, I have to wonder now if we're ever going to close on this house or if I've just been naive."

"What can be done?"

"I don't know. It's a mess because the Kendrickses signed a six-month listing agreement with our company, and they're bound to it. So, whether we get them to a closing or not, they have to stick with us."

"Even if they've been scammed?"

"That's the problem." She let out an exaggerated sigh. "I can't prove anyone has been scammed. At least, not yet." She looked up at me with a hopeful glance. "Maybe this will all be solved soon. Maybe Pfifer will get his funding, and everyone will live happily ever after."

"I hope so, honey."

"Me, too." She gave a little shrug. "But I know you didn't come

176

all the way up here just to talk about that." Brandi attempted a smile. "Come to think of it, I didn't even ask you why you came."

I took a seat and dove into my story, telling her about the FDA issues at McKinley Pharmaceuticals and asking if Scott had ever given her details about HD-387. A worried look crossed her face at once.

"He told me something kind of odd a couple of weeks back."

"What's that?"

"Well, he said that some of the employees at McKinley could end up losing their jobs—and that he somehow felt responsible. When I pressed him to tell me more, he just shut down, changed the subject."

"That lines up with what Bob told me the other day."

"Wow." She shook her head and stared at me. "I don't know what to think about anything anymore. Do you?"

"Nope." I paused a moment, as I tried to figure out how to transition to yet another topic. "Would you mind if I brought up something else?"

"What's that?"

"Scott's father."

The look of surprise on her face spoke volumes. "What about him?"

"He's staying at The Happy Hideaway, out on the highway. Met a guy yesterday afternoon who knows him."

I watched the fear register in her eyes as she spoke. "You're kidding. He's here in town?"

"Yes." I proceeded to tell her about the article in the Savannah paper, and she clamped a hand over her mouth.

"Mom, this is crazy. What does Nadine say?"

"She thinks it has something to do with her political enemies back in Georgia." I offered up a shrug. "Only question now is whether or not Otis is working with them."

Brandi's eyes widened. "Are you saying she thinks they might have had something to do with Scott's disappearance? And that Otis might be involved?"

"Maybe." I shrugged. "Though, to be honest, I've started to suspect everyone who even looks at me cross-eyed."

"Weird thing is, I can't seem to suspect *anyone*," Brandi admitted. "I guess I'm so naive I just don't recognize evil when it stares me in the face."

"You're a very trusting person," I said. "Always have been. But you're smart, too. Don't underestimate yourself."

Brandi let out a little sigh, then shifted directions, talking in detail about Scott and eventually asking my honest opinion about the wedding. "We should just cancel it, don't you think, Mom? I mean, it's the only thing that makes sense. People are going to spend their hard-earned money to fly in from out of state, and it won't be fair if we can't give them what they came for."

Mother-of-the-bride tip: Don't ever let the bride-to-be forget how much she is loved by all.

"They're coming for *you*," I stated. "They love you—and Scott—and they'll want to be here to lend their support." I closed my notebook and stood to give her a hug. "We're not canceling anything yet."

In spite of the way things looked, in spite of the chaotic twists and turns, I had every reason to think there would be a ceremony this coming Saturday night. And—if I had anything to do with it—the groom would most certainly be in attendance.

Smoke Gets in Your Eyes

Wednesday morning dawned cold but clear. Unfortunately, my mind was still clouded. With only four days left until the wedding, I needed to make a decision about the vendors. Should I cancel or simply let them know what was going on? If I did so, how would Brandi react? After our conversation yesterday, the very last thing I wanted to do right now was upset her further.

I needed advice, and I needed it quickly. Mom, Dad, Nadine, Brad, Warren, and I met for our usual around-the-breakfast-table powwow. Only, this morning's agenda was different. We came into "said meeting" on a more somber note. I could tell everyone was struggling, simply from the looks on their faces.

"Problem is," my mom started, "you've got folks like Janetta Mullins actually making purchases in preparation for a wedding that probably isn't going to take place."

I shook my head the minute the words slipped out of her

mouth. Had she really said, "probably isn't going to take place," or had I only imagined it? *Good grief, Mom. You've given up. You don't think there's going to be a wedding, do you?*

"What difference does it make?" I argued.

My mother gave me a puzzled look. "What, honey?"

I tried to hide the irritation in my voice as I spoke, but it was difficult. My insides seemed to be wrestling with my tongue. "What difference does it make if she buys food or not? We've already paid her for it, haven't we?"

"Well, yes. . ."

"Then let her buy it." I crossed my arms and leaned back against the chair. "I still say we're better off that way. Can you imagine how difficult it's going to be to pull off a wedding when Scott returns if we put a stop to the process now?"

"Of course, but. . ."

"You've all lost hope, haven't you?" I looked around the table for a show of support but only found disheartened expressions on each face.

After a moment to reflect, I dove back into my impassioned speech. "I'll do this," I agreed. "I'll call each of the vendors and let them know exactly where we stand. I'll offer them the option of backing out, but I won't ask for any refunds—and I won't give up hope. You can take away anything you like, but you can't take away my hope." I stood and placed my hands on the back of the chair, gripping it like a weight lifter on steroids.

One by one, everyone at the table stood along with me, in a show of support.

I kissed Warren and sent him on his way. My parents headed off to the supermarket because we'd run out of grits—*heaven forbid!*—and Nadine and Brad set off for my home office—Devin's new domain—so that she could spend the morning catching up on political strategies by phone with her campaign manager. Finally, finding myself alone in the kitchen, I began to make the necessary calls. Might as well start with the toughest one first. Malcolm Pfifer.

Hmm. It seems I'd forgotten to add his number to my new cell phone. I'd have to remedy that by calling Brandi. *Hmm* again. Maybe I'd put him off till last. I didn't want Brandi to know what I was up to quite yet. Didn't want to stir the waters.

I started with Janetta. Surely she would offer the strongest support.

"Girl, I don't give a rip what anyone is saying," she told me after I fully explained the situation. "I'm going to plan for a party as if there's going to be one. We're having Italian food Saturday night, one way or the other."

"Are you sure you're going to be up for it, after cooking all day Friday for the church's banquet?"

"This is what I do, Annie!" She let out a little laugh, then grew more serious as she said, "Listen, I don't mean to make light of what you're going through. And I know I'm a new Christian and all. . .but I just have this feeling in my—my. . ."

"Your feeler?"

"Yeah." She giggled. "I know in my knower it's all going to work out. Don't know how, that's for sure. But I am confident. And you can be, too."

Wow. After talking to Janetta, I felt my confidence growing. I hung up from our conversation, then punched in the number for the Be Our Guest wedding facility for a heart-to-heart chat with the facility's owner-slash-wedding coordinator, Julia Holt. After hearing our story, she was taken aback. I probably should have given her some advance warning, but her response was all hearts and flowers, pun intended.

"We don't usually offer a refund," she explained with great compassion in her voice, "but I'd be willing to consider giving back half of what you've paid if the wedding doesn't take place. Then again, Valentine's Day *is* our busiest day of the year. We've got two other ceremonies planned for earlier in the day, and there was a waiting list for the night slot. So if you *do* have to cancel. . ."

"I'm sure we won't." I spoke with the same degree of confidence I'd heard in Janetta's voice just moments before. "We have every reason to believe there is going to be a wedding on Saturday night, and it's going to be the prettiest Valentine's celebration anyone at your facility has ever seen, I can assure you."

After wrapping up my conversation with Julia, I moved on to Pastor Miller, who offered nothing but the utmost love and support. He assured me that his wife—known among all our friends as the best cake decorator in the county—would still bake the most divine wedding cake we'd ever seen.

Pastor Miller did have one question that took me by surprise—something I hadn't thought about. "What should we do about the Friday afternoon rehearsal?" he asked, after letting me ramble awhile. "Should we just leave a little extra time for it on Saturday afternoon?"

"I guess so," I said with a sigh. *Don't forget to call Leonardo's to let them know the Friday night rehearsal dinner is off.* It conflicted with the church's Valentine's banquet anyway. Not that I had any plans to attend "said banquet," but several in the wedding party might opt to go, now that the evening had been freed up.

"I'm here for you, Annie," Pastor Miller said. "Regardless."

Somehow, "regardless" didn't sound as frightening coming from the pastor's mouth as it did coming from my father's. Still, it did leave me feeling pretty conflicted.

Mother-of-the-bride tip: Never use the word regardless *when speaking to the frenzied bride-to-be. Choose your words carefully.*

Next, I telephoned the company responsible for the chocolate fountain and brought them up to speed. Then I called the seamstress responsible for altering Brandi's wedding dress. I knew my daughter hadn't had the courage to pick up the beautiful beaded gown, though the alterations had been completed days ago.

"I read about Scott's disappearance in the *Gazette*," the seamstress said. "Has there been any news?"

"No, I'm afraid not."

I swiftly changed gears, thanking the woman for her work on the dress and assuring her I would be by later in the day to pick it up and pay her.

I telephoned Brandi's hairdresser, Norah, at The Liberty Belle, Clarksborough's one and only salon, just to bring her up to speed. She'd already heard the news—"Not *just* the *Gazette* version," she said with great gusto, "but the Sheila scoop, too." *Great.* At least the national papers hadn't thought to call Sheila. *Yet.*

Thankfully, there was no florist to call. Brandi had opted for silk flowers, which I'd lovingly crafted into bridesmaids' bouquets. But thinking about those bouquets got me thinking about the bridesmaids. They needed to be called. I had to make sure they were with Brandi on the night of the previously scheduled but recently canceled rehearsal dinner, just for moral support.

One by one, using the telephone list Brandi had left on the refrigerator, I contacted the members of the wedding party. By the end of the morning, all bridesmaids, groomsmen, flower girls, and/or ring bearers knew to be on standby. They all agreed to maintain their flexibility.

"I feel sure we will have a wedding," I told everyone. Frankly, I needed to hear the words spoken aloud, so repeating them seemed to be just the ticket.

Now, for something even tougher. I began to telephone our out-of-town guests. Several, including many in our family, opted to come anyway. Some would begin arriving as early as tomorrow. Just one more thing to think about.

Finally, when I could put it off no longer, I telephoned Brandi to get Pfifer's number. She gave it to me, and I called him right away. Thankfully, his machine picked up.

I only half listened as his overly cheerful voice rang out. "You've reached Pfifer Photography, Clarksborough's own one-stop shop for all your photographic needs."

He went on to talk about this month's Valentine's Day special, talking about a variety of love-inspired backdrops for the happy couple to choose from, should they make use of his services. When I finally heard the beep, I dove in with my explanation of where we stood, assuring him I'd be in touch. "We still want you to keep Saturday night open," I added. "So I'll drop by in a day or so to give you the additional deposit money."

By the time I hung up, I was exhausted. And hungry. If Sasha hadn't consumed all of my mother's fudge, this would have been the perfect opportunity to track it down and eat every bite.

Still. . . I thought about that dress hanging in my closet. It ached to be worn. And, in spite of every obstacle, I ached to wear it.

I will wear it this Saturday night. And nothing—and no one—can stop me.

I'm a Believer

My parents returned from the grocery store with enough food to feed an army.

"Your brother and sister-in-law will be here tomorrow," Mom reminded me. "Along with the kids and that adorable little grandson of theirs!"

"You know. . ." I snapped to attention, and an immediate panic set in. "I forgot to ask where they're staying. Do you suppose they're planning to stay here?"

"No, darlin', they've made reservations at one of those places out on the highway," she explained. "Didn't want to put you out."

"Ah." I nodded, torn by the emotions running through me. I wanted to spend time with my family. Wanted to relax and enjoy the people coming into town for a visit. And yet I couldn't get rid of this nagging feeling that I still had work to do.

"Mom, would you mind keeping an eye on things for a few hours?" I gave her an imploring look. "I need to drop Sasha off at the groomer's, and then I want to go back to McKinley Pharmaceuticals."

"Didn't you just have the dog groomed?" she asked.

"Yes, but all of that chocolate—and the after-effects—have left her smelling pretty. . .well. . .rank. Don't know if you've noticed. She could use a bath, and I just don't have time."

My mother offered to bathe her for me.

I was grateful for the offer but couldn't take her up on it. "You've done more than enough already," I assured her. "Why don't you and Dad just spend the afternoon resting? I'll drop Sasha off at Coats 'n' Tails and pick her up when I'm done."

"As you like." With the wave of a hand, my mom went back to her task of unloading groceries. She hummed a little song as she worked.

I paused at the office door and gave it a rap, entering only after I heard Brad's welcoming voice. I was surprised to find Nadine sleeping on the sofa inside. Brad looked up from the computer and put his finger to his lips. "She just fell asleep," he whispered. "She hasn't slept in nights, so I'm not bothering her."

"I won't, either." With a forced whisper, I went on to explain that I'd be gone for the next couple of hours and, with a nod, was on my way.

I bundled up in my warmest duds and then braced myself for the inevitable. Once outside, I shivered against the afternoon cold, quickly wrestling Sasha's puppy car seat into place. "C'mon, girl." I lifted her up, and her tail wagged merrily. "You're going to have to stay put," I admonished. "No foul play today." She settled right down in her seat, and soon, we were out on the open road.

I stopped off at the home of the seamstress and picked up Brandi's dress. After I'd hung it up in the backseat, I found myself glancing at it in the rearview mirror. Even in the plastic bag, it seemed to taunt me. *Will there be a wedding, or won't there?* I did my best to push all negative thoughts aside and remained focused on the road.

Minutes later, I pulled into the parking lot of Coats 'n' Tails and was horrified to discover they'd closed early.

"I don't believe it." I slapped myself in the head—now a common remedy to life's problems. According to the note on the door, they'd had a death in the family. I couldn't exactly fault them for closing over that, now could I?

With a sigh, I turned back to the car, placing the dog, once again, in her car seat. "Looks like you're stuck with me," I said with a woeful shrug. "Like it or not."

Again, her tail bebopped back and forth, and her head leaned against the seat edge. She didn't seem to mind, but I certainly did. This changed everything. What in the world would I do with a dog—even a small one—when I arrived at the pharmaceutical company?

Less than twenty minutes later, I faced the problem head-on. I couldn't leave the little darling in the car. It was too cold outside, and I, for one, didn't want to run the risk of something happening to her. But neither could I take her inside, could I?

There seemed to be only one solution. The familiar silver-haired guard in the tiny shack at the entrance to the property looked warm and toasty. Was that a space heater I saw? Yes, he would surely agree to keep an eye on my lovable pooch for a few minutes while I visited with Bob Kendricks.

Fortunately, I found Mr. Clark to be a dog lover. He took to Sasha—and the idea of watching her—right away.

"Gets kind of lonely sitting here all day," he explained as he jotted down my license number once again. "Might do me some good to have someone to talk to for a change."

Okay, then. I placed my little darling in his outstretched arms, promising to return in twenty minutes or less. Then I headed off to find Bob.

After checking in with the gal at the front desk and receiving my visitor's pass, I located Bob—with the help of some of his coworkers—in the lunchroom. He sat alone, staring out of the window. I could hardly make out what was on the other side, the frost was so thick.

"Late lunch?" I asked.

"No. I'm on a break. Just needed time to myself."

I gave him a sympathetic look. "Is it helping?"

"I'm not sure what will help at this point," he said. "Seems like everything I touch falls apart."

"What do you mean?"

He spent the next several minutes telling me. His house situation. His job. Everything seemed to be unraveling at once. I wasn't sure what to say, so I opted just to let him carry the weight of the conversation. I don't really think he wanted my input, anyway—only someone to talk to.

Kind of like that lonely security guard I had just left Sasha with.

In a hushed voice, Bob dove off into a lengthy story about the fate of the pharmaceutical company, and I took careful mental notes.

"What does your gut tell you about HD-387?" I asked, finally.

He looked up with a shrug. "It's in the final testing phase, and it's going to get the necessary approval. And I'm not even so sure that's a bad thing anymore. I mean, it works really well on most people. It's a good medication. Lots of lives will probably be saved because of it."

Singing a little different song today, eh? Kendricks had certainly shifted gears since the last time we'd met, and I couldn't help but wonder about the change in his thinking. Had he really resolved himself to the idea that the medication *should* garner FDA approval, or was he simply trying to convince himself, now that the deed was nearly done? Worse yet, had someone at the company worked overtime to persuade him, to bring him around to their way of thinking?

"What about all that stuff you said before, about higher-ups at McKinley keeping folks in the dark?" Even as I said the words *in the dark*, a shiver ran through me. Heavens! Maybe that's what Scott was referring to in his text message. Maybe he was so concerned about patients being left in the dark that he sent out a frantic message, in order to save lives? If so, I needed to move, and move fast!

"Look. . ." Kendricks leaned in a bit closer, his voice a hoarse whisper. "You're gonna have to keep your voice down. And don't gesture with your hands when you speak." He nodded toward a camera on the wall to my right. "They've got every room in this place under surveillance. The last thing I need is for folks to think I'm up to something."

"Sorry," I offered.

He let out a lingering sigh. "No, I'm sorry. I don't mean to take out my frustrations on you. I'm just so confused." He leaned back in his chair, not saying a word for a minute or two. "You know. . ." he said finally, "I forgot to mention something the other day."

"Oh?"

"Yeah. A lot of those patients I told you about—the ones in the clinical trials. . ."

"Like the guy in the letters?"

"Yeah." Bob took on a faraway look. "They're out of options."

"What do you mean?" I pulled out my notebook and began to take notes.

"I mean, they're terminal. They're going to die. And they don't particularly care if the research drug they're offered meets FDA standards or not. They're just looking for something to give them hope—even just the tiniest glimmer."

Kind of like what you're looking for right now.

"They're reaching out for something—anything. Taking the medication—risky as it is—is preferable to the alternative."

My goodness, we're somber today. I'd never seen him like this and wasn't sure I knew what to make of it. With my www .investigativeskills.com know-how in place, I did take note of the fact that he hadn't looked me in the eye once since I'd arrived. Not once. I couldn't tell if he'd given up—wearied by life's woes—or if he might be hiding something.

"Can I ask you a question?" What I was about to say didn't exactly come from my list, but the Holy Spirit seemed to be shifting me in another direction altogether. Perhaps the reason for today's visit was going to turn out to be considerably different from what I'd first thought.

"Sure." He gave a limp shrug.

"Are you a believer?"

He now made direct eye contact with me—for the first time since I'd walked in the door. "Believer—in what? The drug, you mean?"

"No."

"The company?" The look of confusion spoke volumes.

"No." I sat across from him and stared into his eyes, focusing on the exhaustion I found there. "What I'm getting at is this—are you a Christian?"

Immediately, Bob's face contorted. "I'm a *scientist*."

"Okay. . ." I wasn't sure what that had to do with anything, but I kept my lips clamped. I could see he wasn't quite finished with his explanation.

"I work with facts and figures." The sudden passion in his eyes took me by surprise. "Statistics. Logic. Reason." He gave me one of those looks that said, *Don't you get it?* Then he shrugged. "I haven't really given any thought to the existence of a God since the three or four times I found myself in Sunday school as a kid. Not sure I ever will. And just so you know, Scott and I have already had this little chat a dozen times or more."

I bit my lip and prayed a silent prayer for help from above. "I'm not here to try to convince you," I said. "I just want you to consider the fact—and it is a fact—that your world is crumbling. Things are falling apart. You said it yourself. And you don't seem to have an answer for how to pull the pieces together. There's no prescription you can take. No clinical trial you can join."

Kendricks pursed his lips but remained silent.

"Maybe there's a reason for that," I argued. "Maybe it's not yours to figure out. Maybe it's too big for you to handle on your own."

"I'm not sure where you're headed with this."

"Just trying to ease another fact into that equation you're working on in your head," I explained. "There's a God-shaped hole in your heart, and until you fill it, you won't find the answers you're looking for—with the job, your house, or your wife."

"I really don't think this is any of your. . ."

At that moment, a movement at the door caught my eye. I looked up to see a wide-eyed Mr. Clark staring down at me.

"Um, ma'am. . . ," he started.

I flew out of my seat, knowing what he was about to say, even before he said it.

"Your little dog is. . .well, she's vamoosed."

"Vamoosed?" I looked around, half expecting to find her right there—close by. Maybe she'd tracked my scent. Dachshunds were hound dogs, after all.

"I opened the door of the guard shack to write down a license plate number," Mr. Clark explained, "and she shot out. I've looked everywhere for her."

Bob stared at me, clearly stunned. "You brought your dog with you?"

"Long story." I headed for the door but turned back just as I reached it. "Look, I didn't mean to upset you, especially with all you're going through. But I do hope you'll think about the things I brought up. I wasn't trying to overstep my bounds."

He shrugged and waved me on my way. "Think nothing of it," he said. "It's going to take a lot more than a simple conversation to convince me there's a God."

Mr. Clark immediately put his hand to his heart. "Oh, Mr.

Kendricks. There is a God. I know, because I've met Him!"

The good-grief-what-have-I-gotten-myself-into expression on Kendricks's face was almost enough to make me forget about the missing dog.

Almost.

CHAPTER 24

SOMETHING'S GOTTA GIVE

We searched for Sasha for nearly fifteen minutes before I located her outside Scott's office door. What she was doing there, I couldn't say, except that she'd likely picked up his scent and wanted to offer assistance. *Good girl, Sasha. You're the best hound dog on the planet!*

I could hear the *thump, thump* of her tail against the wooden floorboards and reached to snatch her into my arms. As I did, Mr. Clark made his breathless appearance, breaking into a smile the moment he saw us.

"You found her!" He reached to scratch Sasha behind the ears, and she nuzzled her head into his palm.

"I found her. She can be a very naughty girl at times, but I've never seen her run away before."

He gave a shrug. "It wasn't like she was running way. More like she was on a mission."

"Ah." I didn't confirm or deny his suspicions. At this point,

Sasha craned her neck to lick my cheek.

"Sure, *now* you're well-behaved," I said to the little mongrel.

"Why do you suppose she stopped here?" Mr. Clark asked.

"I guess she's picked up on Scott's scent." I pointed to the name on the door. "He's my son-in-law."

"Oh!" Clark gave me a knowing look. "Scott Cunningham is your *son-in-law*? Isn't he the one who. . ."

"Yes, and I should have said soon-to-be son-in-law. The wedding is supposed to take place this Saturday evening."

"Oh, yeah." He scratched his whiskery chin and stared me down. "I know Scott, all right, and I've been following the story in the *Gazette* for over a week. I feel like I have a vested interest, since he worked here and all."

Goodness. Could you please stop talking about him in the past tense?

Clark snapped his fingers, and his face lit up. "I know who you are now! I talked to your two daughters the night they found his car down the street."

"Yes, that's right."

"No wonder you've been coming and going so much." He shook his head and leaned against the wall. "Your poor family. You've been through so much. I've been praying for you—all of you."

"Thanks so much."

"This whole thing is so strange, but then. . ." Mr. Clark looked down the hall to make sure no one was listening in, "everything around here has been strange lately."

"Oh?" I gestured for him to walk toward the front door, and he headed off that way, taking my hint.

Within minutes, the two of us—well, three, really, if you

counted Sasha—were jammed into the tiny guard shack, with the space heater blowing madly to keep us warm. I drilled Clark for answers, but he seemed hesitant to share.

"I'm trying to locate my future son-in-law," I explained. "So anything you can tell me would be helpful."

"Well, if you put it like that." He let out a lingering sigh, and I could practically see the wheels turning in his head. "There've been whispers for months now," he said finally. "The whole company is going belly-up if they can't get this latest drug marketed. Stocks have been pretty high so far, but that's only because the new drug has been talked up so much. But if it doesn't get the necessary approval, those stocks will plummet. So it won't just be the employees who suffer."

"That coincides with what I've been told." It also gave me a bit more information to work with. *Stocks, eh? I hadn't thought about that.*

"They're going to start with those at the bottom of the totem pole, I guess." He let out a sigh. "I suppose that means I could be the first to go."

"Surely not," I said. "I would think working security at a company that produces top-secret prescription drug products would put you at the top of the list, not the bottom. So don't fret. And you said you're a believer, right?"

"Yes, I am."

"So you know that God is your source anyway, not this job."

"True, true. It's just that, well. . ."

"What?"

"Thing is. . ." He looked around, as if he half suspected someone to walk up on us. "I'm not so worried about myself. Might sound crazy, but I'm equally as concerned for the McKinley family as I am the employees. They aren't bad people. I've known some of them since I was a little boy. Old Man McKinley was a friend of my father's. He's a great guy. I can't imagine he would intentionally hurt anyone."

"Even to save the company he loves?" I queried. "People are funny when it comes to their pocketbooks."

Clark shrugged. "I don't know. I just can't imagine it. McKinley could shut the place down tomorrow and go on living well. I really think he's worried about the employees. He doesn't want to see any of them lose their jobs."

"Maybe." I jotted down a few notes, then looked up into Mr. Clark's eyes. "Anything else strange going on?"

"Well. . ." He rubbed at his whiskery chin, and I sensed his hesitancy once again. "I've been plenty worried about Bob Kendricks. He's been acting a little. . .irrational lately. I know he's worried—like everyone else—but he's been acting mighty strange. Sometimes I say hello to him, and he acts like he doesn't even hear me. It's like he's here physically, but that's about it. Does that make sense?"

"Unfortunately, yes." I took a deep breath and made the decision not to reveal any of Kendricks's personal woes to Mr. Clark, friendly or not. That was one line of professionalism I refused to cross.

I slipped my sleuthing notebook into my purse and looked my new friend in the eye. "Thanks for your help." I extended my hand, and he shook it warmly.

"Happy to be of service."

I'd just started to leave when something caused me to turn

back—an afterthought, really. "If you don't mind my asking," I said, "The name *Clark*. . . Are you in any way related to "the" Clarks—founding fathers of Clarksborough?"

He gave a hint of a shrug. "Yeah. My great-great-grandfather was the first mayor. Our family has been here for generations."

"Wow." I was impressed, though I couldn't help but wonder how he'd ended up working in a guard shack at McKinley Pharmaceuticals. I didn't ask. A skilled supersleuth knew better than to make a willing informant uncomfortable.

"I love Clarksborough, PA," he said with a smile. "Always have and always will. There's just something about having a town named after you that puts a smile on your face every morning."

I smiled now. "Do me a favor," I said as I reached down to pick up my dog. "Come to Brandi and Scott's wedding this Saturday night, at seven o'clock. It's at the Be Our Guest wedding facility. We'd love to have one of our 'founding fathers' there."

"But. . ."

"No buts. There's going to be a wedding—and you're going to be my guest. I can't think of any better way to thank you for your help with Sasha today."

As if to thank him personally, my canine companion wriggled out of my arms and into his. She licked him all over his face, but he didn't seem to mind.

"Okay, okay!" He smiled as he placed her back in my arms. "I'll see you there."

As Sasha and I pulled away from the pharmaceutical company, I glanced in my rearview mirror and waved to Mr. Clark, who seemed sad to see us go.

I glanced over at the pup and let out a little giggle. "Well," I said, "I think he likes you! Funny girl! You didn't get your bath, but somehow you still came out smelling like a rose."

She wagged her tail, then leaned back against the seat and closed her eyes.

Yep. Crime solving was hard work. For people—and for dogs.

CHAPTER 25

WIPEOUT

I returned home to a chaotic scene. Nadine paced the living room, cell phone in hand, eyes filled with tears. I could hear her end of the conversation but had to wonder who was on the other end of the line. Whoever it was sure had her stirred up.

"What's happened?" I asked Brad. "Is it Scott? Is he. . . ?"

"Nothing to do with Scott." Brad let out a sigh, then looked at his wife. "She's on the phone with her campaign manager. Things back home are worse than ever. I think she's looking at pulling out of the race. It's all just too much for her."

"Oh no!" I looked at my darling southern sister and couldn't help but feel sorry for her. It would take a lot to bring down someone as strong as Nadine Cunningham. I couldn't imagine she would give up. I trembled with anger, wishing I could do something to make things right again. "What have they done now?"

"Several prominent pastors in our area have come out against her in a rather public way," Brad explained. "A couple even bought some airtime on one of the local television stations to get their point across."

"But why? I would think the Christian community would embrace her, especially in light of her work with the homeless."

"Ironically, that's what has them riled up. They're saying her ties to the homeless shelter are suspect, that she's using the poor for political gain."

"Whatever in the world would make them think that?"

"I don't know." His brow wrinkled as he continued on. "I guess it's my fault. I thought it would be a good idea to have some photos done to showcase her work at the shelter, so a few weeks ago, we took some great shots of her—working in the kitchen, leading worship, that sort of thing."

"What's wrong with that?"

"On the surface, nothing," he said, "but the media made it sound as though she only went down there—to the shelter—for the photo shoot, like she doesn't really work there on a regular basis."

"All they have to do is talk to the director, right? Or the people staying at the shelter."

"They're going to believe what they want to believe. Those journalists just swept in, drew some misguided conclusions, and then wrote their articles. They didn't care if they hurt her. They were just looking for news stories. And speaking of which. . ." He shook his head, and anger flashed in his eyes.

"What?"

"Apparently that journalist—the one who interviewed Otis— managed to get another story out of him. Otis spent quite a few years on the street—a self-proclaimed drunk—and he must've bared his soul to this reporter. It was all in there, every word."

"But that's *his* story," I argued. "How could anyone possibly hold that against Nadine?"

"As crazy as it sounds, *supposed* members of the Christian community, at least the vocal ones, are saying she's a hypocrite—that she claims to work with the homeless, the alcoholics, the down-and-outers but that she ousted her husband for the very same thing."

"But that's not true," I argued. "Otis left her. She didn't even know where he was, right?"

"Right. But try convincing people of that." Brad shook his head, and I could see the anger in his eyes. "Maybe we deserve this—Christians getting involved in politics and all. Maybe we're just setting ourselves up for a fall." He sat and raked his fingers through his hair.

"No one deserves this." I pulled off my coat and draped it across the back of the couch. "Especially not someone as good—genuinely good—as Nadine. It's not right."

Brad plopped down onto the sofa, then leaned his head back and rubbed his brow. "We expected this from her opponents, but from the local churches? That's the part that kills me. Our own brothers and sisters in the Lord are turning on us—not even giving us the benefit of the doubt."

I couldn't help but smile as he said the word *us*. Clearly, he was taking her campaign very personally, and that warmed my heart.

"There's nothing worse than having people come out swinging, especially when those swings are coming from within the church," I said with a sigh. "But—inside the church or out—I've discovered that some minds are like concrete."

"How's that?"

I gave a little shrug. "Completely mixed up and permanently set."

"Ah."

"People believe what they want to believe. And sometimes even staring the truth in the face makes no difference. But I always try to remember what the Bible says—everything exposed by the light becomes visible. The truth always comes out. Always. It's just a matter of time."

Even as I spoke the words, I realized something profound. The truth of Scott's whereabouts would eventually make itself known—whether I slaved away at finding him or not. God was in control. And He would eventually shine His light on the situation, revealing everything that needed to be made visible.

After Nadine finished her call, we went into the kitchen and sat together, sipping mugs of piping hot Earl Grey tea—heavy on the cream. I let her do most of the talking. She appeared to have a lot on her mind.

"I'm just so dis-*cour*-aged," she said. "So beaten down. There's so much goin' on at once that I can't tell one thing from another anymore."

Hmm. Sounded a lot like what Bob Kendricks had said.

"One thing I learned years ago," I told her, "was that you shouldn't make a life-changing decision in the heat of the moment. Let the moment pass; then make your decision."

"I don't think I can wait any longer." She melted in a puddle of tears, and I reached my hand across the table to squeeze her fingertips.

"You can wait," I assured her. "You have to wait. This isn't the time. You have too many other things going on. It's all muddy right now. I'm sure nothing is making much sense."

"I just have to wonder. . ." She shook her head and grew silent.

"Wonder what?"

"I'm not saying I'm havin' a crisis of faith," she said, "but. . ." Her gaze shifted out of the window.

"Honey, you're struggling. Nothing wrong with that. All believers do—especially when things happen that seem to be out of their control."

"That's just it," she said. "I'm the kind of person who always has everything under control. I keep things in perfect order—all of my ducks are always in a row. Everyone who *knows* me knows that. But these things. . ." She lifted her hands up in defeat. "The things that have happened over the past couple of weeks are totally out of my control. I can't fix them." Her next words were so quiet I had to strain to hear them. "I'm not used to that. I can usually fix just about anything. That's what I am—a fixer."

"I know you are, hon." I squeezed her hand. "But if we could fix everything ourselves, why would we need God?"

She let out a lingering sigh and then turned to face me. "I know, I know. And I have to admit it's frustrating, realizin' I can't make things happen the way I want them to. I have to give that over to God, really. Maybe. . ." She shook her head, and tears flowed down her cheeks. "Maybe I need to admit that I'm really mad at *Him* right now."

Bingo.

She leaned her head down onto the table and began to weep. As she did, I heard the front door open, and within seconds, Brandi and Candy joined us in the kitchen. "What's happened?" Brandi asked with fear oozing from every pore.

I just shook my head and mouthed, "Politics. I'll tell you later."

Brandi sat next to Nadine and encouraged her to open up and share her heart. The tears began in earnest at that point.

You know, I've discovered something about women. Whenever two or more are gathered together and one of them begins to cry, the others in the room are destined to join in. Within minutes, Brandi was in a puddle. Then she and Nadine took turns, each sharing their fears, their doubts, their true feelings. Candy, as always, played the role of mother hen.

Just about the time I finally got them calmed down, my mother staggered into the kitchen, still groggy from her mid-afternoon nap. She took one look at the swollen, red-rimmed eyes of the others and went into panic mode. She was a good minute or two into an animated round of questioning before I was able to convince her nothing had happened—nothing significant, anyway. In spite of my assurances, her eyes filled with tears.

"I'm sorry." She dropped into a chair and leaned her head into her hands. "I don't know what's wrong with me today. I'm so emotional. I think I'm just exhausted."

"We all are." I knew that was contributing to the tears but didn't know what to do about it. None of us had rested much over the past couple of weeks, and the weariness was taking its toll.

Another few minutes were spent in quiet conversation. Then, as we wrapped up, the other ladies decided to go into the living room to join the men. I had just stepped in line behind them when the telephone rang. Fear kicked in as I reached to answer it. To be honest, I was tired of answering questions about the wedding and fending off reporters. I'd had my fill of it, in fact. I was pleasantly surprised to hear Sheila's voice on the other end of the line.

Her opening line took me by surprise. "Are you at the end of your rope, Annie?"

"Excuse me?"

"I figured you must be," she said, "because I felt a tug."

"Wow." Was this woman discerning, or what? "Yeah, I'm at the end of my rope. You have no idea." I went on to explain the day's events, starting with Bob Kendricks' somber revelations, Nadine's political woes, Brandi's heartbreaking conversation, and my mom's emotional outburst.

"When you reach the end of your rope, you've got to tie a knot and hang on," Sheila responded. "At least, that's what I always say."

"I'm not sure how to knot this one," I acknowledged.

"Then let God handle that for you," she said. "You can't fix everything, Annie."

"Good grief. That's what I just told Nadine. I told her if we could fix everything we wouldn't need God."

"Well, that's true," Sheila said, "so I'll amen your words. But I honestly think there's more to it than that, especially where you're concerned."

"What do you mean?"

"If you're spending all your time trying to fix something that isn't yours to fix, then you're wasting valuable time you could be spending doing something else. Like praying, for instance. Or resting."

A lingering sigh escaped my lips. "I know you're right."

She dove into a motherly lecture, most of it focused on my need for sleep. By the end of the conversation, Sheila had made her point. I *was* exhausted, just as she'd said. I needed rest—not just four or five hours of sleep, but a serious night's sleep.

As I hung up the phone, I set a plan in motion. I would go to bed early tonight, and I would do my best to lay down the burden of Scott's disappearance—at least for the night.

A short time later, the doorbell rang. I opened the front door to find Sergeant O'Henry standing on my front doorstep with a large manila envelope in hand. For half a second there, I almost thought he'd been snooping in my underwear drawer. My heart flip-flopped at the very thought of it.

"Well, hello," I said. "Would you like to come inside and warm up?"

"Sure." He stepped inside the house, reached inside the manila envelope, and pulled out a photograph, which he dangled in front of me. My eyes filled with tears at once as I looked at the photo of Brandi and Scott at the fair—in their outdated wedding gear.

"Ah. Okay." I took it from him and put it into my purse, trying not to focus on the whirlwind of emotions that had just taken hold of me. To be honest, I didn't want to think about the photo. There were too many memories attached, too many unachieved dreams lingering.

Thinking about that picture did serve as a reminder that Pfifer had never returned my call. I hated to talk to the man but needed to get it over with, one way or the other. I would have to remember to call him later to give him the scoop on the wedding.

If I ever figured out what "said scoop" was.

CHAPTER 26

BLOWIN' IN THE WIND

After Nadine's less-than-positive description of her ex-husband, I expected the man to be half ogre, half derelict. So when a surprisingly clean-cut Otis Fuller showed up at my door on Thursday morning, I hardly knew what to think. I stood in the doorway, cold air freezing the tip of my nose, too stunned to say anything for a moment.

"Hello." He extended his hand.

I stared up, up, up at the man with the deeply jutted chin and thick eyebrows, unable to think clearly. "You're. . ." I pointed but couldn't seem to finish my thought. *So, this is what Big Foot looks like.* Just for fun, I glanced down at his feet. Yep. They were huge.

At once, Sasha appeared at my feet, growling like a maniac. I swept her into my arms and did my best to calm her before she scared the neighbors. Or our new guest. Then again, she had only recently chased this very man across my lawn in an attempt to save her family. I couldn't really blame her for growling at him now, could I?

"Otis Fuller." He continued to hold out his hand. "And I owe you an apology."

"Y–you do?" I took hold of his hand, which swallowed mine whole. *This would explain Scott's size 12 wedding ring. He takes after his father.*

Otis gave me an apologetic look. "I'm sure I scared you out of your wits last week with that incident in your backyard."

Ah. "Yes, actually. I wasn't sure what to think."

"I'm really sorry. I didn't think about the fact that I was trespassing. I shouldn't have run like that. I think I just panicked."

Um, me, too.

"Sure hope I didn't hurt your little dog. I was just. . ." His hands began to tremble, and he stuck them in his pocket. "I was just looking for my ex-wife. I thought she might be staying here."

"She was. I mean, she is."

"Ah."

I continued to stand frozen in place—quite literally—until he finally asked if he could speak to Nadine.

"She just borrowed my car to run to the post office. Her husband is. . ." I pointed lamely toward the living room, realizing at once just how odd that must sound to the man. "Would you like to come in and wait?" *Heavens, I hope Nadine doesn't kill me for this.*

"Thank you." He stepped inside, looking about as comfortable as a long-tailed cat in a room full of rocking chairs.

I led the way into the living room, where Brad sat with Nadine's laptop in hand. He looked up, and I couldn't help but notice the curiosity in his eyes. Confusion turned to shock—*or is that horror?*—as I made introductions.

"Brad"—I gestured toward our guest—"this is Otis Fuller. He's Nadine's. . ."

"I know who he is." Brad stood, albeit slowly, and extended his hand. Otis shook it with fervor.

"It's great to finally meet you," Otis said. "I've wondered about you for years—what you looked like, how you all were getting along."

I could see the "well-why-didn't-you-write? Why-didn't-you-call?" look in Brad's eyes, but to his credit, he kept his questions to himself. I gestured for Otis to take a seat on the couch and offered him a cup of coffee.

"Are you sure?" He looked up at me with the most pitiful expression I'd ever seen—almost as if he felt he didn't deserve a cup of coffee, based on his past sins.

I shrugged and tried to play it cool. "It's no problem. I was just going to offer to refill Brad's cup, anyway."

No sooner did I have it in hand than I bolted to the kitchen. My thoughts whirled around in my brain, like pieces of fruit in a blender. Nadine's two husbands were in my living room, and Nadine was off at the post office. Should I offer the fellows coffee and conversation or hide in the bedroom till she came home and skinned me alive? I knew, based on an intense early-morning girlfriend chat that things still weren't going well for her, campaignwise. She was nearly ready to give up, in fact. I'd done my best to encourage her to keep going. But what would she think of me now?

Just then, my mother made an entrance, dressed in a rather over-the-top Valentine's Day outfit. I could definitely tell Sheila had worn off on her. Either that or she'd been watching the

Home Shopping Network again.

"Wow, Mom. You look. . ." *Ornate? Goofy?*

"Like she's ready for love." My father swept in behind her and took her in his arms. They made a little circle around my kitchen, waltzing from appliance to appliance.

And to think, I'd almost slept in this morning.

"You two are certainly. . . chipper today."

Dad gave my mother a devilish wink. "We're not spring chickens, but we still have our moments."

"And it is February, after all," my mother said. As if that explained everything.

I decided to shift the conversation in a different direction. "So, what are you two lovebirds up to this morning?"

"Reporting in for duty, Agatha Annie!" My mother saluted me, and I couldn't help but chuckle. *Warren, I'm going to hurt you for sharing that nickname with my mother. On the other hand. . .*

"Mom, I have just the job for you." I quickly explained the situation going on in the living room, and her eyes lit with delight.

"Ooh! Sounds like fun."

I handed her the coffee cups, and she trotted off in that direction.

My father turned to look at me with panic in his eyes. "Annie, what am I supposed to do with Otis? I've never even met the man."

I gave him an innocent shrug. "How do I know? Just hold him at bay till Nadine gets here."

He shook his head and followed after my mom. I made myself busy in the kitchen. Washed the breakfast dishes. By hand. Cleaned the countertops. Three times. Took out the trash. Contemplated waxing the floors and rearranging the pantry.

All the while, I prayed—prayed for the Lord to reveal His will in this situation—and prayed that my friends and family would forgive me for getting us all in over our heads with this sleuthing madness.

Finally, I heard Nadine at the front door. My heart felt as if it hit my toes and then ping-ponged back up to slap me in my double chins.

From off in the distance, Nadine sang a worship song at the top of her lungs—probably something she'd heard on the radio in my car. It came to an abrupt end midsentence, and I knew the moment of truth had come. Should I slip out the back door now or barrel into the living room to put a stop to any potential bloodshed?

I opted for none of the above. I just stood alone in the kitchen and prayed for a positive outcome. After a while, curiosity got the better of me, particularly when no screams or shouts transpired. I eased my way down the hallway and into the living room, surprised to find everyone seated, chatting peacefully. Nadine, who'd landed in the wingback chair, looked up at me with a please-help-me-out-here look in her eyes.

I leaned against the edge of her chair and listened intently as Otis spoke.

"I spent twenty years battling addiction." He paused a moment, his gaze shifting to the ground. "Actually, I wasn't battling it for most of those years. I was given over to it, and to be honest, I really didn't care. I cared about very little during that season of my life."

Nadine remained painfully silent. My mother, however, seemed intent on getting to know this man, problems and all. "So tell me," she prompted him, "what made you want to give it up?"

"I lived for years as an addict," he said. "I didn't care about anyone or anything else but me. Me, myself, and I."

"A man wrapped up in himself makes a very small package," my mother said.

"You're right," he agreed. "And I guess that's where the change started—when I reached the point where I didn't even care about myself anymore. I guess it was about three years ago," he said. "I'd landed in an ICU ward with alcohol poisoning. Not the first time. More like the twenty-first."

Whoa.

"The doctors told me—just like they always did—that the next time would probably be my last time. I'd stopped believing them long before, but this time, I had a closer call than usual. Low blood sugar led to seizures, and my body temperature dropped to a dangerously low point. I guess you could say I was at my lowest in every conceivable way—physically and spiritually."

"Sounds like you needed a miracle." My mother's sympathetic voice tugged at my heartstrings nearly as much as his story.

"Yes, but I sure didn't deserve one. I'd never done one thing in my life to warrant anything good from God, that's for sure." At this point, Otis's gaze lifted to Nadine, who stared at him intently, not uttering a word.

"So, what happened?" My mom, never one to give up easily, encouraged him to keep talking.

"I'd bargained with God a million times, made a million promises I knew I wouldn't keep. But this time I knew something was different. This time, when the social worker came by, then the chaplain, then a fellow from AA, I just felt. . ." He paused a moment to get control of his emotions. "I just felt hope. For the first time in years."

"The Bible says, 'Hope deferred makes the heart sick,'" my dad threw in. "You can take a lot of things away from a man, but there's nothing worse than trying to take his hope."

Wow. I'd just said the same thing, hadn't I? Losing hope was a terrible thing.

"It's funny you should say that," Otis said. "That's the first scripture I memorized when I started going to meetings." He looked up at Nadine with a pleading look in his eyes. "I've been clean and sober for two years, nine months, and eleven days. But being sober wasn't enough. Repentance is one thing; restitution is another."

She continued to stare, not saying a word.

"It would be one thing for me to just make a phone call and say 'I'm sorry,' and then let it go," he said. "But from what I've read in the Bible, there's more to it than that. I have to do right by you—and Scott. I had to come and do this in person." At this point, his words became quite passionate. "I once heard a preacher say there were twelve words that could mend any relationship."

"Really?" That certainly got my attention. "What are they?"

Otis held up his fingers—one by one—as he recited them: "I was wrong. I am sorry. Please forgive me. I love you." He now turned his attentions to Nadine, and I could see the pleading in his eyes.

I wasn't sure for a minute how she would respond. She'd been through a lot over the past few weeks—everything from political scandals to a missing son. What would this Bible-study-leading, homeless-shelter-working woman-of-God say to her now-sober ex-husband?

We all sat in silence, just staring at her. For a good twenty seconds. Then thirty. When she finally did speak, it seemed to take all of us by surprise.

"I've wanted to hate you," she said, as she turned to face Otis. "Tried really hard, in fact. The first few years after you left, I think I actually managed. But when I came to the Lord. . ." She shook her head and looked Otis straight in the eye. "I had to do business with God about the unforgiving spirit I'd harbored." She hesitated a moment, then shifted her gaze to the ground. "It wasn't easy. I've known plenty of women who've never forgiven their ex's. But I can see how bitter they've become. I didn't want to be like that. Besides, I had our son to raise."

"A son who's never known his father." Otis hung his head in shame.

"Scott has known the love of both an earthly father and his heavenly Father." Nadine looked over at Brad with a reassuring smile. "And he's done a better job of forgivin' you than most could. We have Brad to thank for that."

Brad offered up a weak shrug, and I marveled at his ability to keep his thoughts to himself—especially in light of everything going on around him.

Otis looked up with tears in his eyes. "I came here—to Clarksborough—at Scott's invitation. He reached out to me, and I was ready to take that first step and meet him. Then, when I got to town. . ." He shook his head, and tears started to flow. "When I got to town, I went to his place right away. A neighbor saw me knocking and told me what had happened. I—I couldn't believe it."

"How much do you know about Scott's disappearance?" Nadine asked.

"I know that he's been gone since the last day in January," Otis said, "and that's only because I read the local paper."

"Speaking of papers. . ." She gave him a stern look, but his expression remained unchanged.

"What?" A look of genuine concern filled his eyes.

Nadine swept into business mode, putting on her let's-just-get-right-to-it voice. "I do need to address the issue of the journalist you've been talkin' to."

"W–what?" He looked up with a puzzled expression on his face.

"You told our story to a journalist from Savannah."

"I'm not sure what you mean. . . ." He shrugged, clearly confused.

Nadine looked up at Brad. "Would you get that paper, honey?"

He sprang into action, and in less than a minute, Otis held the paper in his hand. "Oh no!" He read a few lines and then looked up, dark creases etching his brow. "I know what happened here." He set the paper down, a look of realization on his face.

"Folks from Milby to Savannah seem to think they do, too, now that they've read this story," Nadine said. "So, would you mind telling me exactly what gave you the idea that spilling your guts was a good thing?"

"There's this guy at the motel," Otis spoke rapidly, as if he needed to get this story off his chest. "We have breakfast together every morning."

"Stale muffins and coffee?" I asked.

Otis looked at me, amazed. "How did you know that?"

"I have my sources."

The look of wonder stayed on Otis's face as he continued. "Anyway, this guy kind of befriended me. We got to talking, and I shared my testimony. I never dreamed. . ." He shook his head, clearly distraught. "I had no idea he was anything other than just a random stranger in need of a friend. In fact. . ." He paused and pursed his lips. "I really thought maybe he was struggling with an alcohol problem, too. Thought I was helping him in some way."

"This guy is chubby and kind of short, right?" I asked. "Has a scraggly beard? Blondish-colored hair?"

"Yes. That's right. Though. . ." Otis's lips curled up. "I can't really judge his height. Everyone seems short to me."

No doubt. I turned to face Nadine with a sigh. "Well, I've met this journalist twice now, though I only just put it together in my head. I saw him once at the airport snapping photographs of us."

"W–what? Why didn't you say something?"

"I wasn't sure enough," I explained. "But then, I saw him again at the motel the other day. I even stopped to chat with him when you and Brad went out to the car to look for your purse. I didn't recognize him as the same fellow from the airport because he hadn't shaved—and I'd only seen the guy at the airport from a distance. But I know now it had to be the same man. In fact. . ." I looked at Otis with a hint of suspicion. "I gave him the note with the information that led you here today."

"Heavens to Betsy!" Nadine leaped to her feet. "That means he probably followed you here. He knows where we're staying."

"I'm sure he's known that all along." I did my best to console her. "He's pretty savvy. He followed you and my mom to the Burger Barn, remember? But let's don't jump the gun or think that he's going to do something crazy."

"Maybe he already has." Nadine leaned her head into her palms. "Maybe—just maybe—he's the one responsible for Scott's dis-appearance. He's got to be working for my opponents. Got to be."

"We'll get to the bottom of this, if it's the last thing we do."

I reached to pat Nadine's arm. "I'm going to call O'Henry right away, and we'll have his patrol car parked in our driveway. I challenge any reporter—good, bad, or otherwise—to try to bother us while he's here."

I'd just reached to grab the telephone when it let out a loud ring, startling me. I almost hurled the crazy thing into the air out of sheer fright. Once I composed myself, I looked at the caller ID and realized I didn't recognize the number. Never mind that. With everything that was going on, I needed to take every call. I answered and was stunned to hear Tomi Yu's voice on the other end of the line.

"Mrs. Peterson, I had to call you," he said. "That man—the one I told you about? He came into the restaurant again today. Second time this week."

"Was he asking about Scott?" I pulled out my notebook and started to take notes.

"Yes. It was so strange. Said he'd read about Scott's disappearance in the paper and wanted to know if I'd heard anything else. He seemed like a nice enough guy, but something about him just left me with an uneasy feeling. He's kind of nosy. It was almost like he wanted to know what people were saying about Scott's disappearance. He was overly interested."

"What did this man look like, again?"

"Hmm. Just kind of average," Tomi said. "Like I said before. Not terribly tall. Light brown hair." He chuckled. "Of course, I can't be sure of his height. Everyone seems tall next to me." Ironic, considering what Otis had just said.

Are we talking about the man at the motel, perhaps? "Did he have a beard?"

"No. He was clean-cut."

Could've shaved.

"Anyway, he paid for his takeout order, had a long chat with me, and left in a hurry."

"Odd. Very odd."

As we ended the call, I thanked Tomi for this latest tidbit of information. I couldn't help but think this somewhat-average-looking man held the key to my investigation in the palm of his hand.

Now. . .to track him down.

MY FUNNY VALENTINE

Late Thursday night, I struggled to fall asleep. I thought about that photo O'Henry had just returned to me, wishing my heart didn't twist in so many directions every time I looked at it. I pondered the contents of the letters Bob Kendricks had passed my way. They'd been bothering me for some time now. I wondered about the information Tomi had just given me. And I agonized over the situation with the reporter at The Happy Hideaway. He had obviously *wanted* me to know who he was and what he was up to. After all, he had called out to me that afternoon, offering up information about Otis on his own. Did he want to be caught? I tossed around in the bed till the sheets were twisted all around me.

Finally, out of sheer frustration, I rose and took an over-the-counter sleeping pill. A short time later, I dozed off. The dreams came fast and furious in vast Technicolor array. I tried to sort them out when I awoke the next morning, but the grogginess from the medication proved a problem. Still, one thing did make sense. With only thirty-six hours till wedding time, we were in crunch mode. I needed to do something, anything. But what?

I leaned back against the pillows and spent some serious time in prayer. Then I rose from the bed and picked up the telephone to call Sheila, to let her know I was coming by the church to drop off half a dozen casserole dishes various ladies had brought to my house. To be honest, I needed Sheila to myself for a while. If anyone could help me shed some light on all this, she could.

Less than an hour later, cup of Earl Grey in hand, I joined her in the spacious fellowship hall of the Clarksborough Community Church, where she was putting together red and white floral centerpieces. After just a few minutes, Sheila looked over at me with pain in her eyes. Her words surprised me.

"I want you to know that I kind of feel like a traitor, going through with all this." She gestured around the room, and I understood her meaning at once.

"It's not your fault." I gave her a sympathetic shrug, then reached for a bundle of silk flowers. Perhaps helping would ease my frustrations. "You've had this Valentine's banquet planned for months—and you're going to be a great MC. Besides, there's no reason the whole church should suffer, just because we're. . ." I couldn't finish.

Sheila continued putting together the centerpieces, but I could sense the tension in her voice as she spoke. "The Bible says we're to mourn when our brothers and sisters mourn and celebrate when they celebrate. It just feels wrong to be celebrating when you're. . ."

She never said the word *mourning*, but I saw it in her eyes.

"It's just not going to be the same," she continued. "Nothing's the same right now. Especially if you and Warren can't come." She looked up and clamped a hand over her mouth. "I'm sorry. I'm not implying that you *should* come, just that I'll miss you."

I gave a woeful shrug. "I know. And under any other circumstances, I would come. But I just can't—too many people asking too many questions. And besides. . ." The tears started to flow in earnest as the truth hit me square in the face. "I g–guess I'm just now g–getting it—that th–there's really not going to b–be a wedding. All this time I thought. . ." I shook my head in defeat. "I guess it doesn't matter what I thought."

She swept me into her arms and, in her usual Sheila-like way, began to comfort me. "Of *course* it matters. Your faith has been remarkably high all the way through this. And you know what I always say: A bend in the road is not the end of the road. . .unless you fail to make the turn."

I couldn't help but chuckle. "Don't ever change, Sheila. I don't think I could take it." I lifted an awkwardly made centerpiece for her approval. "What do you think of this?"

"Great! Those red silk roses look so real I can almost smell them from here."

My heart twisted within me as I thought about her words. I'd said the same thing to Brandi about the bridesmaids' bouquets just a few short weeks ago. And now. . . No, I wouldn't do this to myself. Not today. I forced a smile and gestured to a nearby table. "Where would you like it?"

She looked around the messy fellowship hall with its boxes, decorations, and ribbons strewed about and shrugged. "Any of the tables will do. But let's get the cloths on them first."

After taking a swig of my now-lukewarm tea, I helped her put red cloths on each table. Good thing Brandi wasn't here to see all this Valentine decor. She'd have a meltdown, for sure. With a sigh, I realized the truth—I was pretty close to a meltdown myself, especially as I faced the cheerful Valentine decorations.

From across the room, my cell phone rang out. I sprinted over to grab it from my purse. I was startled to hear Malcolm Pfifer's voice on the other end of the line.

"Mrs. Peterson?"

"Yes?"

"I'm sorry it's taken me so long to get back to you. I've been extremely busy this week. I, um. . .well, I noticed that you didn't drop off the additional deposit I requested. I hate to bring it up, but. . ."

"Right, well, there's a reason for that. . . ." I dove off into an explanation, but he seemed undaunted.

"As I said, I'm not trying to be rude, but you've kind of put me in an awkward position," he explained. "Tomorrow is Valentine's Day. Valentine's Day—one of the busiest days of the year for those of us in the photography business—and I turned down several other offers for tomorrow night so that I could shoot this wedding for your daughter. I had the opportunity to do a school dance in Philly and a banquet for a large church in Quakertown. That's why I opted to adjust your deposit amount—to cover my losses."

"Well, yes, but. . ."

"I don't want to sound harsh, especially in light of what you're going through." Here he paused, and his voice took on a softer, more agreeable tone. "Look, I really don't want to be unreasonable. I guess I'm just disappointed, is all. I was really looking forward to this shoot. I was there the night Scott and Brandi got engaged, after all, so it meant a lot to me. And it's probably too late to get another gig now."

I did my best to sound calm as I spoke. "Leave tomorrow night open for our family, Mr. Pfifer. We have every reason to believe there's going to be a wedding." I was all business now. "So, just tell me what to do with the additional deposit money. Should I bring it by your studio, say. . ." I glanced at my watch. "around 2:00?"

"I'm not at the studio today," he explained. "It's under construction. Has been, for more than a week now. That's why I've been away from the phone the last few days."

"Well, tell me what to do."

"I guess you could drop a check in the mail," he suggested. He gave me his home address, which I jotted down on the back of a receipt. We ended the call on a pleasant enough note, but I turned to Sheila.

"I don't think you need to send him one red cent," she said. "But that's just my opinion. No point in paying the man for a service he isn't rendering."

"But what if the wedding does happen?" I argued. "What if. . ." Here I dissolved into a puddle of tears. There would be no wedding for Brandi and Scott tomorrow. The way things were going, my daughter would never have a husband.

And I would never be Scott's mother-in-law.

Mother-in-law.

Strange. For whatever reason, I found myself focusing on that word once again. It'd been days since I'd thought about it.

"Hang on there, girl." Sheila drew close and slipped an arm

around my shoulders. Right away, I dissolved into a new puddle of tears.

"I'm tired of hanging. I'm just plain exhausted."

"Everything is going to turn out fine," she whispered. "I can feel it."

"I wish I could," I whispered. "I don't know if anything will ever be okay again."

She allowed me to grieve over the situation for what seemed like a very long time. Then I dove back into my work, a decorating diva with a hot-glue gun in my hands. At some point, I reached to grab the now-cold cup of Earl Grey tea for another sip. Somehow I managed to catch it with the back of my hand, knocking it over. The plastic top popped off and tea went everywhere, covering the tablecloth and splashing on the centerpiece. I mopped up the mess, pulling up a pile of soaked white napkins. All the while, something bothered me, though I couldn't put my finger on it. Something was wrong. I could feel it. But what?

Suddenly, as my hand hit a small metal object, I realized the truth of it. *Heavens to Betsy.* There, underneath the puddle of napkins, sat my new cell phone.

Soaking wet.

YAKETY YAK

When I finished up at the church, I headed over to Mobile Mania—soggy phone in hand—to ask what could be done about it. *Again.* I wasn't sure what the guy behind the counter would say to me—or about me—but I didn't really care. This time I'd paid extra to have the phone insured. They would have to give me another one. Right?

I waited in line behind several unhappy customers, listening as they exchanged not-so-pleasant pleasantries with the lone customer service rep—a guy whose name tag boasted JOE KERR.

Sheila always said you could tell a lot about a person from his name, but I did my best not to let that distract me today. This guy didn't seem the happy-go-lucky sort, and I was certainly in no mood to joke around, either. He didn't even look up as I approached the counter. A mumbled, "Can I help you?" was all I got from him.

"Yes." I gave my warmest smile. "I purchased a new phone last week. One week ago today, in fact."

"Yes?"

"And I've, well. . ." I opened it to show him the odd mixture of colors on the screen, then gazed up into his eyes with a shrug.

Now he glanced down at me with a sympathetic smile. "Really? So soon?"

"Yeah. It was the Earl Grey tea."

"Gets you every time." He gave me a sympathetic look. "I lost one to a cup of Caramel Mocha Frappuccino last Christmas."

"Wow. Seems to be an epidemic," I said. "But thank goodness for that insurance, right? I should be able to replace it at no cost, if I understood correctly."

"Maybe." He gave me a suspicious once-over that sent a little shiver down my spine. As he did, a funny look came over him. "Hey, I know you. You used to go to the gym every morning, right?"

I cringed at the words *used to* but offered a nod in response. "Yeah, when I had time."

"There just don't seem to be enough hours in the day," he agreed.

"You have no idea."

Joe snapped back into business mode right away, possibly in response to my pensive stare. "Do you have your receipt?" he asked.

As I reached to fish it out of my oversized purse, Scott and Brandi's engagement photo popped out. I gripped it and stared at the two happy faces, doing my best not to cry as emotion suddenly took control of me.

"Everything okay?" The fellow gave me a curious look.

"Yes, I'm just a little sad today."

"Well, it's Valentine's weekend—a hard time of year for a lot of us." He offered up a kindhearted shrug, and I could read him like a book. Valentine's Day had left its mark on Joe Kerr, to be sure.

As he rustled up another matching cell phone for me, I stared again at the photo, in some ways, as if for the first time. The quality wasn't very good; that was for sure. The coloring was off, and so was the centering. Every time I looked at it, I came closer to believing Malcolm Pfifer was better off investing in houses, not focusing on a career in photography.

"Hey, I have a picture like that." Joe pointed to the photo in my hand.

"Really?" I looked up at him, curious.

"Yeah. My girlfriend and I. . ." He paused and shook his head. "My *ex*-girlfriend and I had our pictures done at the Fall Festival." He fetched his wallet and opened it to show me a small photo of his ex-girlfriend.

You know, I've discovered that everyone is beautiful if you squint a bit.

As Joe put his wallet back in his pocket, I turned the photo of Brandi and Scott so that he could have a better look. "Meet my daughter and future son-in-law."

"Hey, that guy looks familiar." Joe's brow wrinkled as he stared at the photograph.

"Well. . ." I hated to bring it up, but he'd already started. "I'm sure you've seen this picture in the papers for the past couple of weeks. He's been missing for thirteen days now."

"Yeah"—he snapped his fingers—"I heard about that. The Runaway Groom story."

Everything within me cringed, though I couldn't blame him for assuming Scott had run away. I still wrestled with the same possibility. Probably, before everything was said and done, half of Clarksborough would think the same thing. "We aren't sure what happened to him."

"Sorry about that." Joe went to work on the new phone, pulling it from the box. "Well, I hope you find him."

If Scott didn't return—and soon—Brandi would face the rest of her life alone. The man in this photo might fade from our memories as quickly as the photo itself.

A shiver ran down my spine as I contemplated that possibility. What if Scott simply never reappeared? What if no one ever heard from him again? What if he, like his father before him, simply went off, down his own road, never to be seen or heard from again?

I put the photo back in my purse with a sigh. "Guess I didn't need to be looking at that, anyway." I snapped my fingers as the memory hit. "But it does remind me that I need to go next door and drop off a check."

"At Pfifer's Photography?" Joe's left eyebrow elevated slightly.

"Yes. Malcolm Pfifer was supposed to shoot the wedding tomorrow night. But now. . ." I didn't finish, simply because I wasn't sure what to say next.

"That's one weird guy."

"What do you mean?"

"I dunno. The first time I met him was at the festival. Then, of course, I've seen him coming and going from that place he calls a studio next door."

"That place he *calls* a studio?"

"Well, he's there a lot, but I never see any customers over there. Not many, anyway."

"Oh, right," I explained. "That's because the studio has been under construction for the past couple of weeks. He just told me."

"Ah. I wondered what was up," Joe said. "He's been in and out more than usual—and always with food in his hands. I thought for a while he was living in there." A playful smile followed. "Thought maybe his wife kicked him out or something."

I offered up a shrug. "I haven't got a clue. I just know he's been out of business for a while during the construction. Least, that's what he told me."

Joe handed me the new phone. "Do you need me to show you how to operate this one?"

"Nah." I couldn't help but grin. "It's the same one I bought last week, remember?"

"Ah yes. Would you like me to transfer the data from the old phone to this one so that you don't have to reenter the phone numbers? I think the chip is salvageable."

"Could you?" *Praise the Lord.* "That would be great."

As he moved the data from one phone to the other, I contemplated his words. Valentine's Day was a sad day for many people. I'd never really thought about it until now. Maybe all the events of the past couple of weeks had something to do with the season. It was a thought, anyway.

Moments later, I said my good-byes to Joe.

"See you at the gym," he called out.

"Sure thing." It wasn't exactly a lie. I did hope to make it back—one day.

As I walked out of the building, I glanced in the front window of Pfifer's Photography Studio. The silver tinting on the windows made seeing inside almost impossible. *That's odd. Just last Saturday, I could see inside to the beautiful wedding photo. Now. . .* Seemed strange that he would've had the windows tinted just to hide the fact that the place was under construction.

I reached into my purse to pull out my checkbook, cringing as I made out the check to pay the balance on our deposit. I hated to give the guy any more money, but he did have a point. . . . He had given up other business to keep the evening free for us. The least I could do was pay for his time.

Sure, I'd agreed to drop a check in the mail, but what was the point, really, when there was a mail slot right here—in the door. I could call him later to let him know, right? With things going the way they were, I'd never remember to mail the check anyway. Might as well drop it off with a note, then follow up with a call.

I scribbled a few lines on a scrap of paper I'd found in my purse and opened the oversized mail slot. Right away, the undeniable odor of spicy food shot up my nostrils. *Hmm.* Maybe his wife really *had* given him the boot. Maybe he'd taken up residence inside this darkened room. That would explain his sour mood. Maybe he was holed up inside his store even now, counting his losses. Maybe I should just knock and. . .

Nah. I'd drop the check in the slot and head off on my merry way, new phone in hand. After all, I had places to go, people to see.

CHAPTER 29

ALL SHOOK UP

Friday night was a tough one. Instead of gathering together with an elated wedding party at Leonardo's, our whole family, along with several bridesmaids and groomsmen, met in my living room for a quiet evening together. It wasn't a planned, staged event. On the contrary, we never even announced we'd be together. But somewhere between the hours of seven and eight, over thirty people came knocking at my front door, including my brother and his children.

My mother was delighted, naturally, but that still didn't serve to lift the dark cloud that hung over the group. Happy as we all were to be together, we knew very well that we were nearing the end of the road. Likely, there would be no wedding tomorrow. At least, that's the way things appeared tonight.

Ironically, Brandi was the last to arrive. She entered with red-rimmed eyes, offering up apologies for her tardiness.

"There's such a mess going on at the office," she explained with a shrug. "And my boss had to make an emergency trip out of town, so I've been on my own."

Others in the room greeted her with hugs and kisses, but she eventually found herself in my arms. Once there, she leaned against me and began to cry. I managed to nudge her out of the room and down the hallway, sweeping her into the safety of my bedroom. We needed some mother-daughter time.

We cuddled up next to each other on my bed, and she wept as much as she had when she'd lost her teddy bear at the age of three. I didn't interrupt, at least not until she'd pretty much cried herself out.

"I never dreamed something like this would happen to me, Mom." She looked up at me with those bloodshot eyes, and my heart broke. "I mean, you hear about things like this happening, but only to other people. You know?"

"I know." The words came out as a whisper, as I was barely able to speak at all.

"I've dreamed of my wedding all my life," she whispered. "I always knew it would be on Valentine's Day. And this year, of all years, Valentine's Day fell on a Saturday. This was meant to be!" She looked up at me with that imploring look I'd come to know.

"I know." Why were they the only two words I seemed to be able to come up with tonight? Perhaps because I only knew what had appeared to be God's will until this point?

"What if he's. . . ?" She buried her face in my arms and wept until we were both shaking.

I shook my head, still unable to admit the worst had happened—at least admit as much to anyone other than myself. "I have faith, Brandi. Faith that God is going to bring him back to us."

"I don't even know what faith is anymore." She shook her head, and I could see a look of disgust in her eyes. "I don't."

Biting my tongue was tough. I wanted to quote the Bible, to tell her that faith was the substance of things hoped for, the evidence of things not seen. But would she receive those words now, current circumstances considered? Probably not. Instead, I reached over to my bedside table and grabbed a tissue, which I pressed into her hand.

"It's not cold feet." She dabbed at her eyes, then blew her nose. "I know that now. Something has happened to him. Something terrible."

I didn't ask what led her to this conclusion. Didn't dare. Instead, I drew her to myself and cradled her in my arms as I'd done so many times as a young mother. Just then, a rap on the door caught my attention. Nadine peeked her head inside, and her eyes filled with tears the moment she spied us on the bed. She joined us right away. There we sat, three heartbroken women, arms wrapped around one another so tightly we could scarcely breathe.

We grieved as we had never grieved before. I couldn't help but wonder if we'd seen Scott for the last time. My heart felt heavier than a stone as I contemplated that thought. Was this what it felt like to lose someone you loved? Did it make your heart feel as if it had somehow been ripped in two? How did you go on after something catastrophic? Was there really life after something this tragic?

Just then, Nadine lifted her head and gazed at us with weary eyes. "They always say it's darkest before the dawn," she whispered. "And we've been through plenty of darkness. More than our share.

So I can't help but think the dawn is coming."

"What do you mean?" Brandi whispered.

"I'm not sure how I know"—Nadine shook her head as she spoke—"but I just know Scott is going to come back to us. I know it."

I know in my knower. That's what Janetta had said. Okay, perhaps now was the time to share the verse I'd struggled over just moments before. I sat up straight and dabbed my eyes with a tissue. " 'Faith is the substance of things hoped for,' " I said, " 'the evidence. . .' " Somehow, I never got past the word *evidence*. In light of all we were going through, the word got stuck on my tongue.

" 'The evidence of things not seen,' " Nadine finished the verse.

"Well, there's plenty I'm not seeing," Brandi acknowledged. "But I don't know that I can even pretend to have faith right now."

"We're in this together." Nadine gripped her hand. "And there are dozens of people who love you out there in that living room. So what do you think about this idea?" Her voice intensified, and her eyes lit up. "Instead of giving in to the mourning, why don't we get together and pray—as a group, I mean. I know your family and friends would love to do that with you."

Brandi, to her credit, didn't argue. But she did give us both a look that said, *What difference would that make, really?* I understood her doubts. I'd had plenty myself. But somehow, seeing the hopeful look in Nadine's eyes made me want to hope again. Want to believe again. Would God really intervene this late, when everything looked hopeless?

I stood up and extended my hand in Brandi's direction. "Come on, babe."

After a moment of hesitation, she joined me. Less than a minute later, we joined the others in the living room. Everyone gathered around Brandi, giving her all of the love she could stand. A few knew to give her a little space, but several—family members, mostly—couldn't seem to keep from wrapping her in their arms.

Nadine and I called a quick meeting with our husbands and put together a plan of action.

"I'll take it from here," Warren said.

He called together everyone in the room, and the place grew quiet at once. "We're going to spend some time praying together," he said. "Asking God to move in a supernatural way—to bring to light any hidden things."

I watched as everyone gathered in a circle and grabbed hands. As the people began to pray, I thought back over everything that had happened in the past two weeks. So many things were still hidden to me. Would God really shed His light on them, even now? In the eleventh hour? Only time would tell.

Just one problem. . . We didn't have much time.

ACHY BREAKY HEART

S heila telephoned early Saturday morning, rousing me from
my slumber. She got right to the point with another one of
her one-word questions. "Well?"

Still groggy, I couldn't think to give her a logical answer. "Well,
what?" I managed.

"What can I do?"

"What do you mean?" I sat up in the bed and scratched my
head. Sometimes the woman made no sense at all.

"How can I help you? What can I do? I feel terrible that
I wasn't able to come to your place last night. The Valentine's
banquet went great, by the way, but it just wasn't the same without
the Peterson family."

"Um, thanks. I think." I looked over at the window, noticing
that it was still dark out. At this point, I turned to look at the
alarm clock on my bedside table. *5:45? What in the world?* "Sheila,
what are you doing up this early?" I muttered, doing my best

not to wake Warren. After all, he'd been up till one thirty in the morning, when the prayer meeting wound down and the last of our guests left.

"The Lord woke me up to pray," Sheila informed me.

"Ah." *Did He tell you to call and wake me, too?* She clearly had no idea I'd been up half the night praying already.

"Rise and shine, Annie," she said. "There's work to be done."

I rubbed my eyes and tried to think straight. "I can rise, and I can shine—but I can't do both at the same time." I offered up a lazy yawn, but nothing more.

"Did you know when it's dark outside, you can see the stars?"

"Um, okay." *Like right now, you mean?*

"It takes a really dark night to see them. Doesn't happen otherwise."

I rubbed at my eyes. "Sheila, are you going somewhere with all of this?"

"Yes," she added, "and you know what they say. It's always darkest before the dawn."

"Right." Nadine had used the same expression just last night.

"It's almost dawn, Annie. I just have the most amazing feeling the light's about to break through. Remember that scripture you always quote—the one from Ephesians?"

"Yeah. Sort of." I leaned back against the pillows. " 'Everything exposed by the light becomes visible. . . .' Is that the one you're talking about?"

"That's the one!" Her voice took on a passionate sound. "Everything exposed by the light *will* become visible, so we have to pray specifically for God to shine His spotlight on this situation so that He can make things plain. Would it be okay if I prayed with you for that very thing?"

"Well, for heaven's sake, I never turn down an offer for prayer. Even at five in the morning."

"Five forty-five."

Sheila dove into an amazing, albeit lengthy, prayer. All the while, I leaned back against the pillows, tossing in an occasional, quiet "Amen" to ditto her thoughts. Even as she prayed, I came fully awake. The early hour didn't matter. What mattered was this: God had something specific for me today—and I'd better get to it.

As she finished, I thanked her profusely, then hung up the phone and slipped out of the bed, heading to the bathroom for a few minutes of alone time—to think and to pray.

Then, suddenly, I knew what I must do. And Sheila, God bless her, had awakened me at just the right time to do it. I tiptoed into the closet and reached for my warmest sweat suit—a dark red one with white accents—careful not to wake Warren. After donning it, I reached for my tennis shoes. I had no intention of jogging—or even walking, for that matter. No, I had something a little more interesting in mind on this bitterly cold Valentine's Day. If only I could accomplish it without waking everyone in the house. . .

I stole down the hallway and eased my way out the front door. The icy morning air slapped me square in the face as I made my way to the car. Once inside, I prayed it would start with no problem. Thankfully, the engine purred like a kitten on the first try.

As I pulled out of the driveway, I prayed a quick prayer for God's will to be done. There were missing pieces to the Absent Groom puzzle—and I would find them. This morning, if I could.

I drove with the headlights on, though the morning sun was

now peeking out from the eastern sky, casting a lovely pink and orange haze over Clarksborough. I made my way through town and out onto the highway, wondering what Warren would do if he knew my plans.

As I passed the Clark County Sheriff's Office, an idea struck. I quickly called Sergeant O'Henry on his home phone and asked for his help. Though groggy, he agreed right away. Afterward, I made one more call for help, and my new partner in crime solving was happy to oblige.

It didn't take long to reach The Happy Hideaway. And, to be honest, I wasn't even sure I'd find my informant here—though I certainly prayed for as much. I waited outside the lobby until the first signs of stirring occurred. Then I made my way inside to join others who'd come in, enticed by offers of a free continental breakfast.

Ten minutes and counting. No luck. Fifteen. Sixteen.

Just as the clock reached 6:30, he arrived—my old pal, the reporter from the Savannah newspaper. He was just as short and chubby as the last time I'd seen him, and he still boasted the same scraggly beard. He carried a newspaper in his hand, and in his bleary-eyed state, he didn't even seem to recognize me. At first.

When I asked if I could join him at his table, he looked up at me with a look of chagrin, as if he somehow knew he'd been caught.

Caught at what, I wasn't so sure. Just caught.

"So. . ." He gestured for me to sit. "What can I do for you this morning, Mrs. Peterson?"

"You know my name?"

"Of course I do. That's my business."

"As a reporter, you mean."

"Sure." He nodded and took a bite of a doughnut. "I knew it wouldn't take long for you to figure me out." He extended his hand for a shake as he introduced himself. "Chris Donnelly."

"Chris." I gave him a pensive look. "So. . .why me? What made you think you'd be hearing from me again?"

He shrugged. "I dunno. You seemed like a smart lady—and when you came in here that morning with Nadine Cunningham and her husband, you were asking questions. Lots of them. Seemed like more than mere curiosity to me."

"Well, you appear to know a lot about me," I ventured. "So I guess you know what I've got on my mind this morning—the reason for my visit."

"For once, I'm clueless." He took a bite of a doughnut and made a face, then plopped it back down on his tiny Styrofoam plate.

"Nadine is running for political office, and suddenly—out of the blue—her son turns up missing. Some might have to wonder if you know more about that than you're admitting."

His cheeks reddened. "I'm just a reporter—hired to do a job." He leaned back against his chair with a smug look on his face, then took a swig from his coffee cup.

"A kidnapping job?" I knew better but had to play this thing out to its fullest in order to get the truth from him.

The fellow's eyes grew wide, and he sputtered on his coffee. "Kidnapping? You think I had something to do with that kid of hers turning up missing?"

"Well?"

He set the coffee cup down and shook his head. "Look, lady, I don't mind doing a little snooping. I don't even mind taking on boring assignments like this one—following a middle-aged woman around all over the country, just on the off chance she does or says something that will affect her campaign, but—kidnapping? Are you kidding me? You really think I'm capable of that?"

"I hardly know you," I said, "so I can't say for sure. But you've put yourself in an awkward position."

"It's just my job. I'm always ending up in awkward positions, but that doesn't make me a criminal." He took another swig from his coffee cup.

"Fine." I stood up and gestured for him to do the same. "If you're a real reporter, then you'll want all the facts, which means you'll have to come with me."

"W–what? Where are we going?"

"To my house. You're going to tell Nadine Cunningham face-to-face what you've been up to, and you're going to apologize to her for using her ex-husband against her. Poor move on your part, by the way."

"Made for a great story." He shrugged. "What can I say?"

"You can say, 'I'm sorry,' " Otis Fuller's voice rang out from across the lobby of the motel, "which is exactly what you're going to say."

"Then you're going to explain to Nadine that you didn't have anything to do with Scott's disappearance," I added.

Chris looked back and forth between us, realizing we had him. "What makes you think I'm going to come with you to do all of that?" He flashed a hint of a playful smile.

"For one thing, Officer O'Henry of the Clark County Sheriff's Office. He's waiting outside in his patrol car to ask you a few questions."

"W–what?"

"That's right." I now flashed a smile. "And when he's done questioning you—if he says you're free to go—he'll be happy to escort both of you gentlemen to my house. I'll meet you there." I pointed to the stale doughnuts. "Don't bother eating anything else. I'm going to be feeding you breakfast. It'll be easier to clear your conscience over a bowl of my mother's grits."

"Grits?" Donnelly's eyes lit up. For a moment. Then he raked his fingers through his hair, and a look of dazed curiosity passed over his face. "This is crazy." He stared out the window at the patrol car in the parking lot. "I haven't broken any laws."

"Except a few moral ones," Otis threw in. "Like the one where you neglected to tell me that every word I'd spoken was going to make it into the papers."

"Freedom of the press," Donnelly argued. "There's nothing wrong with that. And I'm not a kidnapper, that's for sure, so you two are barking up the wrong tree, if that's what you're thinking."

I gave a little shrug as O'Henry appeared in the doorway. "Then a simple conversation with this fine officer of the law will clear everything up," I stated. "In the meantime, I'll look for you back at my house in an hour or so for breakfast. Have a great morning!"

I passed him off with a nod to a more-than-stern O'Henry, then climbed back into my car and headed for the grocery store. I'd promised the men breakfast. Now I had to deliver.

LOVE WILL KEEP US TOGETHER

After stopping off at the local supercenter for groceries, I raced home, anxious to tell Warren about my morning. I arrived home to find my bedroom empty. I heard the shower running and knew he would be out shortly, probably full of questions about my whereabouts. I reached for my notebook to jot down my latest findings. My heart raced in anticipation as I wrote the words.

> *Fact #10: Scott's disappearance has nothing to do with Nadine's run for office. Answers have been slow in coming but will arrive shortly.*

As I suspected, Warren emerged from the bathroom in a state of panic. As he toweled dry, I filled him in on the latest. He could hardly believe I'd been up and running since 5:45 but gave me an admiring smile. "You're really on the job, aren't you?"

"I am." I went on to tell him that we would have several breakfast guests, and he flew into action.

"Good grief, Annie," he said, as he slipped on his jeans. "You went and invited that reporter to breakfast—at our house? With Nadine here?"

"Well, yeah," I admitted, "and I invited her ex-husband, too. And I plan to include all of the kids, as well."

Warren slipped on a sweatshirt and muttered from underneath it as it passed over his head: "What were you thinking?"

I gave a little shrug. "I was thinking that if we got everyone together in one room, maybe Nadine would have a chance to find out personally if her opponents have really been behind any of this or if maybe this guy is just some over-the-top reporter looking for a scoop. And hey. . ." I snapped my fingers as the reality hit. "If this guy is looking for a good story, maybe we can give him one."

"What do you mean?"

"I mean, when we find Scott—and we are going to find him— this fellow can write the story—the real story—and turn the whole political thing around for Nadine."

Warren just shook his head and continued to get dressed. I telephoned Brandi and Candy to invite them to a breakfast feast. If I couldn't offer my daughter a wedding today, the very least I could offer her was a Valentine's brunch, where she would be surrounded by the people who loved her the most. Well, the people who loved her the most *and* her missing groom's deadbeat father, along with a somewhat suspicious journalist who happened to love grits.

I explained the situation in detail to my parents and Nadine. Mom responded in her usual enthusiastic way. "The guy who followed us into the Burger Barn is coming to breakfast?"

As I nodded, I sensed Nadine's fear.

"His name is Chris Donnelly," I explained. "He will be arriving shortly."

"Are you sure this is safe?" Nadine asked. "I don't need any more lies spread about me."

"I have a hunch about this one," I explained. "And I don't think this is going to work against you. I really don't. This guy might just end up being your greatest asset."

"I trust you, Annie," she said, "but I'm still nervous."

"I, for one, think it's a good idea," my father said. "Once this man has a bowl of your mother's grits, he'll spill his guts. I guarantee it."

We all pitched in, and by nine o'clock, we'd prepared a large pan of grits, a full platter of pancakes—chocolate chip and blueberry—mounds of bacon, scrambled eggs, and orange-cranberry muffins. Brad and Warren took care of the coffee, and I heated water for tea—Earl Grey, of course.

O'Henry arrived with Otis and Donnelly in tow at exactly 9:20. I took a moment to make introductions and even offered O'Henry a place at our breakfast table. He graciously declined, stating that he'd better get home to his wife. It was Valentine's Day, after all. Donnelly seemed a nervous wreck, particularly as I introduced him to Nadine. She took his hand when he extended it, but her eyes never met his. And Brad, always the first to protect Nadine, kept a watchful eye on the situation. Strangely, Otis did, too.

"You all take a few minutes to talk," I encouraged them, as I scurried about in the kitchen.

Nadine and Brad disappeared into the living room with Donnelly and Otis on their heels. Within minutes, I stuck my head in the room to check on them. Thankfully, their conversation remained on the quiet side, though I could see Nadine's eyes bulging a bit.

"Just tell me one thing," she said. "Who's paying you to do this to me? Who wants to see me ruined?"

"See you ruined?" He gave her an incredulous look. "Lady, don't you know how the newspaper business works? I work for the paper, not some political candidate."

"So all this dirt you're digging up," she continued, "someone hasn't paid you to find out every detail of my life? You can't tell me my opponents aren't behind this in some way."

"Look." He put his hands up in the air. "If I'm lyin', I'm dyin'. I've been assigned to you over the past few weeks. That's all. The paper has assigned reporters to trace city council candidates in all of the small towns surrounding Savannah, particularly the ones like you who have the best chance of winning. Why else do you think I'd be following you into a burger joint, for Pete's sake?"

For a moment, I saw a glimmer of hope in Nadine's eyes, but then she fired right back at him. "What you're doing is cruel and heartless, particularly in light of what I'm going through with the disappearance of my son."

"Hey, I can't help the timing of all this," he argued, "and I had nothing to do with your son's disappearance. In fact, when I got on that plane from Savannah, I had absolutely no clue why you were headed to Pennsylvania—thought maybe you were going on a vacation or something. And I can assure you, staying at that cheap motel hasn't been a piece of cake. And all to drum up a few facts about your life? If you don't believe me, talk to that cop—O'Henry. He knows I'm clean."

"I think he's being honest about that," Otis threw in. "And O'Henry would agree."

"Donnelly isn't Scott's kidnapper," I offered as I made my way to the sofa.

Everyone looked up at me, and I shrugged. "I have my suspicions about who took Scott, and it's not a mealymouthed reporter from Savannah, Georgia."

"Hey now. . ." Donnelly gave me a pout. "You don't have to be mean."

"Exactly." I gave him a brusque nod. "And that's exactly why I've brought you here this morning—to prove that you don't have to be mean to be a good journalist."

"Would you mind being a little more specific?"

"Gladly." I joined him on the couch. "You've been looking for a story. We're going to give you a story—one of the best you've ever written. Might give you the break you've been looking for."

"Huh?"

"Sometimes it's easier to just come out and ask when you're looking for material. We've got plenty to give you—and it's all good, clean, aboveboard stuff."

"Won't make for very good reading then."

"Oh, it'll be good. Filled with adventure. I dare say, by the time this is all said and done, you'll have your story—and a far better one than you ever thought."

His eyes lit up, and I could see an opportunity for a bit of encouragement.

"You just need some balance in your life, Mr. Donnelly. If

you're going to cover a story, cover every angle."

"Thought I was doing a pretty good job of that," he muttered.

"I'll tell you whatever you want to know," Nadine offered, "but you're going to let me see the story before it's printed, and it can't be slanted."

"Me? Slanted?" Donnelly flashed an exaggerated frown. "I would never. . ."

"No, you won't ever—again," I said. "From now on, any story you write about Nadine—or her run for office—will be as straight as an arrow. And filled with facts, not fiction."

His gaze shifted to the floor, and he muttered a quiet "Whatever," followed by, "What do I smell cooking in there?"

I had to surmise, after a big bowl of my mom's grits, we would find Mr. Donnelly to be an admirable ally.

At that moment, the front door swung open and the girls entered, with Garrett on their heels. After brief introductions, we took our places at the table. I glanced over at Brandi. Of course, I never mentioned her swollen, bloodshot eyes, but they broke my heart. How I longed to present her with a groom this morning. Instead, as she took her seat at the table, I presented her with a platter of her favorite pancakes in the world—chocolate chip. She didn't seem as interested in the food, however, as she was in the men who sat across from her. Even though I'd made proper introductions, I could sense her curiosity, particularly where Otis was concerned.

I did my best to keep the conversation light as we ate, but with so many broken hearts at the table, it was difficult. I know, because I could feel the weight of it as I scurried about from place to place, refilling glasses, and offering seconds on food. How I wanted to scream, "Lord, bring him to us, please!" but I refrained. No, some things were better left unsaid.

We wrapped up the morning meal just in time for another delivery at the front door—yet another wedding present. It served as a reminder that I'd better get back to work—and pronto. After all, I had a crime to solve.

"Go get 'em, Agatha Annie!" Warren's words of encouragement rang out in my ears, encouraging me to forge ahead. I squared my shoulders and prepared for the work ahead. Before this day was over, we would have a wedding. . .if I had anything to do with it.

STOP, IN THE NAME OF LOVE!

Crime solving had its ups and downs, but drawing near to the conclusion—the right conclusion—always gave me a bit of a high. As I cleared the breakfast table, I had the undeniable sense I was on to something, that I just needed to slow down for a moment so all the pieces to the puzzle could come together in my head.

Though my house was still full of guests, I slipped into the office to browse the Internet. Something had been bothering me for days—something that wouldn't leave me alone, even now. I jumped from site to site, looking for information, finally finding what I was looking for. Strange, I'd never contemplated this earlier in the week.

After perusing the Web, I went into my bedroom for some alone time. I allowed my mind to wander back over all of the evidence I'd written in my notebook during the past two weeks. I thought about Nadine and her run for office—how I'd grown to suspect Donnelly, and even Otis, for that matter. I thought about Scott, how I'd originally contemplated the possibility that all of this was just a childish prank. I thought about Malcolm Pfifer, how I'd begun to suspect him of ill will at some point along the way.

Then my thoughts began to shift to the situation at McKinley Pharmaceuticals. I paused to give that matter some serious thought. For the life of me, I hadn't been able to figure out if—or how—the folks at McKinley might be involved, particularly after reading the letters Bob had given me. Had they really, in their quest to protect the company, hidden Scott away long enough to allow the drug to pass FDA approval? According to Bob Kendricks, HD-387 would get the necessary approval this coming week. Did that mean Scott would mysteriously reappear from out of the blue once the deed was done?

Troubling thoughts kicked in at this point, and I couldn't seem to shake them. Something—or maybe *Someone*—gave me the strongest sense that Scott was in trouble. Right now. This very moment. He needed me, and he needed me now.

I stood and paced my room, praying as I'd never prayed before. "Lord, you said that everything exposed by the light would become visible. That's what I ask for now—clear vision to see the truth. Give me Your eyes to see, Father."

Suddenly, my mind went back to that text message I'd received. "Dark. In the dark. The groom's in the dark." I remembered something else, too. Something Brandi had said just last night.

Then, suddenly, I knew what had to be done. I knew in my knower—as Janetta had said—that Scott's whereabouts would soon come to light for all the world to see.

With that in mind, I picked up the phone and called Sheila.

She answered with four words: "Where are we meeting?"

"I'll pick you up," I said. "And bring your flashlight."

"Flashlight?" she echoed. "It's almost noon. Are you sure?"

"Oh, I'm sure, all right."

It took a little doing to convince Warren to let me leave, particularly when I told him Sasha was coming along. He gave me his best please-be-careful look, and I knew he knew my sleuthing antennae had risen. As he kissed me good-bye at the door, he whispered, "Go get 'em, Agatha Annie."

Yep. He knew.

Minutes later, I paused in front of Sheila's house to pick her up. She exited the front door dressed in the most colorful winter coat I'd ever laid eyes on. Her bright pink earrings and necklace were a nice complement, naturally, and her fuchsia lipstick just seemed to cap it all off. Wish I could've said the same thing about the shimmering heart-shaped clip in her hair.

"Where are we headed?" she asked, as she climbed into the car.

I quickly shared my thoughts, and she nodded. "Wow. Not what I was thinking at all. But I'm game. Let's get this ball rolling."

Sasha let out a yip from the backseat and we hit the road, the car completely silent—until Sheila began to pray aloud. She prayed for God's radar to kick in and lead us to the very spot where Scott was. She prayed for his safety. And for our safety. And then she prayed a rather remarkable prayer, asking God to help us pull off the wedding of the century. Tonight. After we located the groom, naturally.

As we traversed a curve in the road, I slowed because the car in front of us—the one with the VISUALIZE WORLD PEACE bumper sticker—was traveling at a snail's pace. "Must be a southerner,"

Sheila muttered. "Obviously doesn't have a clue how to drive on icy roads."

I tried not to take her comment personally, though I'd always be a southern gal at heart. After all, I'd lived in Pennsylvania long enough to figure out how to drive in the wintertime.

As the fellow in the car ahead of us continued to inch his way along, my patience grew thin. Finally, he drew to a near stop in the middle of the road, where he sat for a good ten or twelve seconds before making a left turn. Immediately, Sheila rolled down her window and shouted, "Forget world peace! Visualize using your turn signal!"

I shook my head and chuckled. "Honestly, Sheila. You crack me up."

"Crazy drivers." She reached over and honked my horn, just to give the fellow a final warning as he toodled off down the side road. "He just needs to let his wife do the driving, is all."

We continued on our way, and Sheila turned to face me. "Okay, Annie," she said, "I'm ready. Why don't you start by telling me about what's been going on at McKinley Pharmaceuticals. That's the part that has me confused. I'm dying to know how you came to this conclusion."

I started at the beginning, telling her about Bob Kendricks and how we'd met. I told her about HD-387 and the FDA approval process.

"Some of the patients got really sick while taking the drug," I explained, "but the doctors were never able to figure out if the issues they were facing came as a direct result of the drug or if, perhaps, they might've had those issues on their own. Make sense?"

"Yes. But what's going to happen with HD-387?"

"It's going to get the necessary FDA approval," I said. "And from everything I can gather, it's an effective drug, though not without a few side effects."

"Like any other prescription, then," Sheila said.

"Yes. But I can see why Scott was worried. A couple of the patients had severe reactions. One in particular—John Smith, they called him—had been corresponding with Scott and Kendricks for weeks—shared all sorts of information about his liver functions, as well as the severity of his heart condition—both before and after taking the drug. In the end, at least from what I could gather, Scott had to have concluded the obvious—that John Smith had multiple things going on at once. Too many things. Doctors could never have proven conclusively that HD-387 was solely to blame for the elevation of his liver enzymes—not with so many other issues to consider."

"Ah. I see."

"And all the evidence—good and bad—gets factored in," I explained. "Least, that's what Bob said." I then shifted my attention to talking about Bob Kendricks. I dove into a lengthy discussion of all that he had been facing—both personally and professionally—over the past several weeks. "No doubt, he had a lot on his mind. He's been worried about a lot of different things all at once. But he's been especially fearful that Scott may have been kidnapped because he knew too much."

Sheila continued to stare in disbelief. "I'm still confused. With all that information to consider, how in the world did you figure out that Scott's disappearance had nothing to do with his job at McKinley?"

"Ah." I smiled as I turned my car toward town. "That was easy. And if you'll give me just a minute, I'll tell you all about it."

CHAPTER 33

WHO'S SORRY NOW?

I turned onto Main Street and drove past the Burger Barn, beyond the fitness center, and just past the diner, where the lunch crowd swarmed the place. I eased my way through the noontime traffic till I arrived at Pfifer's Photography Studio. As I pulled my car into the parking lot, I turned to face Sheila. Her expression said, *Well, what are you waiting for?* "So, tell me what's really going on here, Annie. And how in the world did you figure out all of this?"

"I've been suspicious of Malcolm Pfifer from the get-go," I explained. "From what I've been able to figure out, he's no photographer, at least not a professional one."

"He's not?" Her eyes grew wide. "It's a shame you didn't know that before you hired him to shoot the wedding. Could've saved you a bundle."

"No kidding." I drew in a deep breath and then continued explaining. "But Brandi and Scott really wanted him because he's the one who shot the infamous photograph the night Scott proposed."

"Ah, that's right. I remember now."

"It wasn't a very good photo, qualitywise," I said. "I'm surprised no one seemed to pick up on it. I'm sure photography is a hobby for Pfifer, which is why he thought this studio would be a good front for what he really does."

Her eyes blazed with excitement as she asked, "What's that?"

"He's a scam-artist extraordinaire," I explained. "Mortgage fraud, to be precise."

"Whoa, Nellie."

I gave her a brisk nod. "But Brandi was on to him, whether she realized it or not. It was her first contract, and she was a little unsure of herself. But she knew enough to realize Norton and Pfifer had written in some kind of side deal that looked suspicious."

"Norton? Isn't that her boss?"

"Yep. And here's the kicker. She told me just last night that Norton has mysteriously left town. Quite suddenly. It took me awhile to figure out why. It wasn't just that he and Pfifer had run into a hitch scamming people out of their houses. They're also the ones responsible for Scott's disappearance. I'd bet my red hat that Norton and Pfifer are in this together."

"You don't have a. . ."

"Yeah, I know. But if I'm guessing right, Norton has skipped out, leaving Pfifer to hold the bag. My guess is that Malcolm will follow on Norton's heels, if he hasn't left Clarksborough already. That's why I feel such pressure to get to Scott now. My gut tells me Pfifer won't let this go on much longer."

"Annie, this is scary. But I'm still not sure I understand how Scott is involved."

"If I've got my ducks in a row—and I think I do—Scott

must've figured out—through Bob, maybe—that something had gone wrong. My guess is he came to confront Pfifer on that Friday, thinking Brandi might be in some kind of danger."

"Oh, Annie, do you think so?"

"Yes." I paused for a moment before delving into an explanation. "In the dark." That's what I kept going back to. Scott's cryptic text message. He *has* been in the dark—and not just symbolically. If I'm right—and trust me, this is just a guess—he's been in the dark—literally—for two weeks now. Where there's a photography studio, there's got to be a darkroom, right?"

Sheila's eyes lit with the revelation. "Of course!"

"I'd guess that's why Pfifer's studio has supposedly been under construction for the past couple weeks—to keep people out. And I'd be willing to bet Scott's been eating a hefty amount of moo goo gai pan while he's in there. Pfifer's been feeding him well, from what I can gather. Probably trying to gain Scott's confidence."

"Wow. So, is Tomi Yu in on this, too?" Sheila seemed stunned.

"Nah. But Pfifer's been spending a lot of time at Lee Yu's Garden," I told her. "Took me awhile to figure out who Tomi was talking about. Had to narrow down my list, but I got it—just this morning, in fact. Average height. Average looking. Just your average Joe."

"Only this time, our average Joe is an average Malcolm Pfifer," Sheila said. She shook her head, clearly stunned. "I *knew* there was something about that guy I didn't like. I hope you didn't give him any more of your money."

I gave her a little shrug. "Yeah. Dropped it off through the mail slot yesterday. But see—that's where the idea came from."

"Idea?"

"Yes. The idea for all this—coming to the studio. Finding Scott." I paused to look at the heavily tinted window of the photography studio, contemplating my next move.

"How are we going to get in there?" Sheila whispered, as if worried she might be overheard. By whom, I wasn't sure.

"We're not."

"We're not?" Her thinly plucked eyebrows arched. "I don't get it."

"Well, not at first," I explained. "Sasha is going in ahead of us." I eased my way out of the front seat and then opened the back door, reaching in for my crime-fighting companion. The little darling wagged her tail, obviously excited about the possibilities that lay ahead.

"Annie, what are you thinking?"

I pointed to the oversize mail slot a couple of feet from the bottom of the door.

"You've got to be kidding me." Sheila shook her head and frowned. "She'll never fit."

"You don't know my Sasha," I said with a grin. "She's a *mini-dachshund*—and dachshunds are hunters by nature. They've been bred to get in tiny spaces—to root out badgers."

"Still. . ." Sheila looked at the mail slot, then back at the dog, clearly perplexed.

I couldn't help but laugh. "I've seen Sasha wiggle through holes smaller than that. You should've seen her shimmy through the snow and under the fence that day Nadine's ex-husband ran across my backyard."

"Are you serious?"

"Yep. She flattens like a pancake." I lifted the little monster into my arms, and she squirmed in excitement.

"Annie, I don't know."

I nudged the car door closed with my elbow and made my way to the front door of the studio. The CLOSED FOR CONSTRUCTION sign remained on the front door, but I tried the knob, just in case. Nope. It was locked up tight.

Just to be safe, I glanced around, to make sure no one was watching. Not a soul. Sheila was the only one in sight, and what a sight she was. Her eyes were as wide as saucers, and she couldn't seem to stop stammering. "W—what h—happens w—when she g—gets ins—side?"

I gave a little shrug. "Scott will hear her barking, and he'll call out to us."

"How do you know? What if Pfifer has him tied up? What if his mouth is taped? And even if we can hear him, how are we going to get inside to free him?"

"I'll call O'Henry as soon as we know something—or to get his help in retrieving Sasha, at the least—" I said. "So stay calm." I lifted Sasha's floppy ear and whispered a few words of encouragement, then pulled open the metal door of the mail slot to ease her in headfirst. "Here we go," I whispered.

The first few inches weren't so bad, but as Sasha got to about the midway point, her belly got stuck.

"Annie, I *told* you this wouldn't work." Sheila shook her head and began to pace the sidewalk.

Somehow, with a little wiggling and squirming—and a lot of prayer on my part—Sasha made her way through. I knew she had quite a drop to get to the floor below, probably a good two and a half feet, but she made it with no problem. I know, because I peeked through the slot as she landed.

"Go find Scott, girl," I called out. "Go get 'em!"

My canine cohort—God bless her—disappeared from view, and I stood aright with a smile on my face.

"Now what?" Sheila whispered.

I inched my way over to the window, where I attempted to peer through the tinting. I could almost see through, if I squinted. Almost. And I could definitely hear Sasha barking her head off—a great indicator. Just then, a voice rang out from behind me.

"We're not open."

I turned and found myself face-to-face with none other than our one-and-only average Joe—Malcolm Pfifer. He held a plastic bag in his hand, and I could smell the Chinese food right away.

The trembling in my hands began immediately, especially when I heard Sasha let out another yelp from inside the store.

"Oh, hey. . . ," I started.

"Mrs. Peterson?" He gave me the oddest look, as he recognized me. "Can I help you?"

"Yes." I forced a broad smile. "I came to tell you that. . ."

Another round of barking rang out from inside the studio, and Pfifer's antennae apparently went straight up in the air. "What in the world?" He reached into his pocket for the keys. "Is that a dog?"

Once his back was turned, Sheila lifted her cell phone and mouthed the words, "I'm calling O'Henry." I nodded, and she slipped away into Mobile Mania to make her call.

"Oh? Did you hear a dog?" I tried.

I could see Pfifer fumbling with the keys and realized his dilemma right away. If my suspicions about Scott were right and

Pfifer opened the door to the studio, he'd be caught red-handed. If he didn't, he might never get the answer to the dog question.

So, there we stood, just Pfifer and me, talking about the weather, the wedding, and the check I'd dropped off yesterday. I managed to run the gamut with conversation topics, killing off a few minutes. Sasha barked her head off all the while. The spicy scent of food from inside the plastic bag he gripped in his hand was familiar, and I quietly praised the Lord for the information Tomi Yu had passed my way. If not for him, I wouldn't be standing here today.

Finally, when I heard the siren from O'Henry's patrol car off in the distance, I felt relief wash over me. However, as soon as Pfifer heard it, he immediately went into panic mode. He turned to run toward his car, just as Sheila came bounding from the front door of Mobile Mania. She let out a scream as their bodies met in a midair crash. He jerked back, lost his balance quite suddenly, and the container of food spilled out all over the sidewalk.

I stared down at the messy mound of moo goo gai pan. "Hmm. Very interesting."

By the time I looked back up, Pfifer was opening the front door of his car. Just as he slipped into the driver's seat, O'Henry pulled in directly behind him, blocking his vehicle.

Pfifer took one look at the officer, sprinted out of the car, and back toward me. What he planned to do, I couldn't imagine. Thankfully, I didn't have to find out. In a stroke of sheer irony, Pfifer lost his footing on the mound of moo goo gai pan and slid feet first into the studio's plate glass window, which shattered all around him in a thousand pieces.

Sheila began to squeal at the top of her lungs, and I—blame it on my premenopausal state—burst into tears. I was torn between wondering if Pfifer was injured and wondering if Sasha might come bounding through the bits of broken glass. Thankfully, the dog stayed put. Couldn't say as much for Pfifer, who tried to scramble to his feet.

O'Henry and a fellow officer sprang from the car and headed our way. Sheila pointed her index finger at a very messy, shaken Pfifer and shouted, "You have the right to remain silent. Anything you say will be misquoted and then used against you."

"Sheila." I gave her a stern look as I brushed away my tears. "First of all, you're not an officer of the law. Second, that's not how it goes."

She offered up a shrug. "That's how I would have written it."

"No doubt." I pulled out a tissue and blew my nose.

Sheila and I quickly stepped aside as O'Henry and the other police officer drew near. Pfifer's hands went up in the air immediately, and he began to spill his guts—almost as rapidly as that moo goo gai pan had slipped out of the container. He was talking so fast I couldn't catch it all, but I did manage to hear the one thing I needed to know. Scott was, indeed, inside. And very much alive.

O'Henry stopped Pfifer by putting his hand up in the air to silence him. "You have the right to remain silent," the good sergeant quoted. "Anything you say can be used against you in a court of law. You have the right to have an attorney present now and during any future questioning. If you cannot afford an attorney, one will be appointed to you free of charge if you wish."

"See," I whispered to Sheila, "that's how it goes."

She shook her head and, with arms crossed at her chest, whispered back, "I would've skipped the part about the free attorney. With all that money you've paid him, he can afford legal counsel, trust me."

As the officers continued the process of making the arrest, Sasha continued to bark like a maniac from inside the studio. I could tell she wanted us to join her. She'd picked up Scott's scent, just like that day at the pharmaceutical company. *Good girl, Sasha! When we get home, that's two treats for you!*

O'Henry snapped handcuffs on Pfifer, whose gaze had shifted to the ground. Ironically, Sheila's gaze had shifted, too—upward. I found her somewhat hyperfocused on a sign hanging above the studio door.

"I never noticed that before," she said with a smile.

I glanced at it in curiosity, then read it aloud: "PASSPORT PHOTOS DONE HERE." I looked at Sheila with a shrug. "What about it?"

"Well," she responded, "it's just that I always say if you look like your passport picture, you probably need the trip."

I laughed until my sides ached. Leave it to Sheila to put a smile on my face, even now.

"I *do* need a trip," I said at last. "A long one. But Pfifer won't be doing my passport photo; that I can guarantee."

In fact, I could pretty much guarantee the man wouldn't be doing anything of the sort—for the next five to ten years.

I Got You, Babe

O'Henry's partner seated a much more subdued Pfifer in the back of the patrol car. Then, key in hand, the good sergeant stepped over the spilled container of moo goo gai pan and opened the door to the studio. He was the first inside but called out to us after only a couple of minutes.

"You can come in, Annie." His words were laced with excitement, and I knew in my knower an adventure lay ahead.

Sheila clutched her flashlight in her hand and entered alongside me. I tiptoed at first, taking a minute to allow my eyes to adjust to the darkness. The room had been stripped of most of its photography paraphernalia and looked more like a tomb than a business place. I felt sick to my stomach as I thought about the fact that Scott had been here for two weeks straight.

I could hear Sasha whining from the back of the room and headed her way, with Sheila on my heels. In the farthest corner of the room, I saw a door. The whole thing was just as I'd pictured it when I'd contemplated this moment.

"We're coming, Scott!" I cried out. "Hang on!"

"I doubt he can hear you," O'Henry said.

"Oh?" I turned to face him.

"Remember, this used to be a butcher shop?"

"Oh, right." I gave the door a second look. "And that was the meat locker. I remember now."

"Perfect place for a darkroom, after a bit of renovation," O'Henry said. "That's what I'm guessing. Now, you ladies stand back until I call for you."

He tried every key on Pfifer's key ring before finally getting the right one. As the doorknob turned, my heart began to sing. "He's here," I whispered to Sheila. "We've found him!" I could practically see the look on Brandi's face now. Just the thought of it put an unspeakable joy in my heart.

Finally, the door swung open. The amber-colored bulb hanging from the ceiling inside the darkroom was the first thing to catch my attention. The second was the smell. I almost lost my stomach immediately. But as Sheila flipped on the flashlight and I caught my first glimpse of Scott, my stomach took second place to my emotions. I erupted in tears—again.

"Scott!" My heart—only seconds ago filled with joy—nearly broke as I saw my future son-in-law inside the tiny, dark space on a stiff wooden chair. His eyes squinted immediately as the light from Sheila's flashlight hit him square in the face, and then he stood and began to weep.

O'Henry went in first, and I followed on his heels, grabbing Scott and crying like there was no tomorrow. Granted, he reeked—two full weeks of not bathing after consuming too much Chinese food will do that to you, but I didn't care. He wept as loudly as I did, and before long, Sheila joined in.

"Thank God, thank God!" Scott repeated the words over and over again.

I eased him out of the darkroom and into the outer office. The light streaming in from the broken window was more than he could take. He squeezed his eyes shut and even put his hands over them. "It's too much. I can't stand it."

I thought about the scripture from Ephesians, the one I'd been quoting for days—*"Everything exposed by the light becomes visible"*—and I had to smile.

"We never stopped searching for you," I whispered. "Everyone is here, in Clarksborough—your mom, Brad, even your real father."

Scott's eyes grew wide. "You're kidding. Took me forever to track him down, and to be honest, I didn't think he'd come. Never even told Brandi I'd found him!"

"Right. Well, she knows now. They've met face–to–face."

A boyish grin lit his face. "Cool."

"So—your father's here—along with half the country. We've had everyone searching for you."

"How in the world did you find me?"

"That's another story," I explained. "One we'll save for later. Suffice to say, Pfifer led me here. I followed his scent." *Smelled for all the world like Chinese food.*

Scott gave me an admiring smile. "You go, Mom!"

Sasha sprang up and down at Scott's side until he finally reached down and scooped her into his arms.

"I guess I should have added that Sasha played a role in finding you, too," I said. "She prefers to get top billing."

"I'll gladly give her all the attention she needs!" Scott scratched her behind the ears, then planted a big kiss on the top of her head. She responded by wriggling in joy, tail wagging merrily.

Just then, the second officer entered the building and called out to O'Henry. "I searched him, Sarge. No weapons, but I found a plane ticket on him."

"Plane ticket?" We all spoke in unison.

"Yeah. He has a flight out of Philadelphia at four o'clock. Guess this was going to be his last stop before heading out of town."

O'Henry headed over to take a look at the ticket, while Scott, Sheila, and I stared at each other in silence.

"So that's where your money went," Sheila said finally. "He used it to buy a plane ticket."

I offered up a shrug. "It was worth every penny to get Scott back. I'm the happiest woman in the world right now." *But speaking of happy women. . .* I clamped my hand to my mouth, remembering. "Brandi!"

Scott's eyes lit with joy. "Can I use your phone to call her?" he asked. "Mine died when I tried to send her a message that first day." He handed Sasha off to Sheila, who cooed over her like a mother hen.

"Before you call her, could I ask you a quick question?"

"Sure."

I'd wondered about Scott's phone situation all along. "How did you slip the phone by Pfifer in the first place?" I asked, as I passed him my new cell phone.

Scott laughed. "It was pretty easy, really." He pulled out his slender silver phone and placed it alongside my chunkier one in his palm. "See, it's a razor phone. Super thin."

"Still. Didn't he search you before putting you in the darkroom?"

"Yes," Scott explained. "The razor was in my pocket, underneath my wallet. Pfifer patted me down and saw that I had the wallet. He watched me pull it out of my pocket, which I managed to do without budging the phone. He took the wallet. Took my keys, though I'm not sure what he did with my car."

"Car's fine," O'Henry threw in. "We've got it down at the station."

"Ah." Scott nodded. "He took everything—except the phone. I was praying I could get it to work, even for a minute or two. I almost got one message out to Brandi that first day.

"She got it," I assured him, "Though we weren't quite sure what to make of it."

"Yeah. I was afraid of that." He shrugged. "But what could I do? The phone was useless to me after that."

"But you sent me a text message days later," I argued. "How in the world. . ."

Scott's face lit in a smile. "You actually got that? I didn't think it went through."

"I got it." I didn't go on to tell him that I'd dropped "said message" into the toilet at the local diner. I'd bring him up to speed on all that later. "But I still don't understand how you—"

"It was just a God-thing then." Scott shook his head. "I don't expect anyone to believe this," he said, "but the truth is, my battery had been dead for days. Days! Then one day, I took the battery off the back and rolled it around in my hands for a while. There was apparently just enough juice in it to get the phone to come back on for about a minute."

"Wow. A miracle, really."

"Trust me, I prayed for a miracle."

Another thing had puzzled me, too. "Why did you send it to me instead of Brandi?"

"Easy," Scott explained. "I was in a hurry, and your name was at the top of the list. *A* for *Annie* made you the most logical candidate."

"Top of the list, eh?" I couldn't help but smile. "It's been awhile since I've had top billing on anything. Don't tell Sasha." I gave him a little wink.

"Puh-leeze!" Sheila rolled her eyes. "You're a crime solver. You've been written up in the paper with a smashing headline! Heavens, you're pretty much a local celebrity! And so is this lovable pooch!" She gave Sasha another loving pat.

As she began to ramble, Scott flipped open my cell phone and punched in a number I knew had to be Brandi's. When my daughter answered, all it took was one word from Scott for the celebration to begin.

"Baby?"

I could hear her ecstatic screams through the phone. It took at least two or three minutes of talking for him to convince her she wasn't dreaming.

"I'm really here." He spoke in between pauses to let her get in a squeal or a question. "I didn't leave you. I would never do that. I love you. I'm going to marry you. Tonight!"

"Yikes," I whispered to Sheila. "I almost forgot! They're getting married. . ." I looked at my watch. ". . .in less than five hours!"

"Don't fret, Agatha Annie," she whispered back. "If you can

solve the crime of the century, surely you can pull off the wedding of the century!"

I swallowed hard and turned my attention back to the matter at hand. *One thing at a time,* I told myself. *One thing at a time.* After what felt like hours, Scott finished up his call with Brandi, then handed back my phone, grinning ear to ear.

"Thanks." He let out a little chuckle. "I think she missed me."

"That would be putting it mildly!" Sheila said.

"We all did." I wrapped him in my arms once again. "And you'll never know the amount of prayer that has gone up on your behalf."

"Trust me, I was praying, too," he said with a nod. "In fact, I wouldn't have made it through these past two weeks otherwise. Besides. . ." Here, he smiled. "I had a lot of time on my hands. That darkroom made for a pretty interesting prayer closet, just not one I'd like to use long-term."

"Speaking of the darkroom. . ." Sergeant O'Henry gave Scott a let's-get-down-to-business face. "If you're up to it, I have a few questions I'd like to ask you. We've got a few loose ends to tie up before I can let you go."

I grabbed my notebook, anxious to hear all Scott had to say. Yes, indeed, we had a few loose ends to tie up. Yes, indeed.

THE TWIST

The good sergeant pulled open his notebook and said, "Just start at the beginning."

I listened closely to Scott's explanation of what had happened. Turns out, my intuitions had been right.

"I was actually headed to Mobile Mania that Friday morning," Scott explained. "I'd been having trouble with my cell phone for days. The battery wouldn't hold a charge. It needed to be replaced." He shook his head, and I could see the anger in his eyes. "But when I got here, they weren't open yet. I watched Pfifer get out of his car and walk into his studio, and that was all the incentive I needed to have a chat with him about Brandi."

O'Henry looked confused. "He's your wedding photographer, right?"

"Yes, but he's also a client at the realty company where Brandi works. Norton is his real estate agent," Scott explained. "They'd had some problems, and I think I knew in my gut he'd been taking

273

her for a ride. Using her."

"Tell me more about that," O'Henry encouraged him. "What kind of problems?"

I could've filled him in, but I let Scott do the talking.

"Pfifer is a scam artist," he explained. "He's set himself up as a bona fide home investor: buying houses, fixing them up, and then renting them out. Sounds legit, right?"

"Right," we all echoed. I even played along, just for fun.

Scott continued on. "Pfifer had signed a contract to buy a home from a guy I work with—Bob Kendricks."

"From the pharmaceutical company?" O'Henry asked.

"Yes. Bob's a great guy and the last person I'd like to see hurt. With Brandi's help—she was Bob's listing agent—he sold his house to Pfifer—or so he thought. But by that Friday morning, I'd already figured out that Pfifer and Norton, who runs the agency, were stringing Bob Kendricks along, telling him they were going to close any day, but with no real closing in sight."

"What louses!" Sheila interjected her thoughts on the matter.

"I wish you could've seen Bob. . . ." Scott shook his head. "Nearly every day, he'd come into the office, sure there would be a closing that week. But it never happened."

"Bob went ahead and allowed Pfifer—his buyer—to put renters in the house," I threw in. "He and his wife moved into their RV, thinking they could hit the road shortly. Bob said the whole renters thing didn't really raise any red flags because he'd been told a closing was imminent. Said he was happy to have the renters in the house—at least, at first."

"You *have* been working on this!" Scott gave me an admiring smile.

"Yeah." I tried to hold back the smile, but it did feel good to know I'd done my homework.

"I'm sure Bob Kendricks isn't the first man to lose his house to these scoundrels." O'Henry shook his head.

"Right," I agreed. "They've got quite a scam going—tell the homeowner they've got a good contract, pretend they're going to a closing, then let the months drag on."

"All the while, they collect the rent check from the unsuspecting renters; is that how it goes?" O'Henry asked.

"You've got it," I explained.

"It took Kendricks awhile to figure out he had a problem on his hands," Scott added.

"I've been leery of Pfifer from the start," I explained, "and Norton, too. They've been working hand in hand, and Brandi has just been a pawn—someone they could pin the crooked contract on."

"Whoa. This is crazy." Sheila shook her head, clearly upset. "But speaking of crooked contracts, what was that thing you were telling me earlier, in the car—about a side deal?"

"I just read about all this on the Web," I told her. "It's pretty prevalent. Savvy scam artists get the highest possible appraisal on the house, then write up a contract, offering a huge amount more than the house is really worth. The seller is excited, happy to be getting top dollar for his home. But then these crooks write in a cleverly worded side deal, where thousands—sometimes multiplied thousands—of dollars come back to the buyer. And that's what happened in this case. But it's illegal. Fraud. And I think that's what was taking so long. I'd wager to say the mortgage company had caught on and wasn't going to finance Pfifer. Brandi knew her client wasn't able to obtain the necessary financing. She told me so. She just didn't know why."

Scott gave me another admiring smile. "Well, I know who to turn to if I ever want to buy a house!"

"No thank you!" I couldn't help but laugh. After all I'd learned, real estate was the last thing I'd venture into.

"Scary stuff," O'Henry said, as he scribbled down information.

"No kidding." I gave a little shrug. "And I feel so sorry for Bob and his wife. They never knew it was illegal. I don't think Brandi ever figured it out either, though she knew something was off base."

"Well, Norton is her boss," Scott explained, "and I'm sure she thought she could trust him. Crazy thing is, he didn't mind involving Brandi—or Bob—in a fraudulent deal, one that could have ended very badly."

They had no idea *how* badly, so I filled them in. "From what I read on the Internet, some of these so-called investors actually go through with a closing, and the seller—in this case, Bob Kendricks and his wife—ends up going to prison for committing mortgage fraud when they were completely oblivious. Meanwhile, the supposed buyer pays on the mortgage a few months, then skips town, to begin again in a new place."

"I've got to wonder why they haven't been caught till now." Sheila shook her head. "They've probably been at this for years."

"They're just getting sloppy, I guess," Scott said.

"Heavens to Betsy," Sheila threw in. "Could happen to anyone."

"And does. It's a national epidemic," I said.

Scott shook his head. "Every time Kendricks would start talking about the situation with his house, I just felt worse and worse for him. He and his wife didn't know how to get the renters out of their house, once they realized the deal had fallen through."

"I think it hurt their pride as much as their pocketbook," I added. "But I'm sure they're not alone. I wouldn't be surprised to learn that Pfifer and Norton had pulled this scam all over Clark County and beyond."

"All I know is this. . . ." Scott chimed in. "On that Friday morning, when I saw Mobile Mania hadn't opened yet, I turned my attention to Pfifer. Decided to confront him. I wanted to see him stopped, particularly since he'd put my Brandi in the middle of something that appeared to be dangerous. That was really all I knew at the time."

I shuddered, just thinking about it.

"I wanted to hear him say it myself," Scott continued, "so that I'd feel better about asking her to quit her job." He raked his hand through his hair. "If I could change one thing about these past two weeks, I would've called Brandi first, to let her know where I was heading. Then she would've quit her job on the spot—and everyone would have known where I was."

"Hindsight is 20/20," I reminded him. "But you didn't need to worry about Brandi. She's a smart girl. She was suspicious of Pfifer, too. And I'm pretty sure she's almost got him figured out by now. She just never realized that you were on to him."

Scott shrugged and gave me a sheepish grin. "She was so proud when she got that new job at the real estate agency," he explained. "And I didn't want her to feel like she'd failed at it. That's why I kept most of my suspicions to myself. Till that Friday. When I got here to confront Pfifer, Norton was with him. I wasn't expecting that. Between the two of them, they somehow managed to take me down. Before I knew it, they had me tied up and shoved in the darkroom."

"That's awful." Sheila shuddered. "They should both be taken out to the woodshed and. . ."

Scott shook his head. "The worst part of being in that room for these two weeks was knowing that Brandi was still working for that man—that she was still at risk every day. And I could do nothing to save her." He gave me an imploring look. "I've prayed for her every single day."

"She's prayed for you, too," I whispered.

"She told me." He smiled for a second; then his expression shifted again as he finished his story. "The first couple of days in that darkroom were terrifying," he said finally. "Pfifer only came and went long enough to let me use the bathroom and maybe eat a few bites of food. But on about the third day, he seemed to soften a little, even untied me and gave me a little more freedom. I somehow got him talking about his life—and he responded as though we were good friends. I told him some of my favorite restaurants, and before I knew it, he was bringing in food, taking care of me."

"Moo goo gai pan?" I asked.

Scott gave me a curious look. "How did you know that?"

"Oh, I have my ways." I gave him a devilish smile.

"I really think I caught him off guard when I showed up that Friday morning," Scott said with a shrug. "I don't think he went into any of this with a plan or anything like that. And I know he was sorry about messing up my wedding, especially since he'd played a role in bringing us together."

"Then again, there's the issue of that plane ticket," Sheila threw in.

"I guess it's clear now that he and Norton were both going

to skip town on you," O'Henry said. "So it's a mighty good thing your future mother-in-law found you when she did."

I smiled as I contemplated the word *mother-in-law*. Just as quickly, however, a shiver slithered down my spine as I realized that Chinese food out on the sidewalk was meant to be Scott's last meal—ever. Would Pfifer really have left him in the darkroom—to die?

In another breath, the truth registered. My willingness to follow God's leading had probably saved Scott's life. The very thought of it brought tears of thankfulness to my eyes—again.

Scott continued on, oblivious to my revelations. "I'm sure Norton Realty will be put out of business once this hits the papers, which means Brandi will be jobless."

"That's kind of a shame," I said with a pout. "She loves working in real estate."

"She loves *people*," Scott said with a grin. "And I know she'll do well, wherever she goes." He leaned over to stretch his back, and I could see the pain in his eyes.

O'Henry gave Scott a critical once-over. "Looks like you're in need of some medical care. I'm going to have the folks from the hospital take a look at you, just to check you out."

"That's not necessary." I could see the fear in Scott's eyes as he spoke. "I'll be fine. I've been away from Brandi too long as it is."

"Just a quick checkup is all. I insist." O'Henry gave him a fatherly pat on the back.

After a few words of argument, Scott finally relented. But I could tell he wouldn't go easily.

And me. . . ? Well, I had a wedding to coordinate. And quick!

CHAPTER 36

GROOVY KIND OF LOVE

I'd never seen so many people fly into action so quickly. It seemed the whole town of Clarksborough had been crouched, prepared but waiting for the moment when they could shift into wedding gear. Talk about a wild ride!

Janetta was the first to kick off the show. She assured me she could, indeed, still pull off the amazing Italian feast Brandi had planned from the beginning. With the help of her son Jake and my mom and dad, who'd leaped at the idea, they would arrive at the wedding facility at six fifteen with foods prepared and ready.

"The appetizer table will include a variety of cheeses and crackers, as well as a vegetable platter and dips," she quoted from memory. "Dinner will include salad with Italian dressing, bread-sticks, bow tie pasta with Alfredo sauce, chicken cacciatore, cheese tortellini, and Italian meatballs in a Portobello sauce."

Wow. The woman was my new hero. And my parents could hardly wait to assist her with the tasks at hand.

Janetta—God bless her—offered to call Pastor Miller's wife, to see how the wedding cake was coming along. Just one more thing I didn't have to deal with, thankfully.

The next ones to offer assistance were Candy and the other bridesmaids. With so little time left for decorating, someone had to transform the Be Our Guest wedding facility into "Cupid's Wonderland." They took to the task like ducks to water. They located the silk-flower bouquets and centerpieces I had put together months ago, along with boxes of twinkling Christmas lights and an array of candles. My brother and his family joined them, and together they headed off to decorate at warp speed.

I put the groomsmen in charge of tracking down tuxedos. With Scott missing his last fitting, we were bound to have issues, but surely they could work something out.

As for the wedding photos, well, that was another story altogether. I gave Devin and Warren the task of locating a photographer. Didn't matter who—as long as he or she had a knack for working under pressure and wouldn't charge me an arm and a leg. I'd already given "said arm and leg" to Pfifer, who had apparently used it to purchase more moo goo gai pan than should be allowed by law. That and a plane ticket.

Nadine, still fighting off tears of joy, flew into wedding-coordinator gear. How or why she thought to assume that role was beyond me, but I didn't stop her. Didn't dare. She called for a quick run-through of the ceremony, which came off without a hitch. Scott, who'd been swept away by O'Henry to the hospital, hadn't yet connected with Brandi in person—only by phone.

"It's really better this way," I assured her. "According to tradition, the bride and groom aren't supposed to see each other on the wedding day, anyway."

"Hardly seems fair, after everything we've been through," she said with a pout.

After the rehearsal, Nadine escorted Brandi to the bride's dressing room near the back of the wedding facility. Norah from The Liberty Belle arrived moments later to style her hair. The woman was all nerves. Still, she did seem to have a knack for up-dos—French twists in particular. Brandi's hair turned out great. And when the veil was placed on her head, I actually began to weep.

Brandi, who at this point hadn't seen her groom-to-be in over two weeks, was a nervous wreck. She'd taken to stammering and stuttering—and I noticed her hands shook uncontrollably as each hour progressed. "I just can't believe this is happening." How often did I hear those words?

Many times throughout the afternoon, Brandi begged to see Scott, begged to be taken over to the hospital for a quick reunion visit. Then, just about the time we were ready to relent, she changed her mind, stating that she wanted to wait. I knew she longed to sweep him into her arms and hold him there for the rest of her life.

By late afternoon, I realized I had to face the inevitable. For two long weeks, I'd avoided not only the local fitness center but the red dress hanging in my closet as well. I could avoid it no longer. I returned home to get cleaned up and dressed. Before bathing, I eased my way into the closet and looked at the mother-of-the-bride attire. "Beautiful," I whispered. Now, if only I could get it zipped. I racked my brain, trying to come up with Plan B. Perhaps I could find a black-on-red skirt and blouse combination that would work.

After a quick shower, the moment arrived. With Warren's help, I slipped the dress over my head. "Just be extra careful trying to zip it," I encouraged him. "It's going to be a challenge, especially with that nylon zipper."

He reached to tug on the fragile zipper, and I prayed all the while that it wouldn't pop as he eased it up my back. After just a second of two, he gave me a funny look. "What were you worried about again?"

"Well, zip it, and I'll show you," I told him.

"Annie." He turned me around and gave me a curious once-over. "I *did* zip it. It's loose!"

"W—what?" I reached around to the back of the dress to feel for the zipper. Sure enough, he'd zipped it with no problem. "How in the world?"

"You've eaten like a bird over the past couple of weeks," he reminded me. "And you've been running like a maniac 24/7. No doubt you've dropped a few pounds."

"You've got to be kidding me," I muttered. "After all those grits? And not one trip to the gym?"

"Hey, grits are only one hundred calories a serving," he said. "I know. I checked the back of the box."

"Good grief. But all that butter and sugar. . ."

He gave a little shrug. "Must not've made much difference."

I stared at myself in the mirror, amazed at what I saw. Not only was the dress *not* tight, it was actually a little loose. Truly, miracles did happen.

"Looks like you've been on the Gone-with–the-Groom diet," Warren said with a mischievous grin. "Not the best way to lose weight, but effective."

"No kidding."

My wonderful husband stepped back and gave me an admiring glance. "You know, I hate to say this—being the father of the bride, and all—but it's possible you might outshine everyone at the wedding tonight, Annie Peterson."

I giggled and felt my cheeks turn warm with embarrassment. "Hardly. But thanks for the compliment." I gave him a careful once-over. In his tuxedo and ascot, he looked quite regal. "You look pretty spiffy yourself," I said with a wink.

"Why, thank you." He bowed at the waist and took me by the hand. "Come along, Mrs. Peterson. I do believe we have a daughter to marry off."

"Indeed." I gave his fingers a squeeze, then followed him out the door. "I believe we do."

Chapter 37

CHAPEL OF LOVE

I arrived at the Be Our Guest facility at exactly six fifteen and was floored to find the decorating done. I stared in amazement at the exquisite reception hall. Thirty-six round tables—seating ten to twelve each—were adorned with beautiful tablecloths, colorful centerpieces, twinkling candles, and a splattering of red silk rose petals. A dazzling array of Christmas lights hung in swags around the room, and there—just ahead of me—stood the most beautiful wedding cake I'd ever laid eyes on. Quite a feat, I must say. Off to the side stood the tempting chocolate fountain. Man, I couldn't wait to try that out!

I connected with Janetta, who'd set up shop in the facility's oversized kitchen. She seemed to have everything under control. Nothing new there. With a smile on her face, she encouraged me to locate my daughter.

"No working for you tonight, Annie," she said. "This is your night to celebrate. So go find that daughter of yours. I'm sure she looks fabulous."

Finally, the moment of truth arrived. I made my way back to the room where Brandi and her bridesmaids were getting ready. I was scarcely prepared for the sight that met me as I swung wide that door. There, in the center of the room, standing in front of a huge oval mirror, stood the most beautiful bride in the world. *Oh, Warren, you were wrong. No one will outshine this daughter of ours tonight!*

The tears came immediately. I couldn't seem to stop them. I wept out of sheer joy—and a bit of sorrow. How could so many gains and losses swim through my head and heart all at one time?

Brandi turned to look at me. Her beautiful eyes—heavily mascaraed, of course, were filled with tears—tears of joy, I knew. And tears of relief.

"You look. . .amazing." I could hardly get the words out. I wanted to sweep her into my arms and plant tiny kisses all over her cheek, just as I'd done on the day she was born. Wanted to see if her skin still felt as soft as on that first day.

Instead, I gave her a light kiss on the back of her hand and stared in silence. I didn't want to mess up the makeup, and I sure didn't want to add to the already-high emotions in the room.

"I love you, Mom." She whispered the words, but I heard them, loud and clear. "I can never thank you enough for finding. . ." She never got Scott's name out. Instead, she reached up with her hankie and dabbed her eyes. "I've got to stop doing this."

"Before long, all the tears will be behind you," I promised. "Nothing but happy days ahead. Before long, there will be babies to tend to, mortgages to pay."

"Please, please!" She put a hand up in the air and laughed aloud. "One thing at a time! And I don't want to think about mortgages today, of all things!"

I let out a little giggle, realizing for the first time what I'd said. Chances were, she'd never want to think about mortgages—or real estate—again.

I turned my attention to Candy, who stood adorned in her bridesmaid's attire. In that striking burgundy dress, she looked as regal as a queen. "You're gorgeous," I mouthed across the room. She gave me a wink that said, *I'm next!* and the reality hit. We had to do this all over again in just a few short months. *Yikes!*

Well, no time to fret about that now. I made the rounds from one part of the wedding facility to the other, checking on everyone and everything. I could hardly believe what an amazing job everyone had done of pulling things together. Truly, the town of Clarksborough had outdone itself.

Finally, just as the ceremony was about to begin, I searched through the crowd of people for someone in particular.

There. In the fifth row.

"Mr. Clark." I extended my hand. "Glad you could make it. I knew we'd have a wedding, in spite of the obstacles."

He gave me a knowing smile. "I've been praying all week. This whole thing is such a miracle."

"Oh, I know. Trust me. And thank you for those prayers."

I turned to nod at Bob Kendricks and his wife, who sat next to Mr. Clark. I knew they'd spent much of the afternoon in O'Henry's office, answering questions and discussing options regarding the renters in their home. "I'd love to hear *your* take on miracles, Mr. Kendricks," I said. "Still going with that scientific viewpoint, or have the facts led you to another conclusion altogether?"

Bob grinned and reached to shake my hand. "Mrs. Peterson, if there is a God—and I'm still not sure—I'd have to say that He works in mysterious ways, just like people always say."

"Oh, amen to that," Mr. Clark said. "Amen to that."

With a very full heart, I went in search of my new friend—journalist Chris Donnelly. He sat in the back of the chapel with his steno pad open, pen in hand.

"Make sure you get this right," I whispered in his ear. "We're all counting on it."

He gave a brusque nod, then began to scribble as the opening music began.

I gave Mr. and Mrs. Yu a polite nod as they took their seats. As Tomi joined them, I mouthed, "Glad you could make it," to them all.

I then turned my attention to my extended family, offering hugs far and wide. Tear-filled eyes met me at every turn. Tears of joy, of course.

Before long, I was being escorted down the aisle, where I faced my first task—joining Nadine to light the family candles, which sat on either side of the unity candle. I gave her a little wink as the glow of candlelight rose before us. "Love you, sis," I whispered.

"Love you more," she whispered in response.

Everything that happened after that was kind of a blur. I remember hearing the music—Pachelbel's Canon. I vaguely remember seeing the little ring bearer—my grandnephew, Shawn—coming down the aisle with the adorable flower girl at his side.

I'm pretty sure I saw the bridesmaids entering down the center aisle—and the groomsmen, who took their places at the front with the groom.

Ah, the groom.

My gaze landed on Scott, who looked remarkably healthy for someone who'd spent the last two weeks eating Chinese food in the dark. Okay, the tuxedo didn't fit exactly right, but the tears in his eyes were all the proof I needed that he wanted to be here— wanted it more than anything else in the whole world.

Finally, the moment arrived. As the bridal march began, I turned to find my daughter on her father's arm, veil over her beautiful face, and could scarcely breathe. I almost forgot to stand. If it hadn't been for Sheila. . .

Heavens to Betsy. What in the world was Sheila doing with a camera in her hand? Yes, there she stood, center aisle, snapping photos right and left. Surely she wasn't the one who'd swept in to take Pfifer's place. Was she?

A little giggle escaped my lips as the reality hit. Yep. Sheila, ever the chameleon, had obviously offered to take on the role of wedding photographer—and what a great one she turned out to be, at that. She didn't miss a beat. She got a terrific shot of Brandi on her father's arm. She got a tear-jerking one of Brandi laying eyes on Scott for the first time. And she got several more of Warren lifting the veil and kissing Brandi on the cheek. She got a really precious one of Scott taking Brandi's hand in his own.

Still, there was one photo that was bound to take the cake— one that I felt sure we'd never forget. As Pastor Miller pronounced Scott and Brandi husband and wife, Sheila snapped a photo of their momentous kiss—one that lasted a good two minutes.

I wiped away the tears—of laughter and of joy—and had to admit. . . Yep. Some things were just better in person than in a photograph.

CHAPTER 38

'S WONDERFUL

O n the Monday after the wedding, our visitors trickled away
in much the same way our savings had over the past several
months. It nearly broke my heart to say good-bye to Nadine and
Brad, but I knew my sweet southern sister had much work to do
once she arrived back in Georgia. I promised to visit her in the
summertime, even going so far as to say I'd help her with campaign
strategies in the meantime via e-mail.

After arriving home from the airport, I happened to glance
down at yesterday's Sunday edition of the *Clark County Gazette*.
Chris Donnelly had written a terrific article for our local paper,
which he'd also forwarded to Savannah. In it, he had detailed the
story of Scott's kidnapping, painting him as quite the hero. Then,
he shared with readers the truth about Nadine's role as the grieving
mother, putting her in the best possible light. The piece also clarified
a few other things. It set the record straight on Otis and focused on
the real purpose behind Nadine's work with the homeless.

All in all, I thought Donnelly did a terrific job, and I especially loved the part where he went into detail about Pfifer and Norton sharing a cell at the Clark County jail. Priceless. As he left, Donnelly, now an ally, vowed only to print the truth. I sent him on his way with a pat on the back and some encouraging words: *"Just the facts, ma'am. Just the facts."* He seemed to take them to heart.

On page two of the *Gazette*, I found another story of interest. Looked like HD-387, now going by the name of Livell, would soon hit the market. I wondered what Scott would think of its release. Funny, in the midst of all that had happened, I'd forgotten to ask him about it. I'd also forgotten to return the manila envelope to Bob Kendricks. I'd have to do that one day this week. Maybe take the opportunity to talk with him more about the Lord.

To think that only a week ago I'd been in the midst of an investigation and the folks at McKinley had been at the top of my suspect list! The past two weeks had surely been fraught with ups and downs.

And now, today, as I faced my parents to say good-bye, I found myself fighting another down moment. Why was sending them off harder than ever before? Because the events of the last two weeks had suddenly put everything—and *everyone*—in perspective?

My mother embraced me for the longest time as she prepared to leave. "I hardly *ever* get to see you," she said with a pout. "And this sure has been fun."

"Which part?" I asked. "The part where my son-in-law turned up missing or the part where we thought the dog ate Dad's heart medication?" Truly, I could hardly imagine what she'd found enjoyable about this particular visit, except the wedding at the end, of course.

She shrugged. "I knew you would find Scott, Annie. Never doubted it for a second. And I just love being with you, especially when you're going through something tough. That's what families are for. And Daddy had a wonderful time, too."

"Really? Wow." I couldn't help but smile as I whispered in her ear, "Before you leave, check out the bumper sticker I put on the back of your car." I chuckled as I thought about its message: How Many Roads Must a Man Travel Down Before He Admits He Is Lost? I'd slipped it on early in the morning, when no one was looking.

She went back to have a look and seconds later erupted in laughter. My dad was so busy loading the luggage that he never even noticed. I kissed him good-bye, and within minutes, my parents were on their way.

After everyone had left, Warren and I settled down on the sofa with bowls of Moo-lennium Crunch ice cream.

"You know, I just realized we haven't eaten this stuff in nearly two weeks." I stared at the bowl in amazement.

"Wow. Guess we were too busy."

I stirred my spoon around in the bowl. "True." I looked at the dreamy mixture and sighed. "But it's funny that I hardly missed it."

"Yeah."

After a second of contemplating that fact, we dove in headfirst. Man, that ice cream tasted good.

I pulled out the digital camera to look over the photographs Sheila had taken at the wedding. We began to scroll through the photos, one by one, giggling, sighing, and even getting a little misty at times.

"You know, Sheila did an amazing job with these," I confessed. "She's a wonder."

"That she is," Warren said with a smile. "That she is."

Of course, there was that one photo of the bride and groom with their heads cut off. The lighting wasn't great, and all you could see of the happy couple was from the waist down. Kind of reminded me of the photograph Pfifer had taken at the fair—the one that had kicked off this whole ordeal.

But no matter. There were plenty of other good shots to take its place, and I couldn't fault my best friend. After all, she'd been there for me, as always, when I needed her most. And her parting words on the night of the wedding still left a smile on my face. What was it she had said? Ah yes... *"Chaos, panic, pandemonium— my work here is done."* I couldn't help but laugh, even now, as I thought about it. The last few weeks had been plenty chaotic, but we'd managed to find joy in the midst of the chaos.

As we scrolled through the photos, I found one that surprised me. "Look at this!" I said to Warren.

He leaned over and took a peek. "I don't know that guy. Do you?"

"Yeah. He works at the cell phone store. His name is Joe. Joe Kerr."

"Joe Kerr?" Warren erupted in laughter. "I wonder what he was doing at our daughter's wedding."

A chuckle rose up unexpectedly as I contemplated the possibilities. "Oh, I have my suspicions. Sheila telephoned the police from inside Mobile Mania. I'm sure one thing led to another...."

"And she invited a total stranger to our daughter's wedding?"

"Probably." I didn't mind, really. It was probably a good thing for Joe to see a happily-ever-after ending. And on Valentine's Day, no less. Yes, Joe Kerr was certainly a welcome guest at my daughter's wedding. And, if I could think of a way to manage it, I'd invite him to church next Sunday, too.

The longer we looked at the photos, the sleepier I got. I leaned my head against Warren's shoulder and found myself slipping into dreamland. Unfortunately, just about that time, a knock at the door roused me from my near sleep.

I jabbed Warren in the arm in an attempt to wake him. "Are you expecting someone?"

"Nope." He shook his head, yawned, and started scrolling through the pictures once again, picking up where we'd left off.

"That's odd." I eased my way off the sofa and headed to the front door, ready to send my would-be caller on his or her way. To be honest, I just needed rest. Peace and quiet.

I opened the door but couldn't find anyone there. A loud bark rang out, and I looked down to discover a metal crate with a dog inside. Not just *any* dog, mind you, but *the* dog—from the vet's office. "What in the world?"

I noticed a tag on the crate, which I read at once.

Dear Annie,

I just couldn't help myself. This little guy broke my heart with his sad brown eyes. I would've taken him back to Mississippi, but your mother wouldn't hear of it. So we both decided you were the perfect candidate. Enjoy your new friend.

Daddy

"You've got to be kidding me."

At that moment, Sasha appeared at my side, tail wagging—until she laid eyes on the crate. The moment she saw her male counterpart, she began to bark at the top of her lungs. Within seconds, Warren made an appearance, rubbing at his eyes.

"What've you got there?"

"Copper."

"Copper? What's that?"

"It's a dog," I explained. "A dachshund."

"Well, yeah," he said, looking down at the crate, "I can see that. But what's it doing here?"

"It's a he," I said. "He's been living at the vet's office but is apparently looking for a home."

"Oh no! Tell me you didn't."

"I didn't."

"Then what in the world. . ."

I pressed the note into his hands, and he read it with a look of horror on his face. "I can't believe your dad would do this to us." Warren looked down at the little pooch, who'd taken to springing up and down like a yo-yo. "We'll have to take him back to the vet's office. Right?" He gave me an inquisitive look.

"Of course!" I stared down at the little fellow. His tail wagged merrily. And, at this point, Sasha seemed to have taken an interest in him. What would it hurt to let him out of the crate for a few minutes?

With Warren's permission, I dragged the crate into the house and opened it. Copper inched his way out, clearly unsure of his new surroundings. Sasha yipped at him for a minute or two but shortly thereafter went to sniffing him in a getting-to-know-you sort of way. Copper took to her right away, licking her on the ears and wagging his tail all the while.

"Seems like a happy pup," Warren said. "Kind of a shame we have to. . ."

"Yeah." I sat on the floor and let the little guy climb into my lap. He licked me on my cheek, and I let out a laugh. "Take it easy, Copper! That tickles!"

We were about halfway into a lovefest with the new pooch when the phone rang. I answered it with a giggle.

Brandi's chipper voice greeted me with the word I'd grown to love so much: "Mom?"

What joy! Had she really paused from her honeymoon in Cozumel to call me?

"Brandi! Aren't you supposed to be honeymooning?"

"I am." She laughed. "We're having a great time. But I forgot to tell you something before I left, something I think you'll find interesting."

"Must be pretty important for you to be calling me all the way from the Yucatan!"

"It is. I forgot to tell you that I have a new job, starting the day I get back."

"You do?" I mouthed the words "Brandi has a new job" to Warren, and a look of confusion registered in his eyes.

"As we were leaving the wedding facility the other night, Tomi Yu and his parents approached me," she explained. "Tomi is about to leave for medical school, and his parents want to retire."

"Right. Sheila told me."

"So, anyway, they're looking for someone to take over the restaurant. I'm going to be the new manager of Lee Yu's Garden!"

"Woo-hoo!" I began to celebrate aloud, and Copper joined in with raucous barking. Before you knew it, Sasha added her voice to the fray, and the whole room came alive with celebratory noises.

"I just thought you'd like to know," Brandi said with a giggle.

From the other end of the line, I could hear Scott holler out the words, "Moo goo gai pan." They seemed to echo all the way from sunny Cozumel to frigid Clarksborough, PA.

"Tell him he's making me hungry," I said.

"Trust me, Mom," Brandi said, "he never wants to see another plate of moo goo gai pan as long as he lives. I've heard all about it."

"I can't say I blame him there." I paused for a moment and attempted to push back the growing lump in my throat. "Brandi, would you give him a kiss from me? Tell him I love him."

After a second or two, she came back with, "He says he loves you, too. And you're the best mother-in-law in the world."

Ah. Mother-in-law. There was that word, again. My heart sang as I realized the truth of it. I *was* a mother-in-law. Finally. And it felt great!

Still, there was one more thing that needed to be said. "Brandi?"

"Yes, Mom?"

"I don't know if I took the time to say it the other night, but you were truly the most beautiful bride to ever walk down an aisle."

"Amen," Warren whispered, adding his ditto to my comment.

"What are you going to say to Candy when it's her turn?" Brandi challenged.

"Hmm." I took a moment to think about that one. "Can you give me a few months to think about it?"

"Sure. You have exactly four months and twenty days," Brandi reminded me. "So you'd better give it some serious thought—and quick."

"Yikes." Only four and a half months to prepare for Candy and Garrett's big day? "Sounds like I'd better get busy," I said. "We have a wedding to plan!"

"Not me." Brandi's voice took on a dreamy note, and I knew at once she must've turned her attention to Scott. "I think I'm just going to relax and enjoy the view for a while."

Just then, something caught my attention. I glanced over at Warren, who'd settled back against the sofa with a broad smile on his face and a come-to-Papa look in his eye. I couldn't stop the smile from creeping up my face as I gave him my best I'll-be-right-there wink.

What was it Brandi had said again? Ah yes. *I think I'm just going to relax and enjoy the view for a while.* Warren extended his hand—a lovely invitation—and I closed out my call to my daughter with these playful words. . . .

"Oh, me, too, honey. Me, too."

Off in the corner, the two dachshunds cuddled together, clearly content. I giggled as I nodded their way. "Looks like Copper is here to stay," I acknowledged, "whether we like it or not."

"Yep." Warren glanced over at the blissful pups and then gazed into my eyes as I joined him on the sofa. "Love is in the air."

"You can say that again," I teased as I snuggled down next to him.

"Love is in the air," he whispered in my ear.

"Mmm-hmm." A sense of contentment washed over me as he planted half a dozen teensy kisses into my hair. All my anxieties melted away as our lips came together for one of the sweetest kisses we had shared in quite some time.

I couldn't help but close my eyes. . .and enjoy the view.

ABOUT THE AUTHOR

JANICE A. THOMPSON is a Christian novelist who lives in the Houston area. She has authored eleven books and has several more in progress, including a line of contemporary, humorous wedding mysteries for Barbour Publishing.

Janice considers herself somewhat overqualified when it comes to writing about weddings. In 2004, her two older daughters both received proposals within weeks of each other. Janice coordinated both weddings—a lovely Valentine's ceremony in February for her daughter Randi and a festive summer gala the following June for daughter Courtney. The weddings came off without a hitch!

Janice has since coordinated weddings for friends and is thrilled to incorporate many of her adventures into her stories. She's also tickled to be able to include her canine companion, Sasha, in each of her "tails."

If you enjoyed

GONE
with the
GROOM

then don't miss

by Janice A. Thompson
ISBN 978-1-59789-524-8

Wherever Christian Books Are Sold